MURDER IN NIRVANA

CASEY DORMAN

ISBN: 978-1-61296-574-1
PUBLISHED BY BLACK ROSE WRITING
www.blackrosewriting.com

Printed in the United States of America
Suggested retail price $17.95

Murder in Nirvana is printed in Book Antiqua

To my wife, Lai.

MURDER IN NIRVANA

CHAPTER ONE

It was the first murder in the mountain village in more than ten years. Under the indifferent light of a heedless moon and stars, someone had savagely beaten sixteen year-old Manuel Torres, leaving his lifeless body in the same position in which he'd died—arms raised to fend off his attacker, shattered legs crumpled beneath him, face fixed in rictal terror. He had been beaten, strangled, kicked, and bitten. Which blow had been the fatal one had yet to be determined.

By Sunday noon, with Jimmy Litton, the town's misfit and hothead securely behind bars, the talk was only about whether he'd been justified in beating Manuel Torres, the outsider who'd escaped from the local treatment center for delinquents, and if Jimmy should be tried as an adult

That's where I came in.

I'd arrived in the small picturesque village of Shambhala, nestled high in the Santa Ynez Mountains above Santa Barbara, having retreated there to tend my wounds after twenty years in the sanguinary trenches of Los Angeles' high profile legal wars.

My wounds had nearly been fatal.

Coming from the courtroom where I'd just won a favorable

verdict for a rich Hollywood celebrity accused of murdering his girlfriend, I was felled by a massive coronary.

I wasn't the first person to think that money and fame would protect me from the human frailties that plague more ordinary humans. Eighteen hour work days, lunches and dinners composed of equal parts of alcohol and animal fat, and an exercise schedule consisting of extended periods of immobility interrupted by frenzied marathons of running, weight-lifting, and workouts with the heavy bag, had set me up to come crashing down to earth.

The truth was that I had a single blocked artery, which was immediately replaced by some kind of plastic/elastic whatever that practically came with a guarantee. The only problem was that I still had a few more of my own arteries, which had no guarantees. I could live for another fifty years if I gave up fatty foods, cigarettes, nine-tenths of my daily ration of alcohol, and, above all, cut down on stress. It was either give up my lifestyle or get used to the idea of a short life. After three months of ranting, cursing and pouting, I knew I had to make a choice— become better adjusted or leave L.A.

I left.

Shambhala was perfect. For nearly a century the valley had served as a Mecca for religious and spiritual seekers, artists, and writers, most of whom shared a similarly dull lifestyle of sobriety, physical exercise, and organic farming, which I, probably ill-advisedly, decided to pursue. After six months, I'd become leaner and fitter, with the greatest threat to my longevity being the boredom which provided me with a daily reminder of why it had never before occurred to me to become a farmer.

I was on the roof one Sunday morning, trying to shingle a bare spot left over from the last strong Santa Ana wind, when Nils Larsen, Shambhala's longtime Chief of Police, turned into the inhospitably overgrown entrance to my narrow dirt driveway. Straightening up, I tried to massage some of the kinks out of my newly discovered back muscles as the black and white cruiser churned up a small cloud of brown dust while it moved purposefully toward my house.

Nils Larsen took his time unwinding from the front seat of his car. He'd spotted me on the roof and stood waiting, tall and lean, with just the suggestion of a paunch beneath his no-nonsense blue cotton shirt, open at the collar, sleeves rolled in a way that meant business. An old fashioned silver star was pinned to his chest. He was a sixty-year-old Dane, but he looked like he might be playing the part of a Sheriff in a western movie, with jeans and cowboy boots rounding out his outfit. All he lacked was a ten-gallon hat. I descended from the roof and walked toward him. He stared at me with flat, gray eyes, waiting until I came close enough for him to address me in his slow, quiet voice.

"Morning, Brian," he said, extending a sunburned, bony hand.

His grip was firm and curt. I nodded and waited.

Larsen shifted awkwardly from one foot to the other. "Hot day to be fixing a roof."

Nils had something on his mind. He wasn't usually one to hem and haw about a subject. I offered him a beer.

We sat out on my porch with a couple of beers—one of the two per day my doctor allowed me to drink—and I waited while Nils moved in a thoughtful to and fro motion in my oak rocker.

He took a long pull on his beer. "I need a little help."

I asked him what kind of help he needed.

"We had a murder in town a couple of days ago. You probably heard. A kid from that treatment center for delinquents—the *Yearling Foundation*. He got in a fight with a local boy and the kid from the Foundation got beaten pretty badly. One of my patrols found him dead outside the fence to the place the next morning. The local boy's a good kid. Never done anything seriously wrong. He needs a good lawyer."

I agreed.

"The judge here in the district court assigned a public defender. Some kid from Santa Barbara, still wet behind the ears. She's been up to see the local boy. She thinks he did it. Hell, she's got about a dozen cases already and no time for this one up here. The kid's gonna get the shaft unless he gets himself a better lawyer. The DA's tough—just got promoted—an eager beaver. It's gonna take an experienced lawyer to defend the boy." He paused and took another pull on his beer. There were beads of sweat on his nose and forehead. "I was thinking of you."

"That makes me feel all warm and fuzzy."

"I meant I was thinking of you to defend the boy," he said, frowning.

I told him that I was retired.

"I know that."

"Retired means I don't work anymore, Nils." I spoke my words as slowly and clearly as I could. After all, Nils was a country boy.

"He's a good kid."

"I thought the police were more into catching the perpetrators, Nils. How come you're working on this boy's defense?"

Nils face reddened a little. I couldn't tell whether I was making him angry or embarrassing him. "He's a local kid. The boy who got killed is a punk who's being treated at that fancy school for delinquents that everybody thinks is so wonderful. I want the Shambhala kid to get a fair shake."

I didn't want to get suckered into something, but I was curious. "Did the local kid do it?"

Nils's narrowed his eyes. "I thought defense lawyers didn't ask that question."

"I'm not a defense lawyer anymore, remember? Did he do it?"

Nils looked down at his feet. His face looked strained. This case meant something special to him. "I don't think so."

CHAPTER TWO

Nils and I both sipped slowly and pretended we had nothing else on our minds but enjoying of the taste of beer. The problem was he was starting to get me hooked on the case. I didn't want him to know that, although he probably did. I decided my best tactic was diversion. "What's the Yearling Foundation?" I asked.

Nils relaxed a little. "You'd know about it if you were a local," he said. "It's been here about three years. Run by Doctor Francine Stein. She used to be at UCLA. Uses all the latest scientific methods to turn around tough kids from the city. Her kids are the worst of the worst. Murderers, rapists, gang kids. There was a big fuss when she opened up the place. Nobody wanted those kind of kids in their backyard. But there's never been any trouble until now. And the Governor and a lot of other bigwigs have been all ga-ga over the program."

"Sounds like a bunch of bullshit to me. I don't know about any scientific methods that work with gang bangers. She's probably just sucking in a lot of government money and the politicians are trying to take credit for getting something done."

Nils shrugged, probably writing off my opinion as another symptom of my chronically cynical personality.

"So how come one of the kids from this Foundation gets in a fight with a local kid," I asked. "Don't they keep their little hoodlums locked up?"

"A bunch of them got out last Friday night. Came to town and started hassling some local kids in the park."

"And the boy charged with the murder was one of the kids they hassled?"

"I don't know why they singled him out, but they did. It wasn't a good choice. He's a good kid but he's got a temper and he's been in a few fights himself. He made quick work out of the Foundation kid."

"That's self-defense."

"It would have been if that was the end of it. The problem is, both kids walked away from it. Nobody really got hurt. But the next morning one of my men found the other kid—a Mexican-American—dead...beaten a lot worse than when he'd left the fight."

"And the boy who fought him earlier is the natural suspect?"

"He was still hanging around. Said he slept in a shed over on the *Krishna School* property instead of going home. The dead kid was found on the school property too, next to the fence that separates the school from the Foundation."

"What did the local kid say about it?"

"His name's Jimmy Litton. Jimmy said he'd been asleep all night in the shed. Said he didn't see the Mexican kid again after their fight."

"And you believe him?"

Nils shrugged again. "Maybe. The DA doesn't and he's charged him with murder."

"Murder? Sounds to me like the worst it could be is manslaughter, even if the kid admits fighting with the other boy a second time. Could even still be self-defense."

Nils gave me a look as if I'd just stated the obvious—which I had—but his look told me that nobody but he and I probably thought so.

I looked at him skeptically. "So what's the public defender

going to plea?"

"She's trying for manslaughter. The DA's after murder two. I'm afraid he'll get it. He'll cream her in court."

"That's the system, Nils. I take it the kid's family's got no money or he wouldn't have a public defender."

"You got it."

"And you think I'll just donate my time, right?"

"I've got a bit of a contingency fund in the department. We can't afford your full fee, but maybe you could give the public defender a little help. Come up with some local angles, point out the weaknesses in the DA's case." He looked at me sheepishly. "Shit, I don't know, McGowan, the kid just needs some help."

"I know I seem like a simple, honest farmer, working here on my little plot of land, Nils, but I'm filthy rich. I got that way taking on clients who were even filthier and richer than I was… well, richer anyway. Even if I wasn't retired, you couldn't afford me."

His eyes flashed with anger and he leaned toward me with a stony face. "OK McGowan. Sometimes I forget that underneath all that warmth, you're an asshole."

I returned his stare. "You sure as hell seem personally involved, Nils."

His face reddened. "He's just a local kid. The family's kind of outcasts and nobody else in town is gonna lift a finger for him."

"So you come to the other outcast in town. The LA lawyer who hasn't got anything to lose by becoming involved in an unpopular defense."

Nils' stone face cracked a little into a wry smile. "All that's true. But I came to you because you're the best lawyer I know."

"Best *retired* lawyer."

"Right." He shook his head sagaciously then glanced at my roof. "I forgot you're into farming now…and home improvement." He looked at me with his gray eyes and even stare.

"That's right, Nils. I'm a farmer now. After I shingle the roof I'm gonna watch my vegetables grow. That's what I moved here for."

He nodded. "Good for you. I'd thought you might be getting bored."

"In Shambhala? Last week there were the Krishnamurti lectures, next week it's the Strawberry Festival. How could I be bored? I'm afraid of becoming overexcited. I've got my heart to think about."

He gave me a long up and down perusal, squinting his eyes, which, I suppose, helped. "Well hell, I had to try." He started to get up.

"If this Litton kid didn't do it, have you got any idea who did?"

Larsen looked at me squarely. No cop ever admitted he didn't have any clues. "Nope," he said, simply.

"You're not much of a salesman, Chief," I said.

He shrugged. "I haven't got much to sell. Just saving a kid."

"Jesus Nils! Who do you think I am, the Salvation Army?"

He gave me that stare again. Damn! Why couldn't he just write me off as a mean-spirited asshole the way most people did?

I couldn't just give in. I still had some dignity to preserve. "I was planning to finish my roof, Nils. I'd hate to just leave it and get caught by an early storm. Especially if I'm leaving it to do *you* a favor." I thought about telling him about my bad knee which was giving me pains—a sure sign that it was about to rain—but I decided that that was overdoing it.

He shook his head, then got up and walked to the end of the porch and spat lazily into the dust…Gary Cooper-like. "Lawyers," he said. He started across the driveway to the ladder. "Got an extra hammer?"

I stood and hitched up my pants. "Yup."

CHAPTER THREE

The ten by twelve visitor's room in the Shambhala jail contained only a tired, unvarnished table with two unforgiving straight back wooden chairs on either side. A long window, about ten inches high, dirty, and covered by wire mesh, ran along the top of one institutional gray wall. A bank of three bare fluorescent bulbs, each at least three feet long, was attached to the ceiling directly above the table. One of the bulbs flickered neurotically.

Janice Le was only five feet tall and looked about eighteen years old, although I knew she had to be closer to twenty-five. She sat perfectly still and expressionless when Nils and I entered the room. Her client, Jimmy Litton, hadn't been brought in yet. I tried to read the young lawyer's reaction to Nils' having brought me into the case, but she was cloaking herself in Asian inscrutability. Nils had told me she was Chinese, but her name and facial characteristics told me that she was Vietnamese, probably second generation American since her first name was Janice.

Nils introduced us. She smiled politely and stuck out her hand.

Keeping everything formal. That wasn't a good sign.

I decided to act humble and apologetic. It wasn't something I was good at. "I don't mean to intrude on your case, Miss Le, but Nils said you were very busy and he and I thought there might be some details I could work on up here in Shambhala."

Her look was as devoid of emotion as a deceased frying pan and I had no idea what she was thinking. I was glad I wasn't playing poker with this chick. "My caseload isn't too full to give my client all the attention he needs, Mr. McGowan. My office has no budget for an extra lawyer. We do not pay your kind of fees anyway."

Whew! I watched to see if any ice cubes fell out of her mouth. She maintained her polite, frigid smile.

"Don't worry about the fee," I said, smiling sweetly, or as near as I could come to it. "Chief Larsen's department has been blessed with a massive endowment, all of which will go toward my fee. If that's not enough, he's pledged the deed for the police station. I'm thinking of turning it into a bed and breakfast."

Not a flicker on her face. Behind me I heard Nils choking.

"I appreciate your offer, but I will handle Mr. Litton's case myself." She gave me one last glance then turned back to her note pad and tape recorder. I'd been dismissed.

Did I need this?

I walked around the table and sat down in front of Miss Le. I lifted up my foot and examined the sole of my shoe. Then I did the same for the other shoe. She looked at me as if she were confused.

"I thought I must have stepped in something," I said. "That's the only explanation I can think of for why you'd want to get rid of me so quickly. I'm doing this for Chief Larsen. He's trying to help. I've had a lot of experience."

Her eyes were directed at the table in front of her. "I know your reputation, Mr. McGowan. Your cases make the newspapers. I don't want anything like that. This is a simple case. I can handle it very adequately by myself." She stared at her notepad on the table.

I remembered my first job out of law school. If I'd run into me at that time, I'd have been scared shitless. "Where'd you go to law school?" I asked.

She looked up…surprised by my question, then dropped her gaze, as if embarrassed. "Southwestern." It was lowest on the totem pole as far as California law schools went. It was also my alma mater.

"Me too."

She was surprised. For the first time, she smiled a genuine smile. She wasn't very pretty, but there was a delicate earnestness in her manner. When she smiled she crinkled up her eyes, making her look a little like a mechanical doll. The way she nodded her head added to the impression. I could see I'd finally broken the ice.

"How about if I help the chief here investigate a little and let you know what I find out? You don't object to a little extra information from the police, do you?"

She looked down at the table, embarrassed, I thought. "All right.," she murmured softly.

"You'll hold off on entering a plea for awhile?"

Her body stiffened. It was easy for her to slip into rigidity. Her gaze met mine. "I will hold off for a short while."

I gave her my warmest smile. "Good. Now I'd like to meet your client."

CHAPTER FOUR

Jimmy Litton was a tall, skinny kid, with big hands and wide shoulders, which made him look more like a Dane or a Swede than the descendant of dustbowl Okies he was supposed to be. He had that kind of stringy, straw-colored hair that looks dirty even when it isn't. He was wearing a blue workman's shirt and a pair of jeans. The shirt had *Shambhala Police* stenciled across the back in black letters. He was shoeless, his feet in white sweat socks. He cast his gaze around the room without looking up at Larsen, Miss Le or myself, then settled on one of the hard wooden chairs, carefully pulling it out from the table and sitting down across from his lawyer. He raised his head and looked at her angrily, then swung his gaze around and stared at me through suspicious, red-rimmed eyes. His long, thin lashes were anemically pale and his eyebrows straw-blonde like his hair.

Chief Larsen moved over next to the guard who'd accompanied him and said something quietly. The man left by the same door he and Jimmy had entered. "This is Mr. McGowan. He's working for me," Nils announced in a voice that surprised me by its gentleness.

Jimmy nodded. In his eyes there was a flicker of acknowledgment toward the Chief. I continued to get the cold stare. I gave Larsen a look that said he really owed me big-time for this. He just shrugged.

"I'll let you all talk," the Chief said, heading for the door.

"This is a privileged conversation," Miss Lee said, looking at me pointedly. It was an invitation for me to leave with Nils.

"I'd like to at least hear the kid's story about what happened."

"He's given a statement to Chief Larsen. You can read that. Anything further he says is for his lawyer only."

Jesus! She was doing it again. And after I'd gotten all sugary just to win her over. "I'm on your side, remember," I said.

Janice Le smiled at me with mechanical politeness. "I appreciate that, Mr. McGowan. Now please leave us alone."

Jimmy just stared at the table. I didn't have much choice. I gave Miss Le what I hoped was a coldly polite smile… and left.

Chief Nils Larsen was still hanging around when I reached the front desk. He was talking to an athletic looking man in his late twenties or early thirties, dressed in white shorts and a gray tee shirt, lines of sweat darkening the neck and back. Whoever the man was, he was still doing exercises while he talked to the Chief, grabbing one ankle and pulling it up behind him as if to stretch the muscles, twisting his torso every once in a while to loosen another set of muscles. He was in front of one of those convex mirrors that gave a view of the whole lobby and he kept glancing at his own distorted image. Chief Larsen was doing his best to ignore the show. When Larsen saw me coming down the hallway from the visiting area he motioned me over, moving a few feet away from the exercise freak.

"Why aren't you talking to Jimmy?" Larsen asked, looking like a worried parent.

"His lawyer threw me out."

"Christ almighty!" Nils fumed.

"No big deal. I can talk to him later. I'm one of your men now, remember?" I smiled brightly. "Look on the sunny side, Chief. As a cop I can beat his story out of him. As a lawyer I didn't have that option."

"I'll give you a copy of the kid's statement," Nils said. "He basically says he didn't do it. Never saw the other kid after their first fight. He also claims that the other kid didn't want to fight him. The other kids from the Foundation forced the Torres kid into the fight. Jimmy says it was like they were after Torres themselves, then they decided to push Torres into the fight with Jimmy."

"That's bullshit, Nils," the man who was still exercising next to Larsen, while listening to our conversation, said. He stuck out his hand to me. "Richard Detwiler. I'm the DA," the man said, moving closer to Nils and myself. "You're McGowan, the famous LA lawyer who's taken the kid's case, I guess?" He had a self-satisfied smile on his face, like he was either enjoying some kind of private joke or he was demented.

"He's already got a lawyer. I'm doing some investigating for Nils. This case isn't going to make anybody famous. Either somebody else did it or it's manslaughter."

Detwiler was still wearing his sick little smile. "Really? As far as I can see the kid is guilty of murder. That's what I'm charging him with. That's only small-town logic of course. Maybe they do things differently in LA."

It was clear I was talking to an asshole. "Isn't this Yearling Foundation a treatment center for big city delinquents? You're gonna tell me that when some LA gang banger picks a fight with a local kid and then gets the shit beaten out of him, you're gonna charge the local kid with murder?"

"It's not just any local kid, McGowan. Jimmy Litton is a troublemaker. He's been in fights before. And his family is known to hate Mexicans."

"And the rest of the town hates poor rednecks like his family. Gimme a break, Detwiler. Jimmy didn't break into the Foundation to start a fight with one of them. They came into town and picked him out. Besides, Torres was killed later, not in his fight with Jimmy."

"Manuel Torres wasn't just killed," Detwiler answered. "Bill Todd, the Medical Examiner says it's the worst beating he's ever seen. The kid was strangled, kicked, even bitten, and half the blows were delivered after he was already dead. It'd be hard to call that manslaughter. Besides that, the Torres kid was sick. Todd says he had a super high white blood cell count, like an infection, maybe even leukemia." He did another torso-twist, then raised his leg behind him and grabbed the ankle, giving it a few tugs and glancing up at the mirror to catch himself in a pose. I was imagining how easy it would be to sweep the other leg out from under him.

"You're pretty eager to get this kid, aren't you?" I said.

He stopped his gymnastics. His face had lost its supercilious smirk. "I don't like hate crimes happening in my town. I'm gonna make an example of Litton."

"Whether he's guilty or not?"

"Prove he's not."

"That's his lawyer's job, but you could end up looking pretty stupid if she does."

"I'll take that chance," he said, sweeping one arm down to touch the opposite toe, then repeating the movement with the other arm.

"Maybe you're used to it." I observed.

"You're a wise-guy, McGowan. We'll see how smart you are when the case goes to court."

I just looked at him.

He gave me another sick smile then went back to flexing. "I gotta get moving," he said. "I'm starting to stiffen up."

Larsen and I watched as he jogged out of the building.

"Nice technique, McGowan," Larsen said dryly. "You've already alienated the DA. Remember, you're working for the police force on this one."

"Don't worry, Chief. That was just a little psychological

skirmish. Sounds like this case is personal for him, anyway."

"Detwiler thinks that this was a hate crime. The Litton's are known for their racist attitudes. The parents anyway. I told you the family's not really part of the community. People around here don't like people who aren't their kind."

"Only certain kinds of bigotry are OK, huh?"

"That's just the way it is in a small town."

"So what's Detwiler's beef about the racial thing? Why would a redneck who hates Mexicans bother him so much?"

"He's Mexican-American."

"With a name like Detwiler?"

"His mother's Mexican. His father's not."

"And Jimmy's family has a reputation for hating Mexicans."

"Now you've got the picture." Larsen said.

"How come you're so sure the kid didn't do it?"

Larsen chewed on his lower lip. "He's not that kind of kid. I've seen him around, watched him grow up. The town kids have been rough on him. He's learned to fight back, but he's no killer."

I stared at Nils for a few seconds, trying to figure out what was going on with him, why he was so involved with this kid. There was something he wasn't telling me. "I hope you're right," I said.

"You think he's depressed?" Nils asked, his question seeming to come from nowhere.

"Depressed?"

"Yeah. Depressed, unhappy, suicidal. Hell, he's in jail for murder and he's only sixteen."

"How would I know? I didn't even get a chance to talk to the kid.. He didn't look very happy, but who would be?"

"We have a psychologist who does some work with us. She sees some of the kids who are put on probation, works with some of the families when we have domestic violence cases. Maybe she should talk to Jimmy."

"Can't hurt. Can she tell us whether or not he's lying?"

Larsen shrugged his shoulders. "Don't know. She's pretty good. She could probably tell you how to relate to the kid to get him to open up to you."

I smiled at him. "You think my jailhouse manner's gonna need a little work?"

He just shrugged.

"Give her a call," I said. "Bring her in. I'd like to talk to her myself. In the meantime, how about if I start poking around?"

"Where do you want to poke?"

"How about that Yearling Foundation? Sounds like it's a pretty good place to start. I can find out a little more about the boy who was killed and what those kids were doing in town. Then maybe I can talk to Jimmy's parents. Sound OK to you?"

"Sounds fine to me. You gonna have another try at that lawyer?"

"I don't want to crowd her. I'll give her a little room, feed her some information so she knows I'm working *with* her, not against her, and maybe she'll come around. If not, I'm not going to be much use to you."

"You could always take the case yourself."

I knew Nils would finally suggest it. "You keep forgetting I'm retired. I'll help out, but I'm not going to jump in with both feet. My doctor forbade me to enter a courtroom for at least a year."

Nils gave me a resigned nod. "OK. Do what you can."

"Don't I get a badge? Maybe a gun? Whose gonna believe I'm a cop?"

"You're a consultant. You don't get a badge or a gun. Stop by the office and I'll give you some ID that says your working for me."

"How about a cheap suit and an old hat? Squeaky shoes?"

"Buy your own."

CHAPTER FIVE

Secluded in the wooded hills only a half-mile from town, sandwiched between the *Krishna School*, an Eastern religious boarding school, on one side and *La Sol*, a new–age health spa, on the other, the *Yearling Foundation* was a place of mystery to nearly everyone in the Shambhala Valley. Chief Larsen knew more about it than anyone because he'd had to set up a special communication system with the Foundation to alert them if any of their young charges escaped and wandered into town as they had the night of the boy's death. The Foundation had its own security force and they strongly preferred that they bring their own kids back and that Larsen and his police force keep as much out of it as possible. According to Larsen, the Foundation's purpose was to work with LA's toughest street kids and try to turn them into model citizens. How it attempted to do that or how successful it was in fulfilling its mission was anybody's guess, at least anybody in Shambhala. What the Yearling Foundation actually *did* behind its high chain-link fence was not public knowledge.

It was Monday afternoon, but all I'd gotten when I called the Foundation earlier was an answering machine. I'd decided to drive over and pay the place a visit. Nils Larsen had given me a card saying I was a special investigator for his department and he said it ought to get me past the front gate. By the look of the high chain-link fence, topped with rolls of barbed wire, it wouldn't be hard to mistake the place for a maximum security prison. The road ended at a gate made out of the same chain link as the rest of the fence and framed in dull gray tubular steel. There was an electronic locking mechanism of some sort keeping it shut. Just inside the gate was a wooden guardhouse. I beeped my horn and a figure emerged. Whoever it was went back inside the guardhouse and the gate opened. When he re-emerged he held up his hand to indicate I shouldn't come through and walked over to my car.

The guard was tall and muscular, good-looking enough to know it—although his good looks were threatened by his permanently disdainful scowl. I guessed his age as probably in his middle to late twenties. He wore his blond hair long, almost to his shoulders, and bleached. Dressed in jeans and a spotless white tee shirt, he could have been a surfer, except he was built more like a body-builder. He flexed his biceps impatiently while I dug out my official ID card.

"What's your business with Dr. Stein?" the guard asked, holding my ID in one hand while he rested the other on the top of my front windshield. I was driving the Jaguar and I had the top down.

"That's between me and Dr. Stein," I said, glancing up at his hand.

He didn't move his hand. "She likes to know what her visitors want."

"Does she?" I said.

The guard flexed again. "This is private property, mister. The Foundation treats some very disturbed children. We don't let just anyone drive through. I'll need to clear this with the office." He took his hand off of my car and pulled a cellular phone out of a holster on his hip. While he dialed, I tried to figure out what kind of place this was. I could just see beyond the gate house. There was a group of low wooden gray buildings having the appearance of an army barracks. Most of the structures were laid out around the periphery of a large grass-covered yard in the center of which stood a tall white flag pole, Old Glory hanging limply in the still afternoon air. I wouldn't have been surprised to see uniformed youngsters goose-stepping across the grass. Instead, there were three or four small groups of boys, all of them dressed much like the guard, assembled in what looked like work parties near several of the buildings. One of the groups was painting the side of a small shed and another was digging in a garden. I couldn't make out what the others were doing. Each group was accompanied by at least two young men in their twenties or thirties—apparently guards or supervisors.

I listened to the guard asking someone on the other end of the phone where Doctor Stein was. Then he made another call. As soon as he began talking, he glanced up at me, frowned, and stepped far enough away from the car that I couldn't listen in. The conversation was taking a long time. I revved my engine. He punched the off button on the phone. "Dr. Stein isn't in her office right now. You'll have to come back." He handed me back my ID card then re-holstered his phone and stood with both arms at his sides, his muscles tensed.

I asked him whom he'd been talking to.

"Secretary."

"She must have a multiple personality. You made more than one call." I was trying to intimidate him with my acute observational powers. "Which way's the office?" I asked.

"You can't go up there now. Not without Dr. Stein's O.K."

"I just follow this road?"

He looked at me as if I were dense. "I said you can't go up there now." His scowl had become more pronounced.

I hated to be pushy, but I reminded myself that I was on official police business. He was making a mistake to question my new-found authority. He'd made an even bigger mistake by leaving the gate open when he'd come out to talk to me. "Call the doctor back and tell her I'm on my way," I said, jamming my foot down on the accelerator. When I looked in the rearview mirror the guard was staring after me, his cellular phone in his hand. The expression on his face suggested that I'd ruined his day.

The road wound between two buildings. A side road led to a small gray building with a heavy iron fence around it. The fence looked even stronger than the one surrounding the rest of the place, and it separated the smaller building from everything else. There were *keep-out* signs posted on the fence and on the building itself. I kept on the main road until saw a large gray two-story Victorian farm house with a sign that said *Office* over the front porch.

The house looked like it dated from the turn of the century and I suspected that it had been the stylish main residence of what had once been a wealthy mountain ranch. The house's original owner must have been a bit of an eccentric and the architect must have heralded from Transylvania. A porch with an overhanging roof, supported by posts every eight or ten feet, stretched across the entire front of the house. The roof rose to a peak, centered over the middle of the porch, and on either side of the pointed façade were round turrets with tall rectangular windows and crowned with conical roofs, producing the appearance of towers on a Gothic castle. The house was surrounded by a heavy chain-link and barbed-wire fence, but the gate was open and there were no *Keep-out* signs posted. I parked in front of the building. The guard from the front gate evidently hadn't followed me. Maybe he'd gone off to find Dr. Stein. At any rate, from what he'd said, the secretary should be in so I climbed the stairs and entered the front door.

The secretary was in all right and she was a first class knockout. She looked up in surprise when I entered. "Are you

Mr. McGowan? Didn't Jerry tell you that Dr. Stein isn't in?" she asked. She had a nice little-girl voice, and a big smile that looked a little uncertain at the moment. She was sitting behind a functional-looking walnut desk but I had a clear view of her shapely figure, sitting primly on her wheeled secretary's chair.

"Jerry told me Dr. Stein wasn't here. After he let me in I think he went to get her."

She looked puzzled. "Really? He went to get her?"

"He seemed in a hurry to go somewhere. Isn't Dr. Stein on the grounds?"

"Oh yes. She's here somewhere."

"Good, then I can wait for her." I gave her a wink to let her know everything was kosher and sat down on a new-looking, artificial leather couch in front of an oak coffee table on which were several neat stacks of magazines. I picked one up and started to read it. When I looked up, the secretary was still staring like she wasn't sure what to do about me. She wasn't the first to have wondered that, but I winked again to reassure her. "Don't get many visitors, I guess. If they'd heard about you, you'd get a lot more people up here just dropping in."

She blushed, which made her look even more fetching She had that kind of beautiful, milky skin that developed a rosy glow when she was embarrassed. She crossed one shapely leg over the other and flashed her big smile. Her teeth were as even as a set of piano keys and dazzling white against her pink skin. She took one brightly finger-nailed hand and smoothed her long blond hair. "You're not from around here are you?" she said. Her eyes had a soft bedroom quality. At least that's how they appeared to me.

"I am now. I'm new though. Moved up here to retire. I got burnt out in Hollywood." I figured it never hurt to dangle a magic word or two in front of a good-looking woman.

"You're in the movie business?"

The carrot seemed to be working. I told her I was a lawyer;

that lots of my clients were in the movie industry.

Her smile disappeared for a moment. When it reappeared, it seemed to lack some of its former luster. The word 'lawyer' sometimes did that to people.

"That's why you're here? It's about Manuel Torres?" she asked. Her voice had dropped to a hushed, almost-whisper.

"Did you know the boy?"

She lowered her eyes and began straightening things on the top of her desk. "I only know the boys by their names. Most of them I've never met."

"They don't come here to the office?"

"We're off limits to the residents, Mr. McGowan. We have all of the confidential files here and most of the medicines. These boys come from very bad backgrounds. We have to enforce very strict rules."

"That's why the fence is around this building?"

"That's just in case there's ever an emergency."

I wondered what kind of an emergency would force the staff to lock themselves *in* behind a fence.

"Manuel Torres came from a bad background, too?" I asked.

Her soft baby blue eyes were pleading, asking me to stop with my questions. "I can't talk about the residents," she said. "You'll have to ask Dr. Stein about Manuel."

I dropped the subject and went back to reading my magazine. I guess my charm had a short half-life.

CHAPTER SIX

I thumbed through a few more magazines while I waited for the doctor to show up. The magazines were just the usual office collection, nothing to give much indication of what the foundation was about. On the wall above me there were a few plaques; one from the governor acknowledging the foundation's work in the area of juvenile crime prevention, another from the Mayor of Los Angeles, saying much the same thing. It all looked pretty respectable, even impressive.

I heard steps on the front porch and looked up to see a tall slim woman dressed in a white lab coat coming through the door. From the lab coat down, she had long, slim, nicely shaped calves and was wearing a pair of tall dark heels. I dragged my gaze away from her legs and saw a narrow face, striking in its severity. Dr. Stein could have been beautiful if she hadn't looked so austere. She had thin black eyebrows, pale skin, which looked heavily made up in spite of its pallor, and jet-black hair wound tightly in a French braid. Her age was probably somewhere between forty and fifty. She looked at me with a brittle smile. Two steps behind her, Jerry the muscle-bound guard gave me a more menacing look.

"You're an impatient man, Mr. McGowan. Jerry says he asked you to wait at the gate." She kept the brittle smile, but her voice had a teasing quality. I guessed she was waiting to make her own judgment about me.

"Jerry told me to go back home. My business is a little more urgent than that."

Jerry started to say something, but the doctor silenced him with a motion of her hand.

"What *is* your business, Mr. McGowan?"

I told her I was investigating Manuel Torres' death for the police department.

"You don't look like a policeman."

I took that as a compliment. "I'm a special consultant to the department. Chief Larsen has hired me to assist in gathering evidence. He's not convinced that the Litton boy is Torres' killer."

Jerry was still standing at the door, a petulant frown on his face. Doctor Stein gave him an irritated look. "Go back to the gate, Jerry. Let's hope you didn't leave it open again."

The look he shot back at her was a lot more insolent than I would have expected from an employee. It was nothing compared to the daggers he aimed at me. Then he turned and sauntered out, skipping down the porch steps two at a time.

"Nice kid," I said.

Doctor Stein held out her hand. "I'm Francine Stein, Director of the Yearling Foundation. We're all a little edgy today. Manny's murder has a lot of the residents and staff upset...maybe even a bit paranoid."

"Paranoid? About what?"

"We don't like the publicity, Mr. McGowan. Shambhala isn't a very open community. It was difficult to get the people to let us come in here. Now a murder is going to make them think that we're a source of trouble."

"But your boy was the victim, Doctor Stein. Unless you think one of your kids killed him."

She looked startled. "Of course not. Why would you say

that?"

"I don't know. Sometimes I just say whatever comes into my head. Aren't some of your kids killers?"

She was more irritated than startled this time. "You have an abrasive manner, Mr. McGowan. I thought you wanted to find out something about Manuel Torres." She dug her hands down into the big side pockets of her lab coat.

"So I do. I'd like to hear more about your place, though. It's not a secret is it?" I smiled as innocently as I could.

The innocence of her own smile put mine to shame. "Not at all, Mr. McGowan. We don't talk about what we do because we're trying to keep a low profile here in Shambhala. As I said, this is not a very open-minded community, despite its new-age reputation. But what we do is quite a matter of public record, as you can see by the reviews we've gotten for our work." She gestured in the direction of the various commendations on the wall.

"Very impressive," I said. "So tell me about Manuel Torres."

"Let's go into my office," she said.

Dr. Francine Stein's office was comfortable, but certainly not fancy. Her desk was a long redwood library table with no side drawers. Across the room in front of her desk was a large picture window looking out on the property. Behind her on the wall were her medical school, internship, and residency certificates as well as her California Medical License. She was Board Certified in genetics. I was surprised. I'd thought she must be a psychiatrist to run a place like this.

Doctor Stein motioned for me to sit down in one of the large leather chairs in front of her desk. I noticed that her desktop was almost bare—a few papers in her teak 'in' and 'out' baskets on the end opposite the computers, a vase with some dried flowers.—probably symbolic of her brittle personality.

"What do you want?" she asked softly, her voice deep and direct. She stared at me with green eyes that could have been attractive if they hadn't been so cold. She leaned back in her chair and crossed one leg over the other, the lab coat splitting high enough above her knee to show more thigh than a Hollywood starlet would have flashed at a casting interview. Her thighs were as nice looking as her calves. She watched my eyes taking her in and smiled.

"The Yearling Foundation and Manuel Torres. I'd like to hear about both of them…and what happened last night—why those kids were in town," I said.

Her smile thinned a little, then she picked up a pencil and held it between her hands, like a pensive conductor, fingering her baton. "Have you heard of *behavior modification*, Mr. McGowan?"

"You mean carrot and stick, M&Ms and electric shock? *Clockwork Orange* kind of stuff?" I hummed a little Beethoven.

She frowned. It seemed to be the expression that came easiest to her. "That's not really how it works," she said. "No one really uses punishment any more. Punishment has no lasting effect unless it's extremely severe. We prefer to work with rewards and something we call *stimulus control*; changing the conditions that provoke certain behaviors in the first place. Added to that, we use a cognitive approach. We try to alter a child's way of thinking about the world."

"That's what your foundation is about…behavior modification?"

"Essentially, yes. We take the most severe cases and our specialty is modifying aggression. Our kids come from LA's street gangs. They are thieves, rapists, even murderers… the worst. Our only rules are that they have to be under 17 and that we have them for at least two years. During that period we have total control of the child. Everything they receive, from the size of their meals to their access to social contact is contingent upon their behaving in exactly the way we want them to."

"B.F. Skinner would be proud of you."

She smiled indulgently. "We go beyond Skinner. Do you know what causes aggression, Mr. McGowan?"

I gathered that I wasn't supposed to. I offered my opinion anyway. "I'd say being human."

Her smile was almost real. "You're pretty close to the truth. Aggression is built into each of us. Aggression has given those who have the most of it an evolutionary advantage since long before the time when man emerged from the apes. Not uncontrolled aggression, however. Any animal who was indiscriminately aggressive would have gotten itself killed or else destroyed its own young. No, the aggression that the species inherited is very specific. It's turned off and on by internal and external cues. And it can be overridden by other considerations. Apes, for instance, will tolerate a lot more provocative behavior from their relatives or fellow troop members than from strangers. It doesn't pay, evolutionarily, to kill those who are likely to carry copies of your own genes. There are cues for signaling relationships, for turning off aggression when it surfaces in another member of the species, for avoiding situations where aggression might surface. How do you think street gangs keep their aggression focused outside their gang and not on each other? They use colors, names, words, hand and facial signals. It's those cues we work with. We reduce the cues which signal the need for aggression and we teach behaviors which elicit pro-social responses from others. Combine that with some training in reflection and logic and then make every advantage in our mini-society here contingent upon producing behavior that is incompatible with aggression and you have our program." She placed the pencil down on the desktop emphatically. The performance was over. She was still showing a lot of thigh.

"Do you teach them how to tie an ascot and which fork to use?"

She gave me a withering look. "I'm not joking about this Mr.

McGowan. What we do works."

"What happens when they return to the jungle? They're not going to get any rewards for being non-aggressive in South Central or East LA."

She nodded seriously. "That's a problem. We hope they don't return. But if they do, we try to instill some mental blocks against using any aggression at all, a set of internal prohibitions that's strong enough to withstand the temptations of the streets."

"Did Manuel Torres have those prohibitions?"

"He didn't need them. Manny Torres wasn't violent to begin with. He was a gang member and a thief, and very smart, a leader, in fact. But he was not aggressive."

Her description of Torres fit with what Jimmy Litton had told Nils. Torres had been forced into his fight with Litton by the other Foundation kids. I asked her how her kids got out.

"I'm afraid they escaped," she answered. "We misjudged how far along some of the boys were. We only maintain maximum security precautions during the first few weeks a resident is here. After that, they don't try to leave. These boys had recently been taken off precautions. A bit too early as it turned out."

"When they're off of precautions, they can leave the compound?"

She shook her head. "No. These boys have committed serious, often heinous crimes. This is a treatment facility not a prison, but none of the residents is free to leave."

"Only some of them did."

"Yes, they did. They escaped. But we brought them back."

"Except Manuel Torres. He didn't come back."

"No, he didn't." She didn't look comfortable with the direction the conversation was going.

"So what happened to Torres?" I asked.

"I really don't know. He wasn't from the same cottage as the other boys. Our staff didn't know he was gone until the police found him. That's when we heard about the fight."

"And after the fight?"

She shrugged. "Nobody knows."

"The Litton kid says that the other boys forced Torres to fight with him," I said.

She looked surprised. "Why would they do that?"

I shrugged. "That's just what he said. Torres didn't want to fight and didn't defend himself when he did. The other kids pushed him into it."

"I told you Manny wasn't a fighter."

"So why would the others force him to fight?"

"Perhaps Jimmy Litton was the one who forced the fight. It sounds like he's trying to put the blame on our residents."

I couldn't be sure she wasn't right.

"Could I talk to the other kids? The ones from the unit that left?"

She glanced at her watch. "I'm afraid that's impossible. They've been asked a lot of questions already and this is disrupting their whole program. This entire episode, with the police and the DA coming here, has brought back a lot of the cues from the environment I'm trying to get them to forget. They've become more unruly as a result. Most of them will have to repeat the first few weeks of the program just to get them back on track."

"Detwiler talked to them?"

"No, but he was here and they knew it."

I told her that both Detwiler and I would need to interview her students at some point. After all, they were witnesses.

She looked puzzled. "Why both you and the DA? Aren't you working together?"

"He and I have made an arrangement. We both collect independent sets of information. It's sort of like a fail-safe system. That way we don't miss anything. He'll do his interviewing and I'll do mine."

The doctor straightened up. Her tone was even and hard. "You'll have to get a judge's order for that, I'm afraid."

"Fair enough, doc. What about Torres' file? I'll need to see that, too."

"It's a confidential medical file."

"Torres is dead, remember. Besides, if he was sent here by the court, then his file's not confidential at all. It belongs to the court. I work for the police, remember? There are some things we need to know. According to our coroner, the Torres boy had something wrong with him-an abnormally high white blood cell count. Was he being treated for anything?"

For a moment I thought she looked panicked. Then she smiled—sweetly but disingenuously. "Of course, Manny had a throat infection. I examined him the very day he died."

"You do the medical work yourself?"

"I'm a licensed physician, Mr. McGowan."

"A geneticist, according to your diploma."

"You're observant. But I'm a physician, nevertheless."

"Can I see the file then?"

"Not without a court order."

"What are you afraid of?"

She was trying to maintain her cool, but she bristled. "You've got a boy in custody who murdered one of my residents. Isn't that enough? I don't intend to have either Manny's background or the Foundation's medical practices be the subject of the trial."

"Secrets, doctor?" I said, trying my best to keep an angelic smile on my face.

"You can be an irritating man, Mr. McGowan. I think I've given you enough of my time," she said, rising. She smoothed her lab coat efficiently.

Since it seemed I'd worn out my welcome I thanked her and headed for the door. On the way out I slipped the secretary a card with my phone number. Maybe I could still get lucky. She looked up at me with a startled expression, then hurriedly swept the card from the top of her desk. With a furtive glance at Doctor Stein's door, the secretary reached down and scooped her purse from the floor then opened it and dropped my business card inside. She returned to her typing without looking back at me. I had the unsettling feeling that my card was a life preserver I'd just thrown to the young woman, rather than the simple invitation that I'd intended.

When I reached the gate, Jerry had dutifully closed it, as he'd been instructed. He came out of the guard's shed to meet me. I could see that getting out of this place was going to be no easier than getting in. Jerry had a pipe wrench the size of a baseball bat in his hand.

I smiled. "I didn't know you gave souvenirs to your guests when they left."

He scowled back at me. I guess he only had one facial expression. "I don't like somebody making a fool of me in front of my boss."

"You'd rather do it all on your own, I guess."

He stood next to the side of my car, still slapping the wrench in his hand. "It'd be a real shame if this wrench happened to fall on your fancy little car," he said, raising the wrench.

"I hope you're remembering that this is an official police vehicle."

He stopped his motion in midair. Slowly he lowered the wrench. "You're lucky. I could'a creamed you," he said, his face twisted in an angry sneer.

"Really?"

I flipped the inside handle of my door down, unlatching it, and using my shoulder like an NFL blocking back's, I drove the corner of the door squarely into Jerry's groin. He fell backward onto the ground, holding his injured anatomy with one hand and still grasping the wrench with the other. I stepped out and stood over him, then reached down and removed the wrench from his hand. He was still clutching his groin, his legs drawn up into a fetal position, but he held his free hand over his face to ward off a blow.

I slapped the wrench against my palm. "Now, should we work on your attitude or do you just want to open the gate?"

Hatred showed in his eyes, but his fear was stronger. He struggled to his feet and limped across the fifteen foot space to the gate and opened it. I threw the wrench into the bushes and got back in my car. "Hope you don't need to fix anything with that real soon," I said.

"You and I are going to meet again, asshole." Jerry managed to spit out between his clenched teeth as I drove through the gate.

I wouldn't miss it.

CHAPTER SEVEN

The evening had cooled and I sat out on my front porch, flip-flops on my feet and a beer in my hand. The beer was one of the two my doctor allowed me each day. The crickets were making a hullabaloo, but I didn't mind. Above me the stars were clear and luminescent in a way they never were beneath the smog of the city. The whole sky seemed closer and at the same time more vast than it had back in LA. I was enjoying the feeling of solitude. Even when I'd lived in a house that was surrounded by over an acre of fenced yard, I'd never felt alone in Los Angeles. Nobody who lives in a city can forget that millions of other people are always there. From where I was now sitting it was a good mile to the next house. I couldn't see a single light in any direction.

I was about ready to crack open the second beer when my cell phone, which I'd left inside the house, began its musical ring, shattering my illusion of privacy. I ignored it until I remembered I was working. I reluctantly opened the screen door and went inside, finally locating the phone on the nightstand next to my bed.

"Brian McGowan?" it was a woman's voice, deep, but musical and pleasant. She sounded hesitant. "I hope I'm not calling too late. I thought I'd get your voicemail."

"I turned off my voicemail. Gives people the impression that I'm going to return their calls," I said.

"Aren't you a lawyer?"

"I'm retired. Now I'm a gentleman farmer."

"But you're working with Chief Larsen on the Litton case, aren't you? Or have I been misinformed?"

"Farming's been a little slow this year. Who am I talking to anyway? You know a lot more about me than I do about you."

She gave a tiny laugh, hardly more than a catch in her throat, but I liked its sound. "This is Doctor Hillary Smythe. I'm a psychologist. Nils Larsen called me about the Litton boy. Said I should talk to you before I saw him."

I thanked her for calling, made the usual pleasant murmurings, and asked her if she could tell me whether Jimmy Litton was telling the truth about not killing Manuel Torres.

"That's not why I'm seeing him. I'm not a police investigator. Nils Larsen is worried about the boy's depression."

"I'm worried that he may be guilty of murder. That's worse than being depressed."

"It may be, but I'm not going to question the boy for you. I'm trying to help him."

"It'll help him if I can figure out if he's telling the truth."

"Aren't you the one who's supposed to figure that out? Nils said you're helping the police with their investigation."

"I'm working for the police because Nils thinks the kid's innocent and he wants me to find a way to prove it. I'd like to talk to Jimmy alone, but I don't think his lawyer's gonna allow it."

"So you want me to do your questioning for you? You know I can't do that. Jimmy's conversation with me is confidential."

"You can form an opinion. That's not confidential."

"You'll have to do your own police work, Mr. McGowan. I'm concerned about Jimmy's mental health and that's it. Are we clear on that?" Her voice had lost its music, but I still sensed a sensual undertone. I'm good at sensing things like that.

"Perfectly clear, Doctor Smythe. You do your work and I'll do mine." I had an afterthought. She still had a nice voice. "How about if we do lunch, sometime?"

She hesitated. I always take a lack of an immediate rejection as an auspicious sign. "Maybe. I'll have to think about it. I'm not sure that I trust you, Mr. McGowan."

"I'm wounded," I said.

She laughed again. This time it was a nice, throaty laugh that sent my imagination on a little side trip. Now I knew I wanted to have lunch with her. "I'm sure you'll survive," she said. "Like I said, I'll think about it. I'm sure we'll be talking again. Goodbye, Mr. McGowan."

I decided to polish off the second beer that I'd been interrupted from opening when Hillary Smythe had called. I kicked off my flip-flops, leaned back in my antique oak and wicker rocker and dedicated myself to trying to time the squeak of the chair to the rhythmic chirpings of the crickets in the oak grove. I'd just about gotten it right when I was again interrupted by the ringtone from my cellphone.

It was Karin Stengaard, Doctor Stein's luscious secretary. I hadn't known her name until now, but I recognized her little girl voice. My first thought was to congratulate myself on being more charming than I'd thought I'd been and on having the wisdom to have given Karin one of my cards. Then I heard the fear in her voice.

"Are you still interested in Manny Torres?" Karin asked. She was breathing hard and fast, like a frightened bird.

"Sure I am, but what's wrong?"

She sounded a if she was choking back a sob. "I've got to tell someone."

"Tell someone what?"

"About Manny. About what happened to him." She stopped abruptly. "I can't talk. I'm still at work and I don't want anyone to hear me."

I asked her if we could meet somewhere. She suggested the Lonesome Pine Lodge, a bar and grill about three miles down the highway toward Santa Barbara. I remembered passing the place several times. When I'd driven by on a Saturday night, cars had filled the parking lot and were spilling out into the street. It was evidently the place to go when you wanted to get away from the confines of Shambhala' restrictive social life. We agreed to meet in half an hour.

She didn't sound as if she'd been responding to my social invitation, but I scraped the day's beard off my face just in case. I regretfully chugged the rest of my beer, quickly brushed my teeth, combed my hair, and hopped into my car, then tooled off in the direction of the Lonesome Pine Lodge. The night was still warm so I drove with the top down.

CHAPTER EIGHT

From the outskirts of Shambhala, the sinuous two-lane Highway 150 winds down to the coastline at a steep incline. On either side of the road tall pines provide a curtain of dark impenetrability, masking the mostly uninhabited forest that runs for miles along the western edge of the Santa Ynez range. The highway's sharp switch-backs had been designed to lessen the uphill grade for the 1950's behemoths that had been in use when the road was built. Highway 150 is not a route to be driving late at night if you're not familiar with it. The curves have a nasty tendency to leap out from nowhere. My Jaguar handled the curves with ease, although the ominous darkness beyond the edges of the pavement intimidated me enough to cool my zeal with the gas pedal. I cruised, listening to the silence of the tall forest sliding by on either side of me and wondering whether I was headed for a romantic assignation or the rescue of a distressed damsel.

I pulled out of a long left-hand curve and saw the road ahead of me bathed in the yellowish light from the Lonesome Pine Lodge parking lot. The lot was only half full. I parked and went inside.

There was a no smoking ban that extended to bars in California, but no one in the Lonesome Pine Lodge seemed to know about it. Or if they did, they didn't care. I looked around through the smoky gray haze, but I didn't see Karin's pretty blonde head anywhere. A middle-aged barfly, who looked a lot more experienced than I, gave me the once over and let me know she was available, but I wasn't buying. I wanted a seat with an unobstructed view of the bar's front door. I was lucky the crowd was thin because there was an empty booth just off the end of the bar at the back of the place. I could see the front door and the entire length of the bar.

The cocktail waitress recognized a new face in the joint and started with her best come-on until I interrupted her with a disappointing request for a cup of black coffee. It hurt me more than it hurt her. When she returned with my order, I could tell after the first sip that coffee wasn't one of the crowd favorites at the Lonesome Pine. It tasted like the contents of the pot had been cooking down to a thick, bitter sludge since that morning. At least I had something to hold in my hands.

There was no live band, although a tiny billboard at my table announced that The *Junkyard Dogs* would be playing next Friday and Saturday night. Tonight the band stand was dark, the dance floor empty and the clientele pared down to the dedicated drinkers who knew the bartender and each other by name and who told each other that week nights at the Lonesome Pine Lodge reminded them of the old days before the young crowd from Santa Barbara had discovered the place. Mostly they were solitary drinkers, sitting with their elbows leaning on the worn red-leather rim of the long bar, hands guarding drinks, eyes staring at themselves in the mirror, occasionally making small-talk to the bartender or their neighbor. Around the edge of the dance floor there was an occasional couple at one of the tables, and over in one corner a party of seven or eight older folks, all gussied up for a night out, were having some kind of get-together, punctuated every once in a while by subdued laughter.

I was debating whether to have a non-alcoholic brew or to go for the real thing when the door to the outside was flung open and a familiar figure stepped inside. It was Jerry the guard from the Yearling Foundation. His eyes were as wide as saucers and even from the distance of my booth at the end of the bar I could see that his face was white as the bleached T-shirt he wore. He took a quick look around at the crowd, but from the look on his face, not much was registering with him. I leaned forward with my head on my hands and my eyes shaded, like a tired drunk, and let his gaze sweep past me. He took a seat at the bar and ordered a whiskey. When it came, he downed it in a gulp then ordered another, finishing it with the same dispatch. Fifteen minutes after he'd come in, he got up and left.

I waited half a minute then I stepped outside into the parking lot…in time to see a dark Camaro peel rubber as it turned onto the highway and headed down the mountain. I went back inside and waited.

After fifteen more minutes spent thinking about the coincidence of Jerry showing up at the Lonesome Pine Lodge, and still no sign of Karin Stengaard, I began to get a sick feeling in the pit of my stomach. I threw down a couple of bucks for the coffee and hustled out to the parking lot. When I got in my Jaguar I laid some rubber of my own heading up the highway toward town. The dark forest around me looked grim and threatening, the dim pavement a too narrow ribbon of safety. I accelerated into the hairpin curves, hoping that the feeling in my gut would turn out to be wrong. Within a mile I saw the flashing lights of a CHP vehicle and a Shambhala Police cruiser. I pulled numbly over to the side of the road.

I told myself that she didn't have to be dead, but I knew better. I got out and sprinted across the road. There was another Shambhala police cruiser pulling up behind the first one. It was Nils Larsen. Two state cops were leaning into the open door of a red Honda Civic, its nose smashed in like that of a Pekingese, wrapped around the trunk of a three foot diameter pine that had a big split running up it from the point of the car's impact. The cops were just looking. I saw a mass of blonde hair against the steering wheel and a lot of blood.

I heard Nils Larsen's voice from behind me. "What have we got?"

One of the CHP cops stepped away from the Honda. "She's dead, Chief. We got here too late. She must have hit that pine going fifty miles an hour. The airbags didn't work. I'd guess she died instantly." There was a pause. "Her name's Karin Stengaard, Chief."

"Jesus!" Nils swore. He was standing right next to me, but he hadn't noticed me yet. He looked over at me with sad eyes then started when he recognized whom I was.

"Christ almighty, McGowan. What are you doing here?"

I told him about the call from Karin and our planned rendezvous at the Lonesome Pine Lodge. I told him about Jerry.

"You think he had something to do with this?" Nils asked.

"He was spooked about something and if he came from the Foundation, he must have driven right past here.'

"Maybe before the accident. The CHP just happened on it fifteen minutes ago. The car's still warm."

"Jerry came in about twenty minutes, maybe a half hour ago," I volunteered.

Nils was moving around, looking in at Karin's body. I didn't want to see her like that. I kept remembering the bright face, the big blue eyes, the little girl voice.

"She was scared when she called me, Nils"

"Scared of what?" He was still moving around the little red car, examining the rear bumper, looking at the tire tracks.

"I don't know. She said she was still at work so I guess it was something or someone at the Foundation."

"You think it was Jerry."

The truth was I didn't know. It made sense that it was Jerry she was scared of, but maybe I just wanted it to be that way because I didn't like him. "You find something?" I asked Nils. He was on his knees over at the edge of the road.

"It looks as if she was on her brakes when she left the road."

"What does that mean?"

"I don't know. But she hit that tree going awfully fast if she was riding her brakes." The ambulance had arrived and the paramedics were heading toward Karin's car with a stretcher.

"Could someone have pushed her off the road?' I asked.

"There's some dents on her rear bumper, but I can't tell if they're recent." Nils stood up. "If she was going too fast…trying to get to your meeting…" His voice trailed off. "We have an accident on these curves every six weeks or so. She might have just gone too fast." His voice sounded tired. "I've known Karin since she was a little girl. I know her parents," he said. In the flashing lights from the ambulance and the cruisers I could see the pain on his face.

"She wanted to tell me something about Torres, Nils. Somebody didn't want her to. I think Jerry's involved in some way."

"I need more than just that Jerry came into the Lonesome Pine Lodge and looked nervous," Nils said. He stared over at the Honda. The paramedics were strapping Karin on the stretcher. They had her covered with a blanket. Nils stepped back. "I'll have her car checked first thing tomorrow morning," he said. "If this was more than an accident, I'll find the one responsible."

The paramedics were coming by with the stretcher. Nils and I both looked down at it as they passed. A few errant strands of blonde hair stuck out from the edge of the blanket. So long baby blue eyes.

CHAPTER NINE

I awoke the next morning thinking about Karin Stengaard. I didn't know if her death had been caused by Jerry or by anyone else, but I wasn't going to just let it go. My thoughts drifted over to Janice Le. She and Karin [were about the same age. The novice attorney had no idea what she might be dealing with. Even if Karin had died accidentally, the secretary was on her way to tell me something — something about Manuel Torres that she thought had some bearing on his death. And whatever it was, she was afraid to tell me about it while she was still at the Yearling Foundation.

Janice Le was naïve and she didn't appear to be the type who had the wisdom to know when she was in over her head. It was probably a good thing that she wasn't actively looking for explanations for Torres' death, other than that her client did it. It might not be safe for her to be poking around too much. Somebody had something he wanted to cover up and it was possible that he — or she — would go as far as murder to keep the cover up intact. That wasn't going to stop me, but it was probably better that I be the one to become a thorn in someone's side than that it be Ms. Le. I didn't at all mind being a thorn in Jerry's side, or Doctor Francine Stein's for that matter. In fact I was looking forward to it.

I had a quick cup of coffee and headed out to the Litton farm. Janice Le wasn't letting Jimmy talk to anyone with the police department, including me, unless she was present. Interviewing Jimmy's parents, though, was legitimate police business and Ms. Le couldn't demand to come along for the ride. The sky was clear, as it nearly always is in September, and the still air lay hot and dry over the valley like an electric blanket. In these low mountains the hottest months are usually late summer or early fall. I had the top down on my Jaguar as I followed the lazily winding road up the back of the valley. There weren't many houses this far out, just an occasional small farm or house trailer set close to the road. Most of the countryside was wild and overgrown with low scrub and thickets of oak and an occasional solitary pine. As the land rose more steeply toward the mountains, outcroppings of bare rock began to appear. It wasn't a place to grow much, but as I gained enough elevation to look back at the valley, I imagined I could see the Pacific in the distant haze. I was trying not to think about Karin Stengaard.

Jimmy Litton's family lived in a house trailer set on a concrete block foundation and surrounded by a group of ramshackle outbuildings, constructed out of a mixture of wood and corrugated metal. One of the buildings appeared to be a barn and the front end of a rusted out car stuck out of another. A tractor sat out in a field behind the house, pointing up the rocky hillside, as though it had gone as far up the hill as it could go and finally given up.

I waited for the dust to settle, then stepped out of my car. I thought I saw a motion behind the shed that housed the broken down car, but whatever it was disappeared before I had a chance to see whether it was a person or a farm animal. I decided to investigate. A quick look inside the shed told me that the car might not be as broken as I'd thought. Just in lousy condition. It was an early eighties Chevy Malibu with four good tires and needing a paint job and a little body work. It was probably the family transportation.

I was nosing around the car when a foot long two-by-four came sailing in through the door, narrowly missing my head. It bounced across the hood of the car and skittered off onto the floor. It had been thrown hard; hard enough to have caused some serious damage if it had hit me. As it was, it just put one more dent in the Chevy's hood. I waited a second to be sure that nothing else was going to come flying in, then I grabbed the missile and charged out of the shed, ready to teach someone a lesson about two-by-four etiquette. The dirt yard between the buildings was just as empty and silent as it had been when I'd arrived, but I heard something moving behind the shed. I held the two-by-four in my right hand and edged around the building.

The skinny, black and white Guernsey cow didn't look impressed. She raised her head to give me a lazy glance, then went back to feeding on the grass.

Throwing a stick seemed like the kind of thing a kid would do but Nils had said that Jimmy had no brothers or sisters. I looking around a little longer, then threw the two- by-four into the shed and headed for the house. There was a radio or TV going inside. The front door was open but a tired looking screen door barred the entrance. One side of the screen had split from the frame, leaving curled strands of wire, which looked like the frayed edges of an old shirt sleeve. I couldn't see anything inside except part of an entry wall covered in fake wood paneling and darkness beyond that. I knocked on the outside of the trailer next to the door.

The radio stayed on, but I heard a chair scraping and then footsteps. A large, heavyset man, unshaven and wearing jeans and a Raiders tee shirt, which had a yellow stain down the front and sweat rings under the arms, appeared at the door. He had on socks but no shoes and he looked irritated. "Yeah? What can

I do for you?" He sounded like he'd learned to talk listening to country music stations.

"Mr. Litton?"

He narrowed his eyes suspiciously. "Yeah?"

I introduced myself and told him I was with the police department. I asked if I could come in.

He ran his gaze up and down me. "You don't look like no police."

"I'm a special investigator, hired just to investigate this case. Chief Larsen arranged for my services."

"That bastard," the man said. He continued to look me over. Slowly he opened the screen. I stepped inside.

The interior of the trailer house was nicer than I'd expected. After the entry there was a good size kitchen, separated from the dining area by a chest-high counter. A small radio was sitting on the counter, and I could hear Rush Limbaugh's voice coming from it. On the left was a carpeted living room, neat, with a plaid couch and a matching, but worn, recliner facing a low wood and glass coffee table and a TV in front of the far wall. Across the living room were two newer looking easy chairs, both covered in a blue material that looked like terry cloth, and behind them, a hallway which must have led to the rest of the house. Mr. Litton led me into the dining area and motioned for me to sit at the table. "Beer?" he asked over his shoulder as he went to the counter and turned down the radio without turning it all the way off.

"No thanks," I said, giving him a steely-eyed stare. "I'm on duty." I felt very pleased with myself.

"You trying to hang this on my boy?" the man asked, heaving himself into a chair opposite me at the table. A half empty longneck Budweiser was in front of him. There were enough bottles sticking out of the waste can on the floor behind him that it might have won an award at a modern art competition.

"I'm actually trying to get your boy off," I said. "Chief Larsen doesn't think he killed that other boy. But the evidence is pretty much against him. I need to know more about Jimmy." I heard footsteps and turned to see a small, brown-haired, gray-faced lady coming down the hallway. She was wearing a faded but clean flower-print house dress. Her face looked like it might have been pretty once, but too much disappointment and not enough hope had robbed her of all but a memory of her earlier beauty. She stopped and looked at her husband inquiringly.

"Police...about Jimmy," her husband said. He didn't bother to introduce her to me.

I stood. "You're Jimmy's mother?"

She looked cautiously at her husband. His face showed no expression. "Yes," she said anxiously. "Have you talked to him?" She had the same Oklahoma twang as her husband.

"He's fine. I saw him yesterday. I'd like to talk to you both about your son."

She looked at her husband as if for permission. He waved in the direction of one of the chairs. She started to sit and then stopped, looking embarrassed.

"Would you like coffee Mr.....?"

"McGowan...Brian McGowan. No thanks. Your husband already offered me something."

She sat down and they both looked at me expectantly. She leaned forward over the table. He sat back scowling, his eyes narrowed distrustfully.

"Jimmy's being held on suspicion of killing another boy. The DA will decide whether to charge him with murder or manslaughter."

"Murder?" his mother looked stung.

"That's bullshit!" his father said, jutting out his chin angrily. "The kid who got killed was a no-account Mexican punk from that fancy school for delinquents. That Mex started the fight. It's not murder if Jimmy was defending hisself."

"It's more complicated than that, Mr. Litton. The other boy was beaten up sometime after the fight with Jimmy. Your son says he didn't do it, but some of the evidence points to him."

"What evidence?" the father asked. His face still had the belligerent expression but he couldn't hold the focus of his eyes for long. I wondered just how many beers he'd had that morning.

"Mostly that Jimmy was found sleeping not far from the body the next morning and, of course, the earlier fight."

Mrs. Litton inhaled sharply. Her husband snorted in disgust. "That's no evidence." He took a long drink from his beer as if to emphasize his point.

"The DA thinks it is. I'd like to know if Jimmy's been in trouble before. The DA mentioned Jimmy getting into fights. How often did that happen?"

"He's not a bad boy." His mother said. "He hardly ever fought."

"He defended hisself." Mr. Litton said. "That's all he ever did. Why blame Jimmy when he stands up to a damn beaner? Those Foundation kids are gang members. Jimmy was lucky it wasn't him what got killed. Mex kids carry knives. Jimmy ought to be a hero. He's only in jail cuz the fucking DA's a Mex hisself."

"The Mexicans are a problem around here," Mrs. Litton interjected. She looked embarrassed by her husband's comments.

"How so?"

"They've taken all the work. That's why my husband is home."

I said I thought he was home because he farmed the place.

"This place?" he sneered. "This place is all rocks. I grow what I can, but it's only enough to give us a few vegetables and barely keep a skinny-ass cow alive. I work for other people, but these damn Mexicans take all the work. They work for peanuts.

Why wouldn't they? Most of them ain't got houses. They live in the hills. They steal my chickens and rabbits when they want meat. All the money they earn goes to Tequila or gets sent home."

"So you're forced to sit home and listen to talk shows on the radio," I said.

He looked at me suspiciously, trying to figure out if I was making fun of him or not. "A day like today's too damn hot to be working outside. Mexicans don't mind the heat."

This was getting nowhere. "So what about Jimmy?" I said. "You never told me how often he got into fights. Any fights with Mexican's before?"

"Sometimes kids picked on Jimmy," his mother said.

"About what?"

She looked nervously at her husband, who was staring at either the table or his beer bottle. She looked over at me. "We couldn't give Jimmy everything some of the other boys had…clothes, fancy sneakers, things like that. Sometimes they made fun of him."

"Just the little rich shits," her husband growled, "or them damn Scandahoovians …the ones what think they own the town. Jimmy taught 'em a lesson or two."

"You mean he fought them?"

"Damn right." He looked over at his wife then muttered, "when he had to."

"How often?"

"Not much," his mother said.

"A few times," his father added. "We told him not to get in fights. We didn't want him getting kicked out of school."

"How bad is Jimmy's temper? When he's gotten mad, has he ever hurt anyone?"

Mrs. Litton again looked at her husband. He answered for both of them. "Who's he gonna get mad at around here? He gets mad at his mother and I'll box his ears. He knows better than to get mad at me."

I looked at his fat face and dull eyes. "What do you do when he gets mad at you, Mr. Litton?"

He leaned forward, an ugly look on his face. I knew what the answer was and he knew I knew it. He stopped himself before he admitted anything that might get him into trouble. "I told you he knows better." He drained the rest of his beer.

I stood to leave. "Who else besides the two of you is here?"

Mrs. Litton froze. This time her husband looked nervous too. "Just us," he said. His wife nodded her head vigorously.

I scratched my head. "Somebody threw a piece of wood at me when I was looking around your shed. I thought I saw someone run behind it."

"That don't make no sense, Mr. McGowan. There's only me and Ruth. Unless it was one of those Mex kids. Sometimes when the parents is off working, the kids come over and fool around on my property. They're as likely to swipe something as anything else. I wouldn't put it past one of 'em to throw something at you."

His wife still looked shaken by my question, but she wasn't about to add anything to her husband's explanation. There didn't seem to be any point in pursuing it. I thanked both of them and left.

CHAPTER TEN

The Ventura County Public Defender's Office said Janice Le was "out on assignment," so I left my name and number on her voice mail. I had done enough investigating to merit another try at her letting me help with Jimmy Litton's defense. Not that I'd found out anything particularly startling, but I knew I wanted to talk to the kid himself and try to get him to flesh out his story a bit more. So far he sounded like the kind of boy who might have given Manuel Torres a pretty good beating and Torres had been portrayed by Francine Stein as not much of a fighter. The only real anomaly was that Karin Stengaard had implied that something was being covered up about Torres. Maybe the coroner could help.

Before I headed to the morgue to talk to the coroner, I called Nils and asked him what had turned up in the investigation of Karin Stengaard's car crash.

"There were marks on her bumper, but the state police experts couldn't say when they'd occurred, except not long enough ago to have rusted over. We haven't had rain for a month, so that's not enough to tell us anything. Her car was old and not in very good shape and besides the airbags not working, the brakes were nearly shot, so she might have used them but they wouldn't have stopped her car from hitting that tree, not at the speed she was going."

"What about Jerry's car?"

"What about it?"

"Was his bumper scratched too?"

"I sent one of my men out to the Foundation to take a look, but his Camaro was clean. Course he could have pushed her and not left a mark on his car... but we don't have anything to go on, really. The CHP has ruled it an accident."

I still had my suspicions, but I wasn't sure what to do with them. I thanked Nils and told him I was on my way to talk to the coroner.

"I saw his report. You'll be surprised," was all Nils would say.

I never would have guessed that Bill Todd was a coroner. My experience with the kind of physicians who went into forensic pathology was that they usually had no choice. They were such cold fish that no living patient would have chosen to see them. Todd was different. He was a short, stocky to the point of almost being rotund, man of about sixty who listened to me as attentively as if I were describing some mysterious malady that was ailing me.

I asked him to go over his report concerning the manner of Torres' death and then tell me anything else he had found that might be odd or unusual. Since I didn't know what I was looking for, it was hard to be more specific.

Todd told me that Torres had died of multiple wounds, the fatal ones probably being blows to the head, although the kidney damage he had received from being kicked would have killed him, albeit more slowly. He was also bitten and strangled, but the strangulation had occurred after he was dead, although Todd admitted that his assailant might not have known that.

"Bitten?" I asked. Biting wasn't all that usual in a gang fight, but it was usually done in self-defense… to get out of someone's grasp.

"Like an animal would bite someone. But they were human bites, not animal ones… on the neck and hands."

"Could it have been more than one person who did it?" I asked.

Todd stroked his chin, then ran his hand over his nearly bald pate. "I've never seen anyone beaten by another individual this badly. That in itself would suggest some kind of gang beating. On the other hand, the majority of blows were on the left side of Torres' body and head, suggesting a single right-handed assailant. Same thing with the kicks; all from the same side and delivered to about the same area of the body. The pattern of blows suggests one person…a very strong person."

"Really? Jimmy Litton didn't impress me as being particularly big or strong."

Todd cocked his head to the side. "The person who beat this boy was tall…at least six foot two because the blows all had a downward arc and the victim was five eleven himself. I'd say the person must weigh about two hundred pounds. Either that or he's extremely muscular. These blows were delivered with a lot of force." He stopped and thought a minute. "Course whoever did it could have been on something like PCP. I've read that some drugs can increase strength enough to make it seem like the assailant is a lot bigger and stronger than he actually is."

"But not taller," I said. "You told Detwiler this…about the size of the person who beat Torres?" I asked the coroner.

"Sure. He didn't seem to like it too much. Sure as hell weakens his case against the Litton kid. You can bet he's not gonna ask me any questions that would bring this out at the trial. Course it's all in my report."

"How about Litton's lawyer? She been to talk to you?"

He shook his head sorrowfully. "Probably won't either. Public Defenders don't have the time to interview a coroner. They get the report. Sometimes they notice the important things, sometimes they don't. I don't know anything about the Le lady, except she's just a kid and she's new. Let's hope she's sharp."

"Yeah, let's" I echoed.

I wasn't going to rely on Janice Le's perspicacity. Jimmy Litton couldn't have inflicted the kind of damage on Manuel Torres that had killed him and Detwiler was going ahead with the prosecution anyway, or so it sounded. Miss Le was going to be aware of the coroner's findings if I had to read them to her out loud. The coroner's report was the kind of evidence that could garner a dismissal if it was presented the right way.

"Anything else?" I asked.

"I don't know what it means but Torres had some kind of disease, an auto-immune disease of some sort as far as I can tell. It may just have been the aftermath of a bad infection, but I couldn't find any infected tissue. His white count was way up, like his immune system was fighting something, a real bad infection or…"

"Or what?"

"I saw the same thing once when I examined a man who'd had a transplant, liver in his case. He died of liver disease, but his body had rejected the transplant. The rejection had shot his white count way up."

"Torres had had an organ transplant?"

"No, certainly not." Todd looked away, as if he were embarrassed to say what he was saying. "Not in someone as young as he was." He swung his eyes back and stared at me. "He may have had a bone marrow transplant. There were incision wounds on the caudal portion of his spine—his tailbone—they weren't from the fight. They were about a month old.."

"He had leukemia?"

"Possibly. But if it was leukemia, then with a white count like that he should have been near death, not running around getting into fights."

"Doctor Stein said he'd had a throat infection."

Todd shrugged. "I didn't find any infected tissue. But then I was looking for wounds, not infections. She didn't mention a bone marrow operation? Didn't say he had cancer?"

Stein hadn't mentioned anything like that. I told him that she'd said he had an infection and that she'd treated him for it recently. "Wouldn't he have to go somewhere to have a transplant?" I asked.

Todd nodded. "UCLA would be the closest. Only major medical centers do that sort of thing."

"Then there'd have to be a record of it."

"I already checked. Torres was never a patient at UCLA or at Loma Linda That's the other center in this area that does transplants."

"So..."

"So maybe that's not what it was. Maybe it was a biopsy or something. Francine Stein might even have done it herself."

"A geneticist doing surgery?"

"It wasn't much of a surgery. The cut was very small and the bone's near the surface at the place of the incision. Anyway that's not what killed him. And whatever drove his white cell count up wasn't what killed him either. As far as I'm concerned it's just an anomaly. I'm more worried about who it was that beat him this badly. Whoever it is, is dangerous and vicious."

I agreed. I thanked Bill Todd and left the morgue, which was in the basement of the small county hospital on the outskirts of Shambhala. As soon as I got home I gave Janice Le another ring. This time she was in.

Her voice was quietly polite. She told me she hadn't gotten the coroner's report yet. I summarized Doctor Todd's findings for her.

"I appreciate the information, Mr. McGowan. When I receive the report I will examine it closely. I will point out the pertinent parts of the report to the District Attorney." She was telling me to fuck off again.

"Mr. Detwiler could be difficult. He doesn't like your client's family," I volunteered, still trying to engage her in some kind of dialogue about the case.

"I understand very well about prejudice. If Mr. Detwiler can be convinced, I will convince him. I am quite competent Mr. McGowan."

I felt as if I were walking on eggshells. "I don't doubt your competence. I'm just making an attempt to help out."

"Why are you making this offer?"

"There's something about this case that makes me worried. A secretary who was going to give me some information about Manuel Torres was killed in a suspicious accident. I don't want you poking around in dangerous places, especially when I can do that kind of thing just as easily."

She was silent. When she finally spoke, her voice had softened. "I do not understand your concern for me, but I appreciate your kindness. I am Vietnamese, Mr. McGowan. My family escaped Vietnam with only their lives. As a small child I lived in refugee camps in Thailand and in the Philippines. I lived many months on a boat. In America I was raised in a neighborhood in which gangs and local strongmen threatened my parents and me every day. I have survived and become educated far beyond anyone else in my family. I am not frightened by danger. I have learned to live with it."

I'd known enough refugees who had relocated to Little Saigon in Orange County to know that she was right. The Vietnamese who came in the second great wave of immigrants—those who were not from the social and economically elite strata of Vietnamese society—lived a hard life. The gang underworld of Little Saigon was as ruthless as any in the larger cities. To make it out of that environment and into law school and a position like Janice Le was in required a strong sense of will and great deal of toughness. But she was still a very young woman. And I didn't know what or who might want to stop her if she found out too much.

"I believe you can take care of yourself, Ms Le. But I still want to help you. If not for your sake, at least because neither myself nor Chief Larsen thinks your client is guilty. We want to be able to give you the evidence to prove that."

She seemed to be thinking things over. "I will accept your help, Mr. McGowan. I want to look into a few more things myself, then we will talk. I would like to know whatever you have found out."

"You'll remember my warning? I know you can take care of yourself, but we should both be cautious. There may be information, particularly about the Torres boy, that someone doesn't want us to reveal."

"Do not worry. I will be safe."

That sounded as close to agreement as we were going to get. "I'll keep in touch," I said.

"Please do."

CHAPTER ELEVEN

It was mid-afternoon and I was hungry and worn out from trying to convince Janice Le that she and I were on the same side. A year ago I would have fed my weariness and my appetite with a three martini lunch. That was before my heart attack. I went to the refrigerator and took out some cold fruit salad and a bottle of diet fruit drink. Being healthy isn't synonymous with having fun.

I went out on my porch and sat down in my oak rocker, putting the plate of salad on the little matching oak table next to it. As I ate, I thought about how I'd been going to a lot of trouble to find out what happened the night Manuel Torres was killed and the person who knew the most about it, except maybe the real killer, was sitting right there in the Shambhala jail. I called Nils to tell him I wanted to question Jimmy Litton.

"You'd better get your butt over here pronto, then," was Nils' answer. "Somebody tried to break Jimmy out of jail this morning. I've got a dead guard and a nearly ruined cell block."

"Who?"

"I don't know…except he—or they—are destructive and strong as hell."

"His father?"

"Have you met his father?"

"I withdraw the question. What about Jimmy?"

"He's still here. Whoever it was couldn't get into his cell. Almost tore it apart trying, and injured Jimmy in the process. He was unconscious when we got to him. Says he can't tell us anything. No description, no nothing. I'm on my way to talk to him again. You can come along if you get here in time."

"What about Ms. Le?"

"What about her? I'm asking Jimmy about the break in, not about Torres' murder. He doesn't need a lawyer for this."

Nils was right. I hung up, shoved the plate and fork in the dishwasher, and hopped in my convertible to head for the jail.

I had expected to see an ambulance in front of the jail, but I guess they had already removed the body of the dead deputy. I could see the damage to the building as soon as got out of my car. The front door, which was at least three inches of solid wood, was completely off its hinges and a couple of city workmen were trying to lift it from the floor and presumably hang it again. I hesitated while they heaved it upright. Either because of the exertion or because I was waiting to go past them, they leaned the door against the wall and let me pass.

When I reached the Litton boy's cell, he was lying on his bed with a bandage on his head. A very large, pear shaped nurse in starched whites was just leaving the cell. She gave me a look which suggested that she regarded me an unavoidable nuisance and announced, to no one in particular, "He needs to rest, not talk to all of you."

The Shambhala Jail was more like a group of small private rooms than it was like the kind of cell block you'd find in a big city. Each cell had a wooden door, reinforced with strips of steel and with a small barred window at head height. The bars had been completely knocked out of Jimmy's cell window and the door badly battered, but it had apparently not given way. I guessed that Jimmy had been struck by one or more of the bars from the window and knocked unconscious. That must have been why he hadn't been able to escape through the open window in the door. Unless he hadn't wanted to escape. Maybe whoever had broken into the jail hadn't wanted to help Jimmy so much as to get to him. Nils looked up at me as I approached the cell. His expression was glum.

"Did anybody see who it was?" I asked.

"Only the deputy who was on duty and he was beaten so badly that he died before we could get him to the hospital. He never had a chance to tell us anything." Nils' eyes showed his sadness.

"How about him?" I asked, nodding in Jimmy's direction.

"He says he didn't see anything. He heard all the commotion and went to the window in his door and the next thing he knew he was waking up on the floor and I was coming into his cell."

"Other prisoners?"

"There aren't any."

"The price of an idyllic community," I said. Nils scowled at me.

"I suppose you didn't see anything?" I asked him.

"The station's across the street. I was in my office. The deputy on duty, Jamison, the one who was killed, buzzed me, but when I came on the intercom, I didn't get an answer. It took me a few minutes before I decided I'd better investigate. When I got here, Jamison was dead, Jimmy was out cold and nobody else was around.

"Whoever it was took the front door right off its hinges," I said.

"Makes me think it wasn't one person," Nils commented.

I was thinking about the coroner's observations. "Or one very strong person."

Nils raised his eyebrows. "He'd have to be a fucking Arnold Schwarzenegger."

"Arnold hang around this town very often?" I asked.

Nils frowned.

"You think they were trying to break Jimmy out, or were they coming after him?"

Nils shook his head. "Can't think who'd want to do either of those."

I looked down at Jimmy. His eyes were foggy and his forehead was already swelling under a large gauze patch that was fastened with adhesive tape over what must have been a nasty abrasion. He probably hadn't faked being unconscious.

"Tell us what happened," I said.

Jimmy's look was still slightly out of focus as he stared up at me. "I got knocked out."

"How?"

He gave me a blank look. When he shrugged his shoulders it seemed to cause him more pain and he brought his hand up to his head and felt the bump. "I don't know. Somebody knocked the bars in on me. I don't know who."

"What did you hear?"

Jimmy dropped his gaze to the floor. "The cop out front yelled. I heard a lot of fighting. Then it stopped. When I went to the window I got hit."

"No voices?"

He shook his head.

"How about footsteps? One person? More than one person?"

"Chief Larsen already asked me that. I couldn't tell. It didn't sound like a lot of people."

I wandered over to the door. Somebody had tried to do the same thing to it that they'd done to the front door. The hinges were bent a little, but they'd held.

"What did they hit it with?" I asked Nils.

"Foot or shoulder, I guess. Nothing that left marks."

"Jesus. That's how they knocked the front door off, too?"

"Looks like it."

"No tools used to open the doors and no weapon used on the guard. Just somebody's strength. And it doesn't sound like it was planned very well. When whoever it was couldn't get in Jimmy's cell, they just left. So we're talking big, strong and stupid."

"And a killer," Nils said, looking with concern at Jimmy. Jimmy avoided looking at him.

"Who would have come after you?" I asked the kid.

Jimmy looked surprised. "You think they wanted me?"

I looked around. "I don't see anyone else here. They tried to bust down your door."

He stared back at me. "I don't know."

"Any idea whether they were trying to rescue you or do the same thing to you that they did to the guard?'

"What, kill me?" The kid looked shocked, as if he hadn't thought of the possibility before.

"Then you thought it was someone trying help you escape?"

He shrugged again. "I don't know. I wasn't trying to escape."

Nils had been listening to everything. "You told us you saw some very large person standing in the shadows at the school, watching Torres and his girl friend."

Jimmy still avoided Nils' eyes. "Yeah," he muttered.

"Big enough to do all this?" Nils asked.

Jimmy looked around like he was trying to come to a judgment about how big someone would have to be to break into the jail and bust the bars out of his window. "Maybe," was his conclusion.

I looked at Nils. He hadn't told me about any large person or about a girlfriend. "We need to talk," I said. It was Nils' turn to shrug.

Jimmy looked tired. I backed out of his cell and walked back down the cell block toward the door leading out to the front desk where the guard was killed. Nils came after me. When I'd passed through the door and was at the front desk I stopped. The two workmen had the door back on a new set of hinges and were tightening up the screws. I turned back to Nils. "What's this about a girl with Torres and some big guy that Jimmy saw?"

"I thought you knew. Jimmy told his lawyer about it."

"His lawyer hasn't told me jack shit."

Nils didn't look at all contrite. "When we picked Jimmy up he was sleeping in a shed on the Krishna school property. We asked him if he'd seen Torres again after their fight. He told us no. Later when Ms. Le interviewed him, he told her that when he was about to go to sleep, he'd heard voices and he looked out and saw Torres with some girl. He thought she was one of the Krishna School girls. They were talking and making out, I guess. Then he saw somebody watching them. He couldn't see them very clearly cuz it was night and whoever it was, was behind some bushes. But he said it was somebody very large. He watched for awhile then the person left. Pretty soon Torres and the girl did too."

"Nice piece of information for you to forget to tell me. Janice Le left it out, too. That means there's at least one witness—the girl—that Torres was alive after his fight with Jimmy. And the big guy is probably the killer. Your coroner says that whoever beat Torres was super strong and big. That's probably who did all this, too."

Nils nodded. "I don't think either Ms. Le or I meant to leave you out. I don't think either she or I believed the part about the big guy in the bushes...until now."

"What about the girl? Have you found her?"

"I was going to go out to the Krishna School today and see if I could identify her. When we found the body, I hadn't heard Jimmy's story about a girl yet."

"Did you ask the school people later?"

"They said they'd check. Frankly, I thought maybe Jimmy'd made it up so I didn't push too hard."

I looked around at the devastation and the blood still on the floor from the dead guard. "I don't think he made it up. And I'll bet that when Bill Todd examines your deputy, he finds that the beating was very similar to the one that killed Torres."

"You mean Torres killer did this?" Nils looked confused. "Why would he come here?"

"To get rid of his only witness."

"Jesus fucking Christ!" Nils swore. Then he looked even more worried. "Jimmy may not be the only witness."

"The girl?"

Nils nodded. "We better the hell get over to that school and find out who she is."

"We?" I asked.

"You're still on the case aren't you?" Nils said. "I just lost a deputy. I'm understaffed. I'll take any help I can get."

"It feels so good to be wanted," I said.

CHAPTER TWELVE

The Krishna School was an attractive complex of Spanish-style, red-tile roofed, one-story stucco buildings that looked more like a Mexican hacienda than a school. In contrast to the dry, brown grass and dust found every place else in Shambhala, the school's grounds were covered by a well-manicured deep green carpet of grass. There looked to be about ten or twelve buildings in all, spread out over maybe four or five acres. Chief Larsen pulled his cruiser into the paved parking lot and we followed a red brick path marked with signs painted with arrows pointing the way to the office. Most of the buildings we passed had large windows, opened wide to let in air. Inside, students in white shirts and short pants, both boys and girls, were having lessons taught by faculty, often dressed in robes, even some of the men. I stopped a minute outside one window to watch a young woman in a diaphanous orange sari as she solved a series of differential equations on a blackboard. Her students looked like they were only twelve or thirteen years old.

Chief Larsen's attention had been captured by something else. He'd wandered a little way down a side path which was so densely covered by brilliant red bougainvillea on either side that it looked almost like a tunnel, and he was standing just to one side of another open window. He motioned me to join him and keep quiet. As I moved closer, I heard occasional heavy grunts and loud thuds coming from inside the building.

I sidled up next to the Chief and craned my neck so I could see inside. Half a dozen young men—maybe sixteen or seventeen years old—were standing in a line. Each one wore a loose fitting pair of white pants, no shirt and no shoes. They faced a man, maybe in his forties, dressed as they were, gray haired, tall, and heavily muscled.

"Watch this," Larsen whispered.

The young man at the head of the line began slowly to circle the teacher. As the youth moved in on the older man, the student began a series of deft feints to the left and right, still circling slowly, hands raised in the air. Then, with a rush, he attacked…a leaping kick, then a straight-arm thrust, and finally a spinning attempt to sweep the teacher's legs from beneath him. With one smooth movement the teacher slammed the student to the floor, jamming his knee on the boy's chest and raising one hand high above his head, poised to deliver the coup de grace. The teacher's arm quivered in anticipation, like an arrow held by an archer's bowstring drawn to the point of breaking. The student's eyes were wide with terror. Nils reflexively began to move toward the window. I grabbed his arm and we both watched the teacher struggle to bring himself under control. Finally he did. Instead of the final blow, the teacher thrust the student aside, barking a short lecture: pointing out where the student had erred in his attack, how the teacher had so easily gained his advantage. The boy scrambled to his feet and anxiously joined the others back in line, a mixture of relief and lingering fear apparent in his eyes.

"I guess they don't just teach non-violence and meditation here," Larsen said quietly.

I nodded. "Some day they're liable to lose a student in one of those lessons. I'd hate to meet up with that big fellow on a dark night."

Larsen looked at me sharply.

"Let's find the office and talk to the headmaster, " I said, moving down the walkway in the direction indicated by the arrows.

"Headmistress," Larsen corrected me. I'd forgotten he'd been here before.

The office was in what looked like the largest and perhaps the oldest of the buildings. It was white stucco like the others, but the wooden porch looked worn by years of traffic going in and out the building's double front doors, which were propped open to let in an afternoon breeze. Years of use had burnished the wood throughout the lobby so that it gleamed like the inside of a fine old yacht. The wide planked wooden floor was covered by a massive, circular oriental rug with a faded abstract design that reminded me of monkeys holding on to each others' tails and balancing small suns on their heads. Old leather covered chairs were scattered haphazardly in small groupings, giving the appearance of a men's club lounge minus the comatose old men and the ashtrays. The walls were covered with framed pictures. They were all of the same person but at various ages, always dressed in the same white pants and shirt, sometimes with a little Nehru hat and sometimes bareheaded, and in the company of a who's who of the world's leaders for most of the last century. In ten yards of wall space I picked out Churchill, Gandhi, Truman, and Kennedy. I stopped looking at that point because an incredibly old looking woman in a flowing red sari, seated at a massive wooden desk in the back of the lobby, interrupted my perusal of the wall by asking Larsen and me if she could help us.

"We'd like to speak to the Headmistress," Larsen said, "I'm Chief Larsen with the Shambhala Police."

The woman rose and tottered toward a door directly behind her. She knocked softly and then, apparently not waiting for a response, opened the door and disappeared inside.

"Who's the guy in the pictures?" I asked Larsen.

"Raja Krishna, the school's founder. He was sort of a philosopher, mystic, religious leader. Pretty well known. He had a lot of influence. Wrote several books. I've read a few, but they're beyond me. He lived till he was about ninety. Didn't die until maybe twenty-five years ago."

"Sure as hell knew everybody important," I said.

"A lot of them came here to visit him. Sort of like a pilgrimage to the master."

"How come I never heard of this Roger guy?" I asked.

"Raja," Larsen corrected me.

"Whatever. I never heard of the guy."

Larsen looked at me deadpan. "You spend a lot of time reading Eastern Philosophy?"

"I see what you mean," I said.

The old woman emerged from the room behind her desk and crept toward us. I resisted an impulse to take her arm and help her into her chair.

"Mrs. Dil will see you," she said in a soft voice. Despite her myriad wrinkles, her face had a warm, youthful glow that surprised me when she got close to us. She led us at a snail's pace into the next room, which turned out to be a large office occupied by a diminutive woman, standing in its center to greet us.

"Chief Larsen!" the woman before us exclaimed. She looked overjoyed to see Nils again.

"Mrs. Dil," Larsen said, nodding, his Gary Cooper poker face having been put on for the occasion. He even looked as if he was sucking in his belly. "This is Brian McGowan, an attorney. He's helping me in the investigation of the death of the boy we found on your property Sunday morning."

Mrs. Dil was a tiny woman. I'd expected the headmistress to be someone who looked like the old woman who'd greeted us in the outer room, but the woman in front of us was dressed in a short-sleeved yellow tee shirt, a skirt that came just to her knees, and a pair of sandals. She had great looking legs, from the knees down anyway, especially since I could tell from her face that she must be in her mid-sixties. Her hair was cut shoulder length and curled under at the ends, a mixture of brown and gray. She didn't seem to be wearing much makeup or making any particular attempt to cover up her wrinkles, but there was something about her face that looked as youthful as a teenager. Her features seemed to be a mixture of Indian and European and she had one of those baby faces that never seems to lose its preteen look, even in old age. Her eyes practically danced, they were so alive. It was as if a mischievous thirteen year old had somehow gotten trapped in a body that was growing old. A female Peter Pan.

She bounced across the room and extended her hand. When she looked at me, there was enough of a teasing sparkle in her eye that I wouldn't have been surprised if she'd winked at me. "Brian!" she exclaimed. "So glad you could visit our school. I hope we can help you in some way."

I had no doubt that she meant it.

She gave Chief Larsen a hug. In fact, I thought she held him a little longer than she needed to. I was starting to see why he'd been so busy trying to strike the right pose. Nils looked uncomfortable with what he had to tell her.

"We've gotten some more information about what went on the night the Torres boy was killed here, Mrs. Dil. We need to talk to you about it, maybe talk to one of your students." He was holding his hat in his hand and shifting from one foot to another like a school boy talking to his girlfriend.

"Now Nils, I've told you to call me Fanny. When you say Mrs. Dil I think my mother-in-law, God rest her soul, just entered the room. You two take seats. What student are you talking about?" She flopped into a big easy chair in front of the desk and threw one leg over the other just enough to show a little more knee.

The Chief swallowed hard and tried to keep from looking at Mrs. Dil's knee. "I didn't know it when I talked to you the other morning, but the boy who's charged with killing Torres says he saw him with one of your female students that night. If it's true, she may be a witness and she might even be in danger."

For just a brief moment Mrs. Dil looked alarmed. Then she gazed at Nils and smiled sweetly. "It's quite true, Nils. One of our girls was with the poor boy on Saturday night. It seems they had been seeing each other for nearly two weeks. I only found out today or I would have called you. The poor child was terribly upset. I think she cared for the boy a great deal. However, she knows nothing about his death."

Larsen took the information with the same calmness as she had given it. "I'll have to talk to her, Fanny. Brian will too."

Fanny Dil nodded. "What did you mean when you said she might be in danger?"

"Someone broke into the jail today. It could have been the person who killed the Torres boy."

"I thought the boy in jail was the one who did it."

"It's not looking that way. Whoever did do it may think that the boy I have in jail is a witness. He may also think that your student is a witness. If he does, she could be in danger."

Mrs. Dil sighed. "Then it must happen. I'm sorry. I wanted to protect her, but the truth is the only real protection. My father often said that."

"Her father was Raja Krishna," Larsen said to me.

"And the girl you want to talk to is his great-granddaughter," Mrs. Dil added, a wistful hint of sadness in her voice.

"Your granddaughter?" I asked.

"She's a wonderful young girl."

"How old is she, Fanny?" I asked. Chief Larsen looked doubly uncomfortable with this new information.

"Fifteen."

"Did you know about her relationship with Torres?"

"No, but she wasn't hiding it. She just hadn't told me. Her father knew."

"And he approved?"

She smiled at my question. "Saraya is fifteen. She can make her own decisions about boyfriends. It's the Krishna way to encourage responsible, critical decision making, not take decisions out of our children's hands, Brian."

"Torres was a gang member, a criminal," I said. "Most parents wouldn't want their daughter seeing a boy like him."

"She said he was nice. Gentle. That's how she described him. She said he was so gentle she was afraid for him. He seemed defenseless."

It sounded as though Torres' behavior was consistent. Both Jimmy and Francine Stein had described him in much the same terms. He didn't sound like the kind of kid who ought to be in the Foundation program, unless the program had changed his behavior.

"Can we talk to your granddaughter?" I asked.

"You can be present when we talk to her, Fanny," Nils Larsen interjected. He had come out of his funk, but he still looked bothered.

"I'd like her father here, too," Mrs. Dil said.

"Is her mother also here?" I asked.

"Her mother died when she was a baby. Her father—my son—raised her, here at the school. I've been her mother, mostly."

Mrs. Dil rang a buzzer on the side of her desk and the woman from the lobby came wobbling into the room. She was asked to bring the girl and her father to the office.

CHAPTER THIRTEEN

In the interim before Mrs. Dil's granddaughter and her father arrived at the office I tried to get a little more information about the school.

"Your father started this school, Fanny?" I asked.

She smiled brightly, seemingly unperturbed by the serious business involving her granddaughter. "In the early fifties. He had lived here off and on from the 1930's. During the second world war he began bringing people here to visit him, holding lectures and seminars. From that, the idea of a school was a natural one."

I confessed that I knew almost nothing about her father.

"He may be one of the most important figures of the last century," she answered. "His ideas and his personal influence on other leaders are what make him important. Intangibles mostly. That's why many people know nothing of him. He also discouraged the development of any type of following. My father was always suspicious of what we now call 'cults of personality'."

"He was a philosopher?"

"That's how he's usually regarded. He saw himself as an educator, a de-mystifier. How did Wittgenstein put it? 'To show the fly the way out of the bottle'…that was my father's goal."

"And the school follows his philosophy?"

"To the extent that he had one. We try to expand children's minds." She glanced saucily at Chief Larsen. "Don't get alarmed Nils. I'm not referring to using drugs or chemicals. That sort of experimentation stopped after the sixties."

"You mean it was part of your program at one time?" I asked.

"Never officially, but we experimented along with everyone else. Some of my father's friends were particularly enthralled with the role of drugs in expanding consciousness. You know the people...Dr. Leary, Mr. Huxley. We tried to incorporate what we called enhanced learning into our program for awhile, but the negative publicity outweighed any advantages. Our program has a simple philosophy, Brian. We push children's mind's to their limits, especially in math, science, and music. We believe these subjects create a foundation for creative, original thinking. We also place very few limitations on how our children learn. Chemically enhanced learning is no longer part of the program, but almost any other kind of experimentation is." Fanny's pride in the school showed in her animated manner.

I was hooked into hearing more. "Experimentation such as...?" I asked.

"Learning through relationships—both platonic and sexual relationships, alternative living arrangements, solitude—any of these may be explored by our students. We also encourage physical activities that expand our children's awareness of themselves and their relationship to their environment. This includes, mountain climbing, skydiving, scuba, even bungee jumping...my favorite, by the way."

I was beginning to see why no one at the school might have been alarmed by her granddaughter's relationship with a delinquent from the Foundation. It seemed that almost anything was OK at the Krishna School. "What about self discipline," I asked. "How do the children learn that they also need to say no to some things in life?" A little voice in my head said, "look who's talking", but I ignored it.

"Usually they suffer the consequences of their decisions. That is the surest way to learn a lesson. We also teach responsibility, however. Responsibility for one's self and to one's community. We are all responsible for one another here. It is our responsibility to allow our friends to be who they are, and to protect them when the world threatens."

I had a flashback to the scene in the karate class. These people were serious about protection.

"Thank you, Fanny," I said. "I think I'd like to learn more. Maybe I'll read one of your father's books." I smiled at her. "Why don't you dress in the Indian garb like the other women here?"

"My mother was an American. She allowed me to choose my attire. From the time that I was a young girl, I thought a sari was something for an old woman to wear. It covers up all the parts of your body you want to show off. I tried it for awhile when my husband, who was Indian, was alive, but it wasn't me. Maybe when I think I don't have anything to show off anymore, I'll start wearing one again. But that's not now." She raised her eyebrows seductively at Nils Larsen and recrossed her shapely legs. Larsen's face reddened a little, but he had a hard time not looking at her legs. Mrs. Dil's eyes sparkled.

I thought about quoting Ghandi, that "love means never having to wear your sari," but then I realized I'd gotten the *Mahatma* mixed up with Ali McGraw.

There was soft knock at the door and it slowly opened. An exquisite teenage version of Mrs. Dil entered the room. She was a tiny creature, with large, innocent looking dark brown eyes, which stared like a fawn's from a soft but perfectly molded dusky face. Coal black hair was drawn back tightly and hung down her back in a thick braid. She wore the short-sleeved white shirt and white shorts that I'd seen on the other students at the school. Her slim dark legs, with their adolescent smoothness, had the same perfect proportions that would stand up to time as well as her grandmother's had. She looked startled to find that the older woman had company.

"I'm sorry," the girl murmured and began to back out of the room. Just then the door opened wide and a tall, muscular man in white cotton pants and a crisp yellow shirt, open at the collar, strode into the room. I recognized him as the instructor in the class on self-defense.

"Saraya, Adamji, come in please." Mrs. Dil motioned for her granddaughter and the man, who I guessed was her son, to enter the room. "We have guests who must ask you questions about the boy who was killed."

The girl immediately dropped her gaze to the floor. Her father looked at his mother with thinly veiled irritation. When he swung his gaze over to Nils and myself he omitted the veil.

"The truth is our greatest protection, Adamji," Mrs. Dil said. Her son nodded, but his clenched jaw told me that he didn't completely agree. Mrs. Dil turned to Nils Larsen. She looked at him a moment with a beatific smile. "Saraya is still grieving, Nils. Remember that when you ask her your questions."

Larsen turned to the girl, who was still looking at the floor. "I'm Chief Larsen and this is Mr. McGowan, Saraya. We only need to know about that night." His voice had the same gentle tone he'd used with Jimmy Litton. The granddaughter slowly raised her soft dark eyes to gaze quietly at Nils.

"I will tell you whatever you need to know," she said, her voice barely louder than a whisper. She gave a quick smile to reassure her grandmother. Her father's gaze darted back and forth between Nils and me, as if he were trying to decide which of us was the greater threat to his daughter.

Nils glanced briefly up at the father, then he turned his gaze on the girl. "How badly was Manuel hurt when you saw him that night?"

"His nose was bleeding, but he said he was all right. I asked him if he needed any medical help and he said he didn't. After a while he seemed to forget about his nose."

"Was he afraid of getting attacked again?"

"He was afraid to go back to the Foundation. He said his friends were trying to force him to fight. He hated fighting."

"He was afraid they would force him to fight if he went back to the Foundation that night?"

"He said he was."

"Was he afraid of the boy he'd gotten in a fight with in town?"

"I don't think so. He said the others had made the two of them fight."

Nils glanced over at me to be sure I was hearing everything.

"Did you notice anyone else when you were with Manuel? Anyone walking by or standing around?"

She looked startled. "No…was someone else there?"

"We don't know," Nils answered. "You're sure you didn't see anyone…standing in the bushes, perhaps?"

Saraya shook her head.

"Are you questioning my daughter's honesty, Chief Larsen?" Adamji Dil asked, a challenging look on his face.

Nils looked embarrassed. "Of course not," he answered, with a self-conscious glance at Fanny Dil.

"How long had you known about your daughter's friendship with the Torres boy?" I asked the father.

Adamji Dil bristled at my question. His back stiffened and he stared at me suspiciously. "I'd known about it for more than a week. Why do you ask, Mr. McGowan?"

I shrugged. "I like to get a complete picture of things." I turned to his daughter. "How long had you known Manuel?"

"About two weeks."

"And you told your father about it, soon after you started

the relationship?"

The girl glanced at her father. He was too busy glaring at me to give her any help. "My father knew about it soon after I began to see Manny," she said.

"You told him about it?"

She hesitated. Truth and loyalty to her father were in conflict. She looked at him again for help.

"I found the two of them together," her father answered for her. "That's how I knew she was seeing the boy. Why are you asking these questions?" I could hear the warning in his voice.

"I told you I'd like to get a complete picture. Did you try to stop the relationship, Mr. Dil?"

"My daughter makes her own decisions, Mr. McGowan. That is how we do things here. I respect her ability to make choices."

"But you also believe in protecting her if her choices begin to threaten her safety. Isn't that also the way you do things here?"

"What do you mean?" he asked, a hard edge creeping into his voice.

"I mean you'd be pretty capable of handling a sixteen year old boy if you wanted him to stop seeing your daughter."

Adamji took a step toward me. "Are you accusing me of something, Mr. McGowan?"

Mrs. Dil was looking curiously at her son. Larsen looked as if he was getting irritated with me. "I'm a defense lawyer by profession, Mr. Dil," I said. "I don't usually accuse people of anything." Of course I was being a cop at the moment, but I was glossing over that point.

Adamji Dil looked at me sullenly without saying anything.

"Do you think my son was involved in the boy's death, Brian?" Mrs. Dil didn't beat around the bush. Her voice was even, not friendly or unfriendly.

"I wouldn't make a judgment like that, Fanny. I'm trying to find out exactly what happened the night that boy was killed.

At least four people knew your granddaughter was with Manny Torres that night; Manny and Saraya, my client, and one more person, someone large who stood in the shadows and watched them."

"You think it was my son?"

"That's what I'd like to find out."

"*Were* you watching them, Adamji?" She spoke with an authority I hadn't heard in her voice before.

Adamji's back stiffened. He looked directly at his mother. "No," he answered softly.

Mrs. Dil's face softened. She smiled at me politely, but the warmth was gone from her eyes. "There. You have your answer, Brian. Now, I think you've asked enough questions. If you need to know more, you can come back again."

She rose and Nils and I did the same. The Chief looked frustrated and he cast a sour glance my way. We muttered our good-byes and Nils and I left the three of them standing in the office.

"Are you just naturally an asshole or do you work at it?" Nils asked as he and I climbed into his car.

"Seems to me you should have been asking those questions. If Jimmy's off the hook, then you need another suspect. A protective father who fights like Chuck Norris sounds like a pretty good candidate to me."

"I'm not gonna accuse Fanny Dil's son of killing the Torres kid. Besides, we're looking for someone who's not very bright, remember? You're not going to tell me that Adamji Dil would try to break into the jail and kill the guard, then knock down the doors with his bare hands?"

I shrugged. He had a point. "Probably not. But I wouldn't eliminate him as a suspect if I were you."

We were silent the rest of the way back to town.

CHAPTER FOURTEEN

I awoke refreshed. After arriving home the night before, all I'd been able to down was one beer and some shrimp salad that I'd picked up from the deli. I dragged myself off to bed and slept like a baby. The coffee smelled good and I grabbed a mug and stepped out on my front porch to survey the new day. That's when I noticed the Jaguar. Somebody had slashed the soft top into ribbons. It looked as if someone had been trying to create nylon confetti.

Finding that your property's been violated always feels as if it were your own person that had been victimized. My reaction was to swear eloquently and profusely until I began to feel foolish for doing something so ineffectual. I shut up, but I stayed pissed, circling the silver sports car slowly, assessing the damage and looking for clues. This was obviously a message but not a very clear one. If whoever did this was trying to tell me something he'd have to be more precise.

The note wasn't hard to find. It was lying face up on the passenger seat, a large muddy stone holding the note in place. I went into the house, fished out a pair of gloves and a plastic bag from a kitchen drawer, then returned and removed the rock, placing it on the floorboard of the car, to be checked, along with the note, for fingerprints later. The note contained only one line, written in large print with a marker: *Keep your nose out of where it doesn't belong.*

"Go to hell," I said loudly, looking around at the edges of the driveway…wishing there was someone on whom I could vent my anger. Even as I spoke, I knew I was shouting into thin air. I pulled myself together and placed the note in the plastic bag, laying it back on the car seat. Carefully, I lowered the softtop on the Jaguar. I'd have to show an insurance adjustor before I could get it fixed. Luckily, there was a Jaguar/Land Rover dealer in town who might have a new top in his inventory. First thing I'd do was to drop by to see Nils Larsen. He ought to be interested in this new development.

The Shambhala Police Department was on a side street downtown, in a one-story Spanish-style stucco building across from the courthouse and jail. It looked like every other police department in small town America, with a cramped lobby filled with posters and announcements—'Fingerprinting is done *only* between 8 and 3 on Mondays, Wednesdays and Fridays' was printed in tall block letters on a cardboard sign standing upright on the counter that ran from one wall to the other about eight feet inside the front door. An overweight, sweating cop, sitting at a desk behind the counter, was occupied with typing something that probably was a term paper for a night school class he was taking in order to get a promotion, but which kept him from paying me any attention for at least two minutes while I stood waiting. When he finally came over to the counter, he gave me a suspicious enough look that I suspected he'd been practicing it. His name tag said *T. Halvorsen*. Reluctantly, he buzzed me through a door that led to a carpeted corridor, the walls of which were lined with pictures of Chief Larsen and other members of his department posing with various local and state luminaries. Larsen's office was at the end of the corridor.

Chief Larsen greeted me with a sour smile. "You're up bright and early. Glad to see you're taking your police work so seriously. Looks like Detwiler's ready to drop the case against Jimmy. The coroner's report and Saraya Dil's testimony finally convinced him…not to mention the assault on my jail. You were right, by the way. The Coroner says it's probably the same guy that killed both my guard and Torres."

"Any leads?" I asked.

"Big, strong, probably stupid. Same thing we had yesterday. Good that Jimmy's no longer a suspect. You can go back to farming."

"Someone slashed the top of my car." I dumped the plastic bag with the rock and the note on his desk.

Larsen eyes widened in surprise then narrowed grimly. "How bad?"

"Ruined it." I pointed to the baggie. "They left a note. Told me to keep my nose where it belonged."

"Jesus Christ," Nils said, shaking his head, the same grim look still on his face. "Why you?"

"I must have made an enemy."

Nils gave me a flat stare. "I wonder how?"

I shrugged. "I'm not sharing any of my secrets."

"Well it's a good thing you're off the case."

"Ms. Le's off the case cuz she doesn't have a client anymore. I'm kinda enjoying being a cop. Besides, aren't you short-handed?"

"You never were a cop, McGowan. You were a consultant. I called you in to try to help Ms. Le with Jimmy's defense. Now Jimmy doesn't need a defense."

"But you still don't know who killed Manny Torres, or your guard. And maybe Karin Stengaard."

"We will."

"I'm an ex-cop," I said. "And I work cheap."

Nils gave me a once over look. "You're really pissed about your car aren't you?"

"Not the car, Chief. Somebody's thumbing his — or her —

nose at us. I can't make sense out of it. Torres and your guard were brutally beaten. Whoever did it was big, strong, and, as you've said, stupid. They didn't even plan how they were gonna get Jimmy out of his cell. It's a wonder they weren't shot by the guard. But if Karin Stengaard was murdered, it wasn't by somebody stupid. And it had to do with Manuel Torres. Something doesn't add up here, Nils. The one thing that's clear is that you've got some kind of vicious killer running around this town. I'm not even sure Jimmy Litton will be safe, once he's out of jail. Are you?"

Nils drummed on his desk top with his fingertips. He gave me a pinched smile, like it was painful to acknowledge that I was right. "I'm not sure Jimmy's safe and if you stay on the case, I won't be sure you're safe."

I could see he was weakening. I added the coup de grace. "Look at it this way, Nils. I'm gonna keep working on this anyway. If I do it officially, then you'll have some control over what I'm doing and you'll know where I am. If I do it on my own, you'll just have to sit in the dark and worry about me."

"Control over you? Jesus, McGowan, you'll say anything won't you."

I smiled. "I *am* a lawyer."

He drew in a deep breath, then let it out of his mouth in a long sigh. "Keep your nose clean and keep me informed. And let me know if you get any more threats. I'm reducing your salary."

"You mean you were really gonna pay me?"

"I have to or its not official. I was gonna pay you a couple of bucks a week. Now I'm cutting it in half."

"Do I get a donut allowance?"

"This is Shambhala, McGowan. Cops eat croissants here. Now where are you headed first?"

I told him I was going to take my car in to get the top fixed. Then I thought maybe I'd talk to the shrink, Hillary Smythe.

Maybe, in her talk with Jimmy, she'd learned something that could be of help.

"She probably won't talk to you. She may still be seeing Jimmy. Just 'cause he's no longer a suspect doesn't mean he hasn't been traumatized by this whole thing."

"I've got something that'll make her talk to me," I said.

Nils looked at me skeptically. "What?"

"Charm."

His skepticism deepened.

CHAPTER FIFTEEN

Hillary Smythe's office was an outside walk-up in a two-story wooden building above an antique shop and a children's toy store. Her nameplate was posted on the side of the toy store next to a stairwell leading up to a second story balcony. An insurance agent and a dentist had offices fronting on the same balcony. It was nearly 11:30 in the morning. Doctor Smythe's door was unlocked.

A bell over the sill jingled lightly when I opened and closed the door. The waiting room was small and there was no receptionist. A brass floor lamp in the corner across from the door provided dim lighting . On one side of the room was a black leather couch and on the other were a couple of cushioned straight backed chairs, both covered in a dark fabric with lines of small yellow flowers running vertically. In front of the couch was a coffee table with various magazines laid out in neat lines, like solitaire cards, so that the title of each showed above the one below. On a smaller table between the two chairs was a card holder filled with the doctor's cards and next to it, two piles of brochures: one pertaining to laws relating to confidentiality and the other to legal limits on client's rights. It warmed my lawyerly heart to see other professionals spending so much effort protecting themselves from being sued. I took one of the cards, skipped the brochures, and sat down on the couch.

The bell over the door tinkled and a tall, slim brunette in a long, soft maroon colored skirt and a loose, violet print peasant blouse, strode purposefully into the room, carrying a steaming cup of coffee. She gave a startled little jump when she saw me, almost spilling her coffee. "Hello. Can I help you?" she asked. I recognized the deep musical voice from the phone.

"Brian McGowan, special investigator," I said in strong, official sounding tones. I stood up and reached out my hand. "I guess you're Hillary Smythe."

"I'm Doctor Smythe. I just stepped out to buy some coffee." She stuck out her hand.

Her skin was soft, but her grip was solid. She gave my hand a perfunctory shake. No lingering touch to mix up the messages. She was smiling politely, but I could see my name hadn't rung any bells. She had that look of someone who was trying to recall where they'd heard of or met someone before. She was a strikingly beautiful woman. Her eyes were a pale green, like a cat's I'd once had. With her dark hair, she had a bit of an Irish look. Her darkly tanned skin looked freshly scrubbed, rather than made up. She even smelled freshly scrubbed…or maybe I was imagining that. Her nose was sharp with a hint of a bend along its bridge, adding character to her face. She had a wide mouth and wore lightly shaded lipstick. Her flowing attire didn't reveal much about her figure except that she wasn't concealing any excess weight. She was slim and straight, with the soft material curving suggestively outward in all the right places.

Suddenly her face lit up in recognition. "You're the lawyer turned gentleman farmer! Chief Larsen hired you to help with the Litton case." There really was a musical quality to her husky voice.

"And you're Jimmy's shrink. I thought we should talk."

She looked confused. "I can't talk about one of my clients. Besides, Jimmy's no longer a suspect. Chief Larsen called me this morning. I'll be seeing him as a private case now."

"So how about lunch?" I asked, deftly changing the subject.

She looked disconcerted for a moment, then glanced at her watch. "I've got about forty minutes before my next appointment."

I held out my arm in a gallant gesture. She suppressed a giggle and took my arm. The bell tinkled as we went out.The nearest restaurant was the Taj Mahal and it wasn't particularly crowded. The maitre d' was actually Indian and he showed us to a nice table at one side of the room, covered with a crisp white cloth, lavender linen napkins, and single rose in a bud vase. We both accepted menus and declined wine. When the waiter returned for our order I picked a shrimp curry with vegetables and Doctor Smyth chose a lamb curry.

"Why are you still interested in Jimmy?" she asked.

"I thought you couldn't talk about him."

"I'm not. I'm asking you questions."

"I thought shrinks were supposed to *answer* questions with questions."

"Not if I ask my questions first."

The conversation was being threatened by our mutual cleverness. "Jimmy may have seen something the night Manuel Torres was killed. He may have seen the real killer. At least it looks like the killer thinks so. Somebody broke into the jail yesterday and tried to get to Jimmy."

"I read about that. I didn't know it was about Jimmy. The paper said a guard was killed."

"Beaten to death. Just like Torres. Jimmy could still be in danger.'

"Really?" She looked worried. "And you think Jimmy saw the person the night of the murder?"

"I know he saw him. But maybe he didn't see him well

enough to be able to identify him. The problem is the killer doesn't know that."

Hillary sat back and mulled something over. She looked puzzled.

"What is it?" I asked.

She shook her head. "Nothing…probably. I can tell you this much about Jimmy. Something was bothering him that he wouldn't talk about. I knew he didn't kill Torres. But he knows something and he won't tell me what it is." She looked fixedly at me, her green eyes shining with intensity. "If he saw the killer, he really could be in danger, couldn't he?"

I nodded. "He'd be safest if he told Nils about it. We could put him in protective custody." I remembered about the jail break-in. "Well, anyway he'd be safer than at home."

"I'll talk to him," she said. She took a look at her watch. The food had arrived and was getting cold while we talked. "I'd better hurry. I've got an appointment," she said.

We both busied ourselves with eating. I was eager to talk more. It didn't have to be about Jimmy Litton.

"This is a funny community," I said, more or less to break the ice.

"I agree," she said, looking around as if she was making her assessment at that very moment, but still working away at her meal. "I'd like to hear why you think so."

"It's very open on the one hand, and conservative as hell on the other. I mean, there's this new-age health spa and the Hare Krishna joint, but Nils Larsen tells me that the local paragons won't accept anybody who's not white, European, and from the right old country. Then you've got this Brave New World institution for delinquents run by a fanatical geneticist."

"It's not a Hare Krishna joint, it's the Krishna School," she said, patiently. "It doesn't have anything to do with Hare Krishna. But Nils is basically right about the people. As far as the Yearling Foundation goes, it's hard to tell what the place is about."

"What do you think is going on there?" I asked.

"What do you know about Francine Stein?" Hillary asked, looking up from her curry.

I shrugged. "She wears short skirts."

She raised her eyebrows. "Stein used to teach at UCLA…the medical school. She was a world-class geneticist. That was only about three or four years ago. Something happened. Nothing public—no scandal or anything—but she left under a cloud. She came up here and joined her husband at La Sol."

"Her husband runs La Sol, the place next door to the Foundation?"

"Owns it. He's also a physician. Only he's not her husband anymore. She divorced him after she'd been here about two years. That's when she started the Foundation. She took half of the land and a pile of money."

"And now they work right next door to each other. Does that create any problems?"

"There were a lot of fireworks at first. Bernie Stein tried to sue his wife, then when that didn't work he accused her of carrying on some kind of secret research when she was at La Sol."

"What kind of research?"

"Bernie's accusations never got that far. He withdrew his accusations almost as soon as he'd made them. My guess is that he realized that he might be in as much trouble as Francine if it turned out she was doing something illegal while she was at La Sol."

"You're thinking like a lawyer," I said. I asked her what she thought of Stein's program at the Foundation. "Does it really work?"

"Who knows? Nobody really knows what goes on there. I heard her speak once and the way she described what they were doing it sounded like pretty standard behavior modification.

Nothing new. She throws in a little evolutionary stuff to make it sound more unique, but the core is basic behavior mod. The stuff works as long as you keep doing it, but it's not going to make any dramatic changes in those kids. Not changes that will survive going back to their old neighborhoods."

"That was my impression, too. I'm glad to hear you agree. So the whole description is a lot of smoke and mirrors."

"And maybe she's doing something else entirely."

"What do you mean?"

"I know it sounds silly, but when I heard her talk I got the feeling that she was just making a lot of noise, a smokescreen to cover up something else."

"The secret research that her husband was talking about?"

"Maybe. But I don't even know what kind of research that was, or if she was really doing it. Bernie may have made the whole thing up."

"I think you're right. Something's going on at the Foundation and it has something to do with Manuel Torres' death."

"What makes you say that?"

I told her about Karin and my suspicions about Jerry.

She looked horrified. "You really think the guard killed her?"

"I don't know. There was no direct evidence of foul play, but it's mighty suspicious that Jerry showed up at the Lonesome Pine Lodge about the same time that Karin had her accident right up the road."

"That's frightening," she said, shuddering. "Could this Jerry be the one who killed Torres and broke into the jail? The one that Jimmy might have seen?"

"I don't know. He fits the bill, physically. But so could lots of people. I don't take him for the one who broke into the jail, but he might have killed Torres."

"But didn't you say that it was Torres murderer who broke

into the jail?"

"That's what I think, but maybe it wasn't. I just don't think Jerry's dumb enough to come busting into the jailhouse empty handed. He used a pipe wrench just to give me a warning."

"This is all very confusing."

"I'm glad it seems that way to you, too," I said.

We got up and headed for the door. She had about five minutes to make it back to her office.

"You'll talk to Jimmy, then? Try to find out what he knows and get him to tell Nils? He seems to have a pretty good relationship with Nils."

"Nils is very protective toward the Littons, at least Mrs. Litton and Jimmy," Hillary said.

"Why is that?" I asked.

"You don't know?" she asked, raising her eyebrows.

"Know what?"

Hillary looked around. We were alone just outside the restaurant entrance by now. "Nils Larsen dated Ruth Litton at one time."

"You're kidding. When was this?"

"The Littons split up for awhile after they were first married, maybe twenty years ago. Ruth and Nils Larsen went out for awhile then Ruth found out she was pregnant with Litton's baby and she went back to him. There was a rumor that she and Nils kept seeing each other for awhile even after that."

"The baby wouldn't have been Jimmy, he's only sixteen. He said he didn't have any brothers or sisters."

"He had a brother. He only lived for a few years. He had some strange disorder then died."

"But Mrs. Litton stayed with her husband. How do you know all this?"

"I'm not telling you anything confidential. It's pretty common knowledge around town. People talk."

"You sure it's true?"

"I've heard it from more than one source. You could ask him."

"I think I'll let sleeping dogs lie. It explains some of his protectiveness about Jimmy, though. I guess he feels some obligation to Mrs. Litton to look out for her son."

"I do too. He's my client." Hillary said. She turned and headed back toward her office. "See you," she said huskily over her shoulder. Did she give me a wink or was that just my imagination?

On my way home I couldn't resist dropping by Nils' office and gloating about having gotten Hillary Smythe to have lunch with me. Nils wasn't as impressed as I'd thought he'd be, but he appreciated that the psychologist was going to try to get Jimmy Litton to tell the police whatever he knew about the figure that he'd seen lurking in the bushes the night of Torres' murder. I didn't say anything about Nils' relationship to Jimmy's mother. Nils had a message for me.

"Janice Le called you. Left a message that it was urgent that you call her today. Halvorsen took the call. He didn't ask her what it was about."

I told Nils I'd thought Ms Le would have dropped the case like a hot potato. She had no official role now that the Litton kid had been released. But then I'd underestimated Janice Le before.

When I returned her call, Ms Le's office said she'd gone into LA for the day. She'd logged out on the Litton case, meaning she hadn't closed it. I left my home number and a message for her to call me whenever she got back.

CHAPTER SIXTEEN

The next morning it was cloudy. During the night I'd heard distant mountain thunder, but there hadn't been any rain. It was only a matter of time. As soon as I finished my first life-sustaining cup of coffee, I went to my garage, hauled out my aluminum extension ladder and was up on the roof. Nils Larsen and I had finished one patching job, but there were still two to go. The shingles were already on the roof, wired together in a half dozen tight bundles. I got down on my knees and began hammering. The breeze was blowing cool and forceful off the distant Pacific, bringing back memories of gusty fall beach mornings, but I knew it would bring the season's first rain in a matter of hours. A line from an old song ran through my head. "…it don't rain in California, but girl let me warn ya, it pours." Fall rains can bring down mountains in California.

I was so intent on working that I didn't see the Shambhala Police cruiser until I heard it stop almost below me. Nils Larsen eased himself out of the front seat. He didn't look up at me but went directly to his trunk and pulled out a hammer and one of those short leather carpenter's aprons with the loops for the hammer and whatever other tools carpenters use. He clambered up the ladder.

"I'll work on this spot," Larsen said, hoisting one of the

bundles of shingles on his shoulder and striding up to the bare spot near the crown of the roof. I would have had to inch my way up there, dragging the load of shingles behind me. We both worked without speaking.

Nils had started after I did, and the area he shingled was bigger, but we finished about the same time. I was hot, but the breeze had gotten stronger and overhead the churning clouds were nearly black. The pines around the house were starting to whip back and forth. I felt the first large drop of rain. In another minute it would be pouring.

"Beer?" I asked Nils.

"Just one," he answered. "Then I got to get back to town. Day like this and we'll have a shitload of emergency calls."

We got off the roof just as the murky sky let go full force. Nils and I sprinted for the front porch. Once inside, I got a couple of beers from the refrigerator, pried off the caps and handed one to Nils. I flopped into a chair. He looked around, then sat down on the end of my couch. "You'll have to go out in this a lot today," I said, just making conversation.

Nils shrugged and took a short pull on his beer. "Anymore threats?"

"Nothing. I've got a rental from the local dealer. My car will be fixed in a couple of days. You know how it is getting an adjuster to look at it. Any luck with the fingerprints on the note?"

"Not so far. Jerry doesn't have a record. We'd have to print him to see if they're his. I'm not sure we've got enough to ask him to do that."

"I'll get you some prints."

"They won't hold up in court…you know that better than I do."

"If it turns out to be Jerry who did it, I might prefer settling things with him myself."

He reached inside his shirt pocket and pulled out a thickly folded set of papers. "Manuel Torres' police record," he said, handing them across to me. I unfolded the papers and began reading.

Torres had been in trouble since he was ten. He'd been arrested six times in six years. Every crime was a violent one. He'd started with torturing animals, then molesting younger children, three assault/robbery charges, and finally he'd knifed someone. Evidently his victim had lived because the charge was assault with a deadly weapon, not murder.

"Jesus Christ!" I said. "This doesn't sound like the same kid everybody's described to me so far."

"What do you think's going on?" Nils asked.

"It's possible that Stein's program changed Torres. Maybe the boy Saraya Dil knew and the one Jimmy got in a fight with wasn't the same kid he used to be when he was on the streets of the barrio. If that's true, then Stein's got a helluva good program. But Stein lied to me. Hell, if she really turned a kid like this around, why wouldn't she take credit for it?"

Larsen just looked at me. The rain was coming down so hard by now that it produced an almost deafening roar. Nils' eyes scanned the room. "No leaks."

"I'm going back to the Foundation. I'll probably need a court order to get Stein to turn over her files to me. But I can sure as hell interview the kids who came into town that night."

Nils pulled another set of papers from his other shirt pocket. "Here's the court order." He hesitated a moment. "Detwiler's got a copy of Torres' record, too. I had to give him one—he's the DA."

"Detwiler and I are on the same side now, aren't we?"

"Whatever you find out becomes his. He'll be the one who eventually builds a case, once we catch somebody."

"So what's the problem?"

Nils shrugged. "No problem. Except Detwiler may not completely trust you. He'll probably want to interview those kids himself. He's not very good at that kind of thing."

"Hasn't got my sensitivity, huh?"

Nils heaved a sigh. "You're probably a better bullshitter. That may be what it takes."

"You always make me feel good about myself, Nils." I looked out at the rain. It was coming down so hard I could barely see the trees across my driveway. "Looks like a good day to visit the Yearling Foundation."

Nils gave me a brief smile and stood up.

"Wait a minute," I said. I went into the bedroom and got a poncho. "Put this on. I've got two of them. I'll get it back later."

He slipped the poncho over his head and stood at the door looking out, as if hoping there might be a break in the downpour. Then he sprinted for his car.

I took a shower and put on some clean clothes, then had a second cup of coffee. Outside, the rain was coming down in big gusty sheets. The water was making small rivers in my driveway. I was glad my house was on high ground. I thought about the roads. This was the kind of rain that washed them out. Then I thought about the Litton's house trailer. I couldn't remember whether it was above or below the land around it. I wondered if Nils Larsen would go out and check on the Litton place.

I suddenly remembered Janice Le. She hadn't returned my call. Maybe she'd forgotten about whatever she'd wanted to talk to me about. Maybe she'd called me before she'd gotten the word that the charges against her client had been dropped. By this time, she probably didn't give a rat's ass about Jimmy Litton or me. Nevertheless, I decided to put in one more call to the young lawyer. After all, her call the day before had been described as 'urgent', so maybe it was important.

Janice Le still wasn't in but my call quickly got transferred to her supervisor. He was a Chief Public Defender named Adam Rooks, with a deep, African-American sounding voice. "So you're the famous LA lawyer, turned small-town cop," Rooks intoned sarcastically. "Ms. Le told me about you. Why are you calling her?"

I told him that she called me with a message that it was urgent that I call her. That's all I knew.

"The Litton case is closed," Rooks said, non-sequiturially.

"So maybe Ms. Le was calling me for a date, or to get my autograph. Why am I talking to you about this? Where's Ms. Le?"

There was a quarter of a minute of silence on Rooks' end of the line. Finally I heard him exhale loudly through his nose. "She didn't come back yesterday and she hasn't been to work yet today. We can't reach her at home."

"You mean she's missing?"

"Not officially. Not yet, anyway. But we don't know where she is. Her log from yesterday says she was going down to LA to talk to the Torres kid's family…maybe some of his friends."

"Did she know that the charges against Litton had been dropped?"

"I don't know. She left early in the morning, maybe before the message got to her about the change in the case. Maybe she got the message and decided to take some time off, though that's not like her. We're checking it all out."

"Well keep me posted," I told Rooks. "I had a threat against me and there's already been one suspicious death of a possible witness in the case. If I were you, I'd get the LAPD out looking for Ms. Le, pronto."

"That's what we're doing. I'll be back in touch." He hung up.

It was probably nothing, but after Karin Stengaard's death, I couldn't help but worry about Janice Le. Any poking around about Manuel Torres seemed to bring either a disaster or the threat of one. I looked out the window. The rain hadn't let up, but the news about Janice Le made me even more anxious to do some more poking around myself. I got out my poncho and made a dash for the rental Range Rover.

CHAPTER SEVENTEEN

The road to the Foundation was intact, although a tumultuous runoff threatened the sides of the drainage ditch that ran along next to it. Angry sheets of rain pounded across the pavement and beat a steady tattoo on the hood of my car as I inched along through the downpour. When I finally reached the gate I honked my horn. Someone stuck his head out of the guard house, then closed the door. In a few seconds a figure came out, covered from head to toe in yellow rain pants and a hooded coat. When he got close I could see it was Jerry. From the guard shed he hadn't been able to tell it was me, since I was driving a new Range Rover instead of my Jaguar. When he got close enough to see me, he began scowling.

Jerry stood there dripping until I rolled down my window. The rain blew in against my face.

"What's the matter, your little car have leaks?" he said, flashing a sick grin.

"I'm here to see your boss, junior," I said.

"I have to call the office," he said, his scowl returning.

I rolled the window back up and waited while he ran back inside his shed to make his call. This time the gate was closed, so I couldn't just drive on through. In a minute Jerry was back, still scowling and with big drops of water dripping off of his nose and chin. I took my time rolling down my window.

"Doctor Stein is in the main office," he shouted over the rain.

"I know the way." I rolled the window up and waited for him to raise the gate. As soon as he had it up I gunned the motor. I didn't look back to see if my rooster tail had gotten him.

A new face—Karin Stengaard's replacement—was at the front desk in the office. She was another blonde, not quite as perky as Karin, but quietly attractive. I reined in my charm. I wasn't going to endanger another pretty face by getting her interested in sharing anything with me. I was thinking that I should have gotten out of my car at the gate and beaten the shit out of Jerry. It was just a passing thought.

"Doctor Stein is waiting in her office. You can go in." The blonde gave me a pleasant smile.

 I nodded politely.

Francine Stein was sitting behind her desk looking out at the rain. She had one long shapely leg crossed over the other to reveal a good four inches of slim white thigh. She was wearing a light wool sweater that had a "V" neck low enough that its edges rested on the curvatures of her breasts. She didn't get up when I walked in.

"Glad to see me?" I asked.

A hint of a smile raised the corners of her mouth. "I was probably a little short with you before, Mr. McGowan. I'm happy you're back so I can make amends." She held my gaze a little longer than necessary, then slowly batted her thick eyelashes.

"I can sense your change of attitude already," I said.

She pointed me to a chair. It was the one that offered me the best view of her legs. I looked. She didn't move. "Perhaps I can just tell you whatever you want to know, Mr. McGowan?"

I gave her a regretful smile. "You can call me Brian. You've already told me your version of Torres' history. It doesn't match very well with this." I took out the copy of the boy's police record, got up, and carefully placed it in front of her on the desk.

She gave the papers a cursory glance. "But that was Torres before he came here. When I spoke to you I was referring to his behavior here. He was among our least aggressive boys. He was no angel, of course, but he kept his behavior under very good control."

"Your program changed him?"

"Perhaps, a little. But Manny knew when it didn't pay to go against the system. Manny was what we call a sociopath, Brian. He always kept himself under control. We never had any difficulty with him, not even at the beginning."

"I'd like to see his file."

Her smile disappeared for just one second. Then she painted it back on. "Certainly; that's why you're here." She punched a button on her phone and spoke to the new girl over the intercom. "Lisa, please bring in Manuel Torres' file, would you, please?"

We sat eyeing each other, waiting for the file. Presently, Doctor Stein leaned forward, exposing more of her cleavage.

"You're an interesting man, Brian."

She must be prone to understatement. "How so?" I asked.

"I understand you're a well-known lawyer in LA. You've defended a lot of movie stars. I also heard you've taken this case for free."

"I like the thrill of police work."

"But you don't need the money?"

"I'm supposed to be retired. This is a favor for someone.'

"Are you married?"

I shook my head.

She was making a heroic effort to crack the brittleness in her smile. "I found it very lonely when I got divorced." She held my gaze for an extra moment. She smoothed her sweater across one breast with her hand. I thought the hand lingered over the breast a little longer than necessary, but maybe that was my imagination.

She was saying all the right things and showing me all the right parts. If we'd been sitting in a bar instead of in her office waiting for a piece of evidence which she'd tried to keep from me, I might have responded. If I hadn't already sampled her personality I might have responded. But we weren't in a bar and I had a good idea about her personality by now.

"Maybe you work too much," I offered, less than helpfully.

Our tete-a-tete was interrupted by a knock on the door.

The new blonde secretary walked demurely into the room, an impersonal smile fixed on her face. She handed the folder to Doctor Stein, like she was an obedient student turning in her homework. Francine Stein watched her latest underling like a jealous diva.

Doctor Stein made a brief show of perusing the chart she was just handed, as though she hadn't seen it for some time. I waited for the show to be over. Presently she handed me the chart. "I'll want a copy of it," I said, thumbing through the pages.

Doctor Stein nodded. She'd come around to the front of her desk where she sat casually on the edge of the desktop, her right foot just touching the floor while she crossed her left leg over the right just above the knee, her pretty calf just inches from my own knee. I took a deep breath and continued reading.

It was a laundered chart. There was almost no mention of Torres' behavior. Whole weeks apparently passed with no notations in the chart at all. In the medical section there was a mention of his being on Ritalin when he arrived at the Foundation eight months earlier, but, other than periodic treatment with iron supplements for anemia and blood tests to monitor the same condition, he'd not gotten any serious medical treatment.

"Kind of a thin chart," I said.

Doctor Stein sat swinging her leg in front of me. "We're more of a school than a hospital, Brian. We don't record everything a student does. The chart contains essential medical information and reports of behavioral incidents. When a student is well behaved, he has very little written in his chart."

"I thought Torres was being treated for an infection. That was why he had such a high white blood cell count remember?"

She was nonplussed for only a moment. "I suppose those reports just haven't been filed yet. I'll see that you get them."

"Anything else that hasn't been filed yet?"

"I'm sure the record is complete, other than that." She kept the brittle smile on her face and she didn't stop swinging her leg, but what friendliness had been there had left her eyes completely. I didn't much care. I was a getting pissed myself. Did she think that I'd be satisfied with doctored files just because she'd thrown in a little thigh and cleavage on the side?

"The autopsy found an incision in the lower spinal column. The coroner said it resembled a wound from a bone marrow transplant. It was only a month old."

She tried staring me down, but she couldn't hold her gaze long enough to do it. Her eyes began to dart around the room. "We have an infirmary, but we don't do surgery here."

"So where'd the wound come from?"

She'd calmed down enough to look me directly in the eyes. "I don't have any idea. Perhaps he'd gotten into an altercation with another student. If so, it went unreported."

"An unreported knife wound in one of your students?"

Her expression became stony. "I've given you the Torres boy's file. Is there anything else you want?" There was a snake-like hiss to her tone.

"I'd like to talk to the students who came into town that night," I said.

"Now?"

"Sure, why not? I'm conducting a police investigation, remember?"

She didn't answer. Instead, she picked up the telephone and told her secretary to send Jerry up to the office. "Jerry will take you," she said curtly.

"The boy with the charm," I said.

"The boys you're going to talk to can be difficult. Jerry can keep them in line."

"Who'll keep Jerry in line?"

She didn't answer.

There was a knock on the door and a dripping wet Jerry came into the room. He brushed back the hood on his raincoat, sending a small waterfall of trapped rainwater down onto the polished hardwood floor. Doctor Stein stiffened but held her tongue.

"Lisa said you wanted to see me, doctor," Jerry said.

"Mr. McGowan wants to talk to the boys in C-3, the ones who went into town the night Manny was killed."

Jerry stared at her as though he hadn't understood her correctly.

Doctor Stein gave him an irritated look. "This is a police matter and Mr. McGowan is working with the police. He has to be given access to the boys. I'd like you to go with him."

It seemed like a lot of explanation to be given to one of the hired help. Jerry looked over at me and smiled, a nice hollow smile that was as malevolent as if he were welcoming me to my own execution. "I'd be happy to," he said.

As Jerry and I were both contemplating what he might have in store for me, the intercom buzzer sounded and the secretary's respectful voice announced the arrival of Richard Detwiler. I thought the look Jerry and Doctor Stein exchanged was that of a couple of kids getting caught with their hands in the cookie jar.

"I'll guess you'll be a regular tour guide," I told Jerry.

Jerry had lost his enthusiasm. He shifted back and forth on

his feet and glumly eyed Doctor Stein.

Detwiler didn't look surprised to see me. "Talked to the kids yet?" he asked anxiously, striding into the room, dripping water everywhere and ignoring Doctor Stein and Jerry completely.

"And you thought I was rude," I said to Francine Stein.

Detwiler stopped and turned to the doctor, his face momentarily flushed with embarrassment. "Sorry," he said. "Good to see you again Doctor. I'm taking charge here. Mr. McGowan is just a consultant to the police department. I think it's best he and I interview those children together."

"Certainly," Francine Stein said, giving me a polite smile that told me she enjoyed seeing me get put in my place.

I smiled back. "You don't have to worry about him," I said, nodding in Detwiler's direction. "I'll make sure he doesn't violate any of your students' rights."

Detwiler glowered at me as I smiled in his direction.

CHAPTER EIGHTEEN

Jerry led us through the downpour toward one of the far buildings. The three of us trudged through the mud and grass of the central yard. Jerry and I both were wearing heavy boots and hooded ponchos, but Detwiler had on his indoor Oxfords and carried an umbrella, which threatened to blow inside out with every gust of wind. I could hear him swearing next to me. When we arrived at building C-3 it was obvious that Jerry hadn't needed to bring us through the muddy field. The paved road that led past the office continued on around to this building. Detwiler looked like he was ready to kill Jerry.

C-3 was set up pretty much like an army barracks. We entered into what looked like a day room or lounge and through a doorway at one end I could see rows of bunk beds where the residents slept in one big dormitory. About a dozen teenage boys, nearly all Mexicans and Blacks, were scattered in chairs and on a couple of couches, watching TV in the lounge. All of them were dressed identically in the Foundation 'uniform' of jeans and a white tee shirt, although a couple of them had their tee shirts off. Most of them wore tattoos, ranging from elaborate snakes and dragons to crudely scratched nicknames like 'Cholo' or 'Spider'. A few had the telltale teardrop markings that advertised that they'd killed a rival gang member. I expected a gallery of hostile, challenging stares when we walked into the cottage. Instead, the teenagers leapt to their feet when we entered, like a squad of Marines reacting to the presence of their drill sergeant. They looked like they were scared to death of all three of us.

Jerry stood there a moment, eyeing the group of them. When Jerry made a sudden movement to remove his poncho, the nearest two kids almost tripped over each other backing away. Jerry didn't seem to notice. As soon as he had his poncho off, he told them that we were there to question them about the night Manny Torres was killed and he wanted them to answer our questions. I took out a piece of paper and a pen and asked Jerry to write down the names of all the kids while Detwiler and I talked to them.

Detwiler had the sensitivity of a telephone pole. He began asking his questions and didn't appear to notice that these kids, who looked like refugees from a grade B movie about gang bangers, were as timid as all hell. I tried out a few different attitudes on them. When I came on quiet and polite, they reacted the same. They didn't do polite so well, but they were trying. When I raised my voice or showed some temper, they practically shrank into the walls. Detwiler's manner, which expressed about as much emotion as a turnip, got the same muted reaction from each one of the kids...and the same story.

All of them had seen the fight between Manny and Jimmy Litton and they all described it in exactly the same way— Manny had said a few things in Spanish and Jimmy went ballistic and beat the shit out of him. Manny was hurt pretty badly, but he wanted to be alone. He left and then Jerry and another guard showed up and brought all of the boys back to the Foundation. None of them saw Manny alive again. The end of each of their stories was punctuated with a fearful glance toward Jerry, who was absorbed in examining his fingernails.

I raised my eyebrows at Detwiler. I wondered if he was

suspicious of the obvious uniformity in the kids' descriptions.

"What?" he said, looking at me. He seemed satisfied with the teenagers' stories.

"Why'd Manny go with you?" I asked no one in particular. Since no one answered immediately, I guessed they hadn't rehearsed an answer to that question. Finally, a small Black kid with the name 'Runt' on one shoulder and a burst of red stars on the other, said Manny had offered to show them how to get past the fence. Runt looked around self-consciously, but he seemed more afraid that I'd get mad at him if he didn't answer than that his cottage mates would do something to him if he did. He said Manny was already planning to leave the grounds that night, himself. He was meeting someone. Runt thought Manny was meeting a girl.

"So how come Manny went with you to the park?' I asked. "His girl friend's at the Krishna School. That's in the other direction." Runt looked at Jerry then at the other kids. They all looked at Jerry. Nobody answered. Jerry gave me a sick smile. I wondered how a candy-ass like Jerry could scare street kids like these. Any one of them, even Runt, would take care of him in less than five minutes if he showed up on their turf in the city. Stein's program had the kids behaving like frightened rabbits.

I took back the pen and paper, carefully avoiding smudging the fingerprints Jerry'd just left on both.

"Let's walk back on the road," I told Detwiler when we left the building.

"Find out everything you needed, McGowan?" Jerry asked, his scowl transformed into an even more distasteful smirk.

I was ready to see if Jerry really was tough enough to intimidate those kids. "Go back to wherever you came from shit-for-brains," I said to him. He and Detwiler both looked startled at my words. Jerry resurrected his scowl then clenched his fists and took a step toward me, his right arm drawn back. If he was planning to throw a punch, he was about a millenium too slow. I stepped forward, grabbed his upraised arm, slipped my head under it, holding onto his wrist, then snapped my head back into the crook of his shoulder while sweeping his legs out from under him with my left foot. He went down like a sack of potatoes.

"Jesus Christ, McGowan," Detwiler screeched. "What in the hell are you doing?"

I had my foot drawn back ready to make my point a second time in case Jerry had some thoughts about coming at me mano-a-mano. I hoped he did. He'd banged his head a pretty good one when he went down and he looked a little woozy. I reluctantly let him struggle back to his feet.

"You're a fucking madman," Jerry managed to say between teeth clenched in pain. He reached up and caught a handful of blood dripping from the back of his head. His clothing was covered with mud. "Shit!' he exclaimed. He backed away, repeating his last comment several more times then turned and stalked off through the mud toward the office.

"You are a madman," Detwiler echoed. I didn't feel like arguing. I was starting to feel my heart pumping a lot harder than it was supposed to.

"Shit," I muttered. "I've got to sit down."

Detwiler's eyes were bugged out. "Jesus," he repeated. "You're white as a sheet. Are you having a heart attack?"

"Not if I can sit down," I said, grabbing his arm for support. I limped over to the stairs leading into C-3 and sat down heavily. If I was white as a sheet it was because I was scared out of my wits. My next heart attack would probably be my last. I didn't want this to be it. I sat there listening to my heart pounding and waiting to see what would happen. Gradually my heart slowed down. Not, thankfully, to a stop.

"I'm too old for this kinda shit," I said, looking up at Detwiler. His face looked like mine must have looked five minutes earlier.

"You all right?" he asked.

"I'll make it. Let's walk back to the cars. I want to talk."

He eyed me warily, like he was waiting for me to keel over. I got up and started walking along the road. I was feeling good, as if I'd proven something by not having another heart attack. Talk about Pyhrric victories.

"Did those seem like tough street kids to you?" I asked as we walked.

"This program's got them under control," Detwiler said, still eyeing me uncertainly.

"Bullshit," I said, ignoring his anxious sideways glances. "They're not just under control. They're altered in some way."

"What the hell are you talking about? "

"I mean those kids aren't normal. It's like something is missing from them. They can be either frightened or calm, but that's it. Where's the anger? Where's the belligerence?"

"That's the point of Doctor Stein's program, McGowan. These kids aren't angry or belligerent any more."

"Nuts! These kids have been castrated. I don't mean literally, but not a one of 'em's got any balls. Fucking Jerry's got them saying just what he wants them to say and afraid to say anything else. For Christ's sake, Detwiler, you're a DA. Have you ever had street kids talk to you like that before?"

Detwiler was concentrating on keeping his shoes out of the puddles in the street. The shoes looked to me like they were ruined already. He walked on in silence for a few seconds. I had the foolish hope that he was considering what I'd said.

"You know what's wrong with you, McGowan?" he finally said.

"I do, but let's hear your version."

"You've got to try to turn every case into some kind of grandstand play. Somebody beat the hell out of Manuel Torres. These kids say it was Jimmy Litton, but we know that Torres was still alive after that beating and that somebody bigger than

Litton attacked Torres a second time. So far we haven't got a clue as to who the real killer is. I know you want to be a hot shot special investigator, but there's no point throwing suspicion on this foundation or Dr. Stein. Who the hell cares if Stein has turned these kids into wimps? That's what she's supposed to do and it hasn't got anything to do with the case except that it makes it less likely that any of them is the killer."

He was a moron, but maybe he was right. These kids might be abnormally passive for young criminals, but that probably didn't mean anything except that Dr. Stein's program really worked. How it could work so well, I had no idea. But the answer to that question was probably irrelevant. On the other hand, I wasn't sure.

I needed to pay Francine Stein another visit. I waited until Detwiler drove off, then I headed back to Stein's office.

I didn't see Jerry, but two of the other guards, a surfer type like Jerry, with blond hair sticking out from under his hood and muscles big enough to bulge out from under his poncho, and a gigantic African-American whose angry glower was as intimidating as his size, were standing like statues in front of the office door. They didn't so much as twitch when I mounted the steps.

"Must hurt to have your feet nailed to the floor," I said.

Neither of them smiled at my clever banter.

"I'd like to talk to Doctor Stein." I said.

"She's not taking visitors," the African-American muttered in a menacing voice.

"Then how come she's at the door behind you?" I said, pointing past their shoulders.

The two idiots turned around to look. I stiff-armed both of them and before either one of them could recover, I was through the door. Francine Stein was standing in the middle of the waiting room. She held up a warning hand which stopped the two embarrassed guards, who were about to yank me back out onto the porch. I didn't want to think what they had in mind for me after that.

"You're becoming a thorn in my side, Mr. McGowan," Doctor Stein said, staring at me coldly.

"It's my personality. I can't do anything about it."

"Jerry says you roughed him up."

I narrowed my eyes and gave her my best macho stare. "It doesn't pay to mess around with a cop…consultant cop, that is."

She just shook her head. "Why are you still here?"

"I wondered about those kids in C-3. What have you done to them?"

Her stare didn't waver, but I could see her right eyelid begin to twitch. "What do you mean?"

"They're too passive. If Manuel Torres was like that, then he wasn't a normal kid when he got killed. He had something wrong with him."

"Those kids are non-aggressive because of our program. That's the idea. I've told you that Torres wasn't an aggressive kid to begin with."

I returned her cold stare. "I don't know what's going on here, Doctor, but I plan to find out."

"That could be dangerous."

"Are you threatening me?"

"We have dangerous residents here. We have very strict security to keep these residents under control. That security is also to keep uninvited visitors off of our grounds…for their own safety, of course."

"Right."

"Accidents happen, Mr. McGowan. This can be a dangerous place to be poking around."

"You mean like Karin Stengaard's accident?"

She didn't show any reaction—just continued to gaze at me with her hard cold eyes. "Accidents happen."

"You think I'll have an accident before I get out of here today?" I asked. I glanced over my shoulder. The two muscle-bound cretins were still visible through the glass pane on the door.

She smiled a thin, straight smile. Her eyes were like two motes of glacial ice. "Not today."

I nodded and backed toward the door.

Francine Stein watched me leave, the thin, cruel smile never leaving her face. I wished the two guards a nice day and drove off. On the way out the gate was open.

CHAPTER NINETEEN

I had Jerry's prints on the paper with the list of names I'd had him collect and my next stop was Nils' office to get him to try to match them to the prints from the note in my car. I thought Nils would be impressed by my cleverness, but his face was like stone when he took the list from me. "They found Janice Le," he said.

I had a bad feeling. "Found her?"

"She's dead."

It felt like a rock had descended to the pit of my stomach. I remembered her small, brave words. And her pride. "Another beating?" I asked Nils.

He shook his head. "Drive-by. Probably not random, though. She was in Torres' neighborhood checking out his background. The damn kid was telling everybody she talked to that she was the lawyer for the boy accused of killing Torres. It looks like some of Torres old gang buddies heard her and decided to go after her."

"I don't believe it."

"What do you mean? You don't believe what?"

"Janice Le wasn't stupid. And she grew up around gangs. She wouldn't have done something to provoke Torres' gang. And nobody would kill her just because she was Jimmy Litton's lawyer."

"Well somebody did. She was talking to his family and his gang. Seems like they'd be the natural suspects."

I shook my head. "It's possible, but that sounds like a fantasy scenario to me."

"So what do you think happened?"

"I don't know, but this is two young women who've died because of this case so far."

"We don't know that about Karin Stengaard. There's no evidence that her death was anything except an accident. Janice Le may have been killed because she was investigating Torres' death, but she was nosing around a very dangerous neighborhood where it's not safe to be asking questions."

Maybe he was right, but I was still uncomfortable. "Do they have any suspects yet?"

"Not yet. Somebody's supposed to let me know when they do. I'll keep you informed."

There didn't seem to be anything else for me to do about Janice Le. The LAPD would investigate her death better than I ever could. Maybe I was trying to tie it into the Torres case because I felt guilty. I felt as if it should have been me asking the questions in the barrio, not a young female attorney on one of her first cases. Only it hadn't been me and it was too late to do anything about it. Anyway, I was tired. I decided to go home and go to bed.

The sound of a car's tires crunching on the gravel in my driveway woke me from my late afternoon nap. I parted the curtains and looked out from my bedroom window. It was Nils. It was dark outside I checked my watch. It was after ten o'clock. I rolled off my bed and put on my shoes. When Nils reached the door I was there to open it for him.

"You sleeping?" Nils asked, looking at my hair, which I guessed must be standing on end from my nap.

"I was rudely awakened by the sound of your car."

"Good," Nils said. "I've got some news for you."

I motioned toward the porch. "Pull up a chair and I'll get a couple of beers."

When I got back Nils was looking at my oak rocker. "It's got a squeak."

"That's part of its charm. What's up? Something about Janice Le?"

Nils shook his head. "Nothing yet. I got the results back on the prints from your car and those you took from Jerry from the Foundation."

"You gonna tell me?"

"They're Jerry's prints. Of course the way you got them, there's no way to use them in court. I could haul him in, but I've got no probable cause to print him officially." Chief Larsen took the beer I held out to him and settled further into the wicker rocking chair. I sat down on the top stair of my porch and leaned against the railing. The storm clouds had blown away, leaving the cool night air crisp and fresh. A high thin mist blurred the stars and put a halo around the quarter moon. The crickets in the old oak thicket were doing double-time sawing their legs together. It was a night for a heavy shirt but still a night to be outside.

"It makes me feel better about pushing him into the mud," I said, "although I felt pretty good about it already."

"Detwiler told me about that. He thinks you're crazy."

"We share a mutual respect."

"You'd think somebody who vandalized a car like that would have a record. Trashing someone's car is a pretty risky thing to do…especially if you're dumb enough to leave a note with your prints on it."

"More than risky. Jerry doesn't like me, but sticking his neck out like that is going way out of his way. What's more, it wasn't just vandalism, it was a threat, remember? About keeping my nose out of places it didn't belong."

Nils looked down on me from his chair. "You think Jerry was trying to give you a message about the Foundation?"

"There's something going on at the Foundation that Francine Stein doesn't want me to find out about. Something that's related to Manuel Torres."

I could see Nils tipping his beer in the dim light. The rocking chair creaked as he leaned toward me. "You mean it might have been Doctor Stein's idea to trash your car?"

"Maybe. Something's going on out there. Whatever she's done to those kids is amazing. I'll bet every last one of them has a history of violence as long as my arm. None of them would raise a finger against anyone anymore. I don't know if she's frightened the hell out of 'em or used drugs on them, or what, but I've never seen anything like it. From the description Saraya gave us of Torres, he was the same way."

"But what would that have to do with him getting killed?"

Nils was raising the same point Detwiler had and I still didn't have an answer. I took a long pull on my beer and held the bottle up to the light coming from the window. I still had about half of it left. On my meager ration of beer, I started measuring after the first swallow. "I haven't a clue," I said. "Maybe I'll visit Francine Stein's husband tomorrow. I heard he made some accusations about his wife doing some kind of secret research."

"I'd take what Bernie Stein says with a grain of salt if I were you. He'll say anything about his ex-wife if he thinks it'll get her in some sort of trouble."

"You know why they split up?"

"Too much ego and not enough room, that's my guess."

"Him too, huh?"

"He's different from her, that's for sure. Kind of a likable guy but a real bullshitter. You'll see." Nils put down his empty bottle and stood up. "Let me know what you find out. Meantime, I'm gonna get the records on all of those Foundation kids. Can't hurt."

"Good." I watched him leave and then went inside. I had one more beer left in my evening's allotment.

CHAPTER TWENTY

Nils caught me by phone the next morning just as I was about to leave the house. He was at the Litton farm and he wanted me there, pronto.

The high mist from the night before had settled into the upper valley as a thin fog, giving the rocky hills, with their squatty oaks and tall lonely pines an eerie appearance, as if the scenery were coming and going. I drove slowly in my rental Range Rover, winding my way up the road to the Litton place. When I saw the little complex with the trailer house and sheds, the fog was just burning off from the heat of the morning sun. Chief Larsen's cruiser was parked in front of the trailer and alongside it a gas company van and another car. Nobody was in sight.

I climbed out of my car and headed for the house, but a I stopped when a young man wearing a gas company uniform came from around the shed that housed the old Malibu. He jumped when he saw me. His face was greenish with his mouth pursed in distaste, like he'd just had to fish around in a bag of old garbage.

"You the lawyer?" he said. He was struggling to straighten out his mouth, but he was losing the fight.

I nodded. I didn't want to ask him what had made him sick.

I had a feeling I'd soon find out.

He jerked his thumb over his shoulder in the direction from which he'd come. "Back there."

I smelled it as soon as I rounded the shed. It was the Litton's Guernsey. It was in several different places in the field behind the shed. Nils was kneeling over the black and white hide, but the body that should have been inside the hide was fifteen feet away… most of the body that is. Three of the hooves were another five feet past the body, tied together with a strand of rope, surrounded by a pool of partly dried blood. The fourth was sticking out of the mouth of the cow's head, which was five or six feet away from the rest of the body parts. Somebody I didn't know was examining the head. He was wearing thin rubber gloves and was poking at the mouth with some kind of instrument. I guessed he was a vet. His shoes were covered with blood.

"She was still alive," the vet said grimly. He looked up and saw me. "Pretty, huh? Fucking sadists." It was a concise diagnosis.

Nils saw me and introduced me to Doctor Jack Lemon, the local veterinarian. I didn't smile at the name. "The gas man found the cow when he came to check the meter this morning," Nils said.

"Where are the Littons?" I asked.

"The old man's throwing up, most likely. He took one look and went back inside. Jimmy and his mom haven't been out."

"What did you mean, she was alive?" I asked the vet.

"When they stuck the hoof in her mouth. They hobbled her, cut the hooves off then gagged her with one of them." He shook his head.

"That's what killed her?"

"No, it was the loss of blood.'

"When did they remove the hide?" I wasn't sure I really wanted to know.

"Can't tell. I hope she was dead by then."

"How many foot prints?" I asked Nils.

"Maybe three or four...could even be more. Hard to separate from the gas man's and Litton's in all this mud. Looks like at least three others, maybe a fourth, all of them smudged."

"Any idea who would do this? Or why?"

Nils shook his head disgustedly. "Somebody pretty sick."

"What's Litton say?"

"Mexicans. That's what he says to everything."

"He say why he thinks Mexicans would do this?"

"Said they're mad 'cuz they still think Jimmy killed Torres."

 "That's bullshit, right?"

Nils thought for a moment. "I suppose it could be a reprisal. But none of the Mexicans around here would have known Torres. It wouldn't surprise me if whoever did this was involved in Torres' murder themselves," Nils said.

"Why?"

"Same degree of violence. Never seen anything like it," Nils said, shaking is head in disgust. "...and I was in 'Nam."

I walked back around the shed. Nils followed me. "Jerry couldn't have done this. Not by himself. Nobody could have," I said.

"Unless they were on something...angel dust or something like that, maybe. I'd guess drugs anyway, with something this weird."

"You think Litton could be right about Mexicans? You got any Satanic cults or anything like that around here?"

"What Mexicans we got aren't weird. There was some cult stuff down in Lompoc once, but nothing around here. This is connected to the Torres case. I just don't know how."

I told him I didn't either. But I thought he was right. "This might be a good time to talk some more to Jimmy. Maybe he'll tell us something more about the mysterious person he saw watching Torres and Saraya."

Nils held out his hand in a 'be my guest' gesture. He and I walked around the shed to the trailer and I knocked on the door. Ronald Litton, Jimmy's father, opened the trailer door. He still looked a little green around the gills, but he had a beer in his hand so I was confident he was treating whatever ailed him.

"Yeah?" he said. When he saw Nils his eyes narrowed in hatred. There was obviously something going on between these two. Maybe Litton knew about his wife's one-time relationship with the Chief.

"Jimmy here?" I asked.

"He ain't here."

I remembered it was a school day. "He at school?" I asked.

"Damned if I know." Litton answered. "That's where he's s'pposed to be. What you want with my boy?"

"We'd like to talk to him," Nils said, soundng more belligerent than I would have expected from him.

"He ain't here," Litton repeated. He gave us each a nasty look, then shut the door.

"He ain't here," I said to Nils.

"Nope," the Chief said, "I guess he ain't."

CHAPTER TWENTY-ONE

Doctor Bernard Stein's *La Sol Spa and Resort* was adjacent to the Yearling Foundation, but on the side opposite the Krishna School. The Foundation's land had originally been part of the spa until the breakup of the Stein's marriage. Before that, Raja Krishna and the non-profit foundation he had set up had owned all of the land and it had remained undeveloped. Stein had apparently acquired the land for the spa from the Krishna Foundation in some type of long-term lease.

The Spanish architecture of La Sol was reminiscent of the Krishna School next door, though the buildings were a little newer. I breezed past the entrance and pulled up in front of the office. My appointment wasn't for another half hour, but I went inside and announced myself to Stein's friendly middle-aged secretary who told me that her boss was running late and I'd have to wait at least an hour. I said I'd wander around and have a look-see at things. She took a motherly interest in me and launched into a verbal tour of the place and when I finally disengaged myself and said I'd just wander around, she stuffed a map and the day's schedule of events into my pocket.

Stein didn't scrimp on the gardening. I hadn't seen anything quite so exotic and luxurious since I'd visited the Huntington Library in Pasadena. The paths that wound between plots of roses and camellias and groves of bamboo, were graveled and newly raked. I heard bird sounds but not much else until two joggers came running by, nodding and telling me hello like we were old friends. Pretty soon other walkers appeared, all headed in a common direction. Most of them were dressed in shorts or jogging outfits and looked about the age of my parents. They all were sporting the kind of self-satisfied, mindless friendliness that reminded me of those people who used to come up to me and shake my hand when I was a kid and attended church. I made a half-hearted effort to smile back.

According to the schedule, the big attraction everyone was headed toward was the lecture and discussion on *Visualizing Health* being held in some place called *Jiddu's Grove*. I followed the crowd. The grove was a stand of oaks forming a rough circle with wooden benches around the inner edge of its periphery. I stood gawking at the fifteen or twenty mostly geriatric cases who were taking seats until a sweet-faced little woman in a tennis outfit grabbed my elbow and began pulling me into the grove.

"Don't be shy, young man," she said. She looked about sixty-five. Her skin, where it wasn't covered by the tennis outfit, was the color of smoked leather and looked about the same texture. I tried to smile politely and dig my heels in, but she was a strong old bird. It was either go along with her or get into what could have been an ugly wrestling match that would have been embarrassing to lose. I tried to fix a smile on my face by gritting my teeth while I reluctantly sat down on one of the benches. I wasn't able to shake the parasitic old lady who held on to my arm until she had sat down next to me.

We didn't have long to wait. I could feel a stirring of excitement among the oldsters and I thought for a moment that someone was going to wheel in a tray of bran and prunes, but instead I was astounded to see a native American in full headdress, leather leggings, and smock, come striding somberly into the center of the grove, rattling a tambourine-like instrument in his hand. He noted my presence with a look of suspicion, but then he directed his gaze more majestically around the eager faces of his audience. "Bemidji Snohomish…may your journey be fruitful," he said. I was sure I'd spent a Saturday night in either Bemidji or Snohomish a few years ago.

William Runningfoot knew how to work an audience. He launched into a polemic against what he called the 'Western' approach to medicine. I wasn't sure where he thought Native Americans came from if not the West, but precision was not particularly important to Runningfoot. According to his version of history, the early Americans were the first race to realize that good health and the ability to overcome illness were based on the same principles. Their secret was not their use of natural herbs and medicines, but their ability to control their health with positive thoughts. According to Runningfoot, that meant seeing themselves as at one with nature. The Native Americans, we were told, had discovered that the mind controlled the body's immune system, something modern medicine was only beginning to admit as it rediscovered these ancient truths. The path to health, as revealed by ancient Native American practices, was to be achieved through positive visualization, the practice of which, coincidentally, William Runingfoot could, with persuasion, teach them. No doubt for a hefty fee.

The elderly faces hung onto Runningfoot's every word. I could imagine them throwing out their pills and vitamins by the truckloads. Runningfoot's message sounded like a bunch of pseudoscientific con artistry to me. When he opened his talk up for discussion I told him so.

"I sensed your negativism," he said. "It is in your aura."

I wanted to ask him how his aura would look if he'd started his day viewing a mutilated cow, but I thought that was being petty. I kept my question simple. "My what?"

"You are not familiar with the Celestine vision, I see." The word Celestine seemed to carry a special significance for this crowd. I could hear it reverberating through the audience.

Runningfoot looked around the group for approval. They looked like they'd all arrived at the same conclusion about me — I was hopelessly mired in a Western frame of mind. I knew it was pointless to go on, but I felt compelled to point out that no early American had probably ever lived as long as anyone in the present audience and that that was without a doubt because of the invention of antibiotics, beta-blockers, and by-pass surgery. As far as I recollected, Runningfoot's right-thinking ancestors tended to be a race that was decimated by widespread diseases even more often than the Europeans who displaced them. I concluded by claiming that in my opinion the only impact Native American practices had had on the health field was confined to the introduction of tobacco, for which I praised them profusely.

Maybe I overstated my case. William Runningfoot zeroed in on my negative aura. He said I was losing valuable energy by fighting against my natural inclination toward health. He could see my energy escaping, like steam from a teapot, I guess. Several old coots in the audience claimed to also be able to see my aura dissipating into the void.

The woman next to me murmured that it was all quite 'Celestine' but at least she didn't try to grasp my arm again. I thanked the group for my new education, decided against letting out a war-whoop, then slipped away and headed back to the office. Stein still wasn't in but that didn't bother me because a short, curvaceous blonde in a bra-less yellow jersey and a tiny pair of white shorts, which looked like they'd been painted on, was lounging in the lobby, reading a brochure on nutrition. She had one smooth, tan leg slung over the other, and was swinging a cute little foot which sported spotlessly clean white running shoes over a pair of pink-topped socks. I stood there with my mouth watering.

"Doctor Stein?" She looked up at me with a pair of bright blue eyes. She had a button nose and a mouth that turned up at the corners, with full lips colored the same pink as the tops of her socks. Her voice dripped with innocence.

"Sorry," I smiled back. "I'm waiting for him too." I raised my eyebrows and looked at the chair next to her. Her smile widened, so I sat.

"Are you staying here?" She'd put her brochure down and was looking up at me with those bright blue eyes.

I told her I was only a visitor. "How about you?" I asked.

"I just arrived. I'm supposed to see Doctor Stein to learn about my program."

"What kind of program?"

"Oh mostly nutrition. I feel healthy, but I want to be sure I'm not putting poisons in my body. I'd like to do some searching also." She drew her elbows in and clasped her hands together in gesture of hopefulness.

"Searching?" I was ready to help in whatever way I could.

"For my spiritual side," she said eagerly.

I nodded, trying to match her eagerness. About a quart of coffee or a handful of amphetamines would have helped. "I'm searching too," I said.

"I knew it!" she clapped her hands together. "I can sense these things. It's almost like…I don't know how to describe it."

"Celestine?" I offered.

"You feel it too!" she leaned closer, excited.

I nodded. "I think our auras belong together."

Her eyes widened. "Really?"

I glanced down at her breasts. They were heaving noticeably faster. "I'm certain of it," I said. Before I could take any further advantage of the moment, the front door opened and a large boned, long-faced man about six-feet tall came striding into the lobby. The secretary nodded in our direction and he spun around to look down at Miss Eagerness and me.

"Bernie Stein," he said warmly to the woman. Until that moment I wouldn't have known it was Stein. He wore a pair of cotton suntan slacks and a blue oxford cloth shirt, open at the collar. His long, angular face cracked into a wide smile, and he extended a bony hand to the cute little morsel sitting next to me.

The woman introduced herself as Malynda Price.

Stein finally turned to me and I told him who I was. His face clouded a little when I said I was with the police. It was comforting to find that another profession got as poor a reception from people as did lawyers.

"Do you mind if I talk to Miss Price first?" he asked. "It'll only take a few minutes to explain her program to her."

I told him to go ahead. "I'll see you again," I told Miss Price. Her walk across the lobby was everything I'd hoped it would be.

CHAPTER TWENTY-TWO

Doctor Bernie Stein spent less time with Malynda Price than I would have and when she came out of his office I had a chance to put in one last good word for myself with her. Just seeing Miss Price again cheered me up enough that it was hard to remember why I'd come to see the doctor. Then I remembered that it was because of his ex-wife.

Bernie Stein didn't have anything good to say about Francine except that she was brilliant. Other than that, according to him, she was a crook and a whore. "She knew what kind of plans I had for this place and it didn't bother her one bit to ruin them by splitting up the land and starting that damned Foundation of hers." Stein talked with big expansive gestures, like he was selling something even when he was complaining about his ex-wife.

"What kind of plans did you have?" I asked, surveying Stein's office. The room was about as different from that of his ex-wife as it could be. Stein's degrees and certificates were there on the wall, as they were in every doctor's office. This Doctor Stein was an internist. On his desk was a loosely organized assortment of Indian artifacts, including a peace pipe, a miniature ceremonial drum, several arrowheads, and a few well-worn rocks. It looked like he'd emptied out the back seat of his car after a stop at *Little America*. The walls of the office were dotted with posters spouting slogans like 'visualize health', 'take control of your body' and 'eat to live'. On one wall hung a five-foot high plastic board on which was written the day's schedule just the way it had appeared on the paper his secretary had given to me earlier.

Stein looked like he wished he hadn't said anything about his plans. He glanced around nervously, as if he might be overheard. "How do I know you aren't working for her? You don't seem like a cop."

I wasn't sure if I should feel flattered or insulted. "Working for her doing what?"

"Seeing if I'm going to sell…if I've had any offers."

"Sell? I thought that you leased the land."

"I don't own the land, but I own the buildings, the plantings, and the license for the health spa. It'd be a valuable acquisition for someone who wanted to expand the operation, like to add a golf course, for instance. But who'd buy the place now that it's half the size it used to be and there's a home for delinquents next door?"

"Your wife owns half the lease and she pulled out her half and ruined a deal for you?"

"Right," he answered, ruefully. He reached into his desk drawer and pulled out a pack of Benson and Hedges. "Mind if I smoke?"

I glanced around at his posters. "Health yourself," I said.

"Talking about my wife always does this to me. Assuming you're not working for her and you're really some type of cop, why are you interested in her?" He pulled a cigarette out of the pack and threw the rest on the top of the desk. Then he pulled a lighter and an ashtray from a side drawer and lit up. I watched jealously as he inhaled deeply and savored the first drag from his cigarette. A powerful air conditioner sucked the tell-tale smoke into a duct in the ceiling.

"I'm investigating the murder of one of the kids from the Foundation," I said.

"What's that got to do with Francine?"

"What's she really doing over there?"

"You mean you don't buy the behavior modification idea?"

"That's part of her program, but what else goes on there?"

His big eyes narrowed cagily. He took a long drag on his cigarette. "I'm not sure what you mean." He'd leaned forward in his chair, waiting for my answer.

"I visited the place and met some of the kids. She's done something to them. Made them passive, frightened. She says its behavior modification. It's got to be something more than just that."

Stein sat back and gazed at me, letting his cigarette burn between his fingers. "Passive? You mean totally non-aggressive?"

"That's exactly what I mean. Like they'd been altered in some way, physically altered, not just taught how to behave."

Stein pretended to be fascinated by his cigarette. I could see the wheels turning in his head. "Suppose you uncovered my ex-wife doing something illegal. Would you go after her?"

"You mean really illegal or just scamming people the way you do here?"

Stein looked insulted. He began to sputter. "What the hell are your talking about? We don't scam anybody here. What we do is on the cutting edge of science."

"Yeah. I listened to one of Chief Runningmouth's lectures. If I was a little old lady who'd read nothing but the Inquirer and Reader's Digest I'd have been impressed."

His mouth twisted into a half smile. "Bill Runningfoot represents a neglected side of medicine…the natural healing his ancestors practiced before they were driven from their land."

I picked up the peace pipe off of the desk. It was made of plastic. "I guess they were driven all the way to China," I said.

He sat up straight and stubbed out his cigarette. He'd dropped the friendly hale-fellow-well-met act. "OK McGowan, so I run a business here. You didn't answer my question. What if you found out my wife was doing something illegal?"

I wasn't sure what he was getting at. "Depends on how serious it was. I'm a consultant to the police department, pulled in for just this case. I'm also a lawyer, which makes me an officer of the court, but I prefer to live and let live. If she's cheating on her income taxes, that's her business. If she's abusing kids, that's something else."

Stein leaned forward, his elbows on the desk. He put the fingertips of his two hands together, drumming them against each other. Whatever he was thinking was giving him a real buzz. "I think I can help you, McGowan. Maybe we can help each other." He flipped through a Rolodex on his desk, then took a pen from his pocket and wrote something on a piece of paper, handing it to me when he finished. "I want you to visit Dr. Wang. This is his number at UCLA. He and my wife used to work together. Tell Wang I told you to look into the research Francine was doing when she was there."

"What kind of research?"

"Go see Wang. Have him tell you what Francine was doing there. If it gives you any ideas, give me a call."

I folded the paper and put it in my shirt pocket. "You know a guy named Jerry who works for your wife?"

Stein's whole face reddened. He was trying to keep his expression bland, but I could tell by the number of times that his Adam's apple bobbed up and down that he was having to swallow something pretty bitter. "Jerry used to work here. What about him?"

"What kind of things does your wife have him do?"

He stared hard at me. "If you mean is he balling Francine, the answer is yes."

I whistled softly. No wonder Jerry acted so confident around his boss. "That's interesting, but it's not what I meant. Was he ever involved in anything violent when he was here?"

Stein's eyes flashed. "Only when I threw him off the place, and my wife along with him. It was lucky that Adamji was here. He had to flatten Jerry with a few kicks to get him to let go of my throat."

"Adamji Dil?"

"His family holds the title to this property."

I had a sudden thought. "Was Adamji involved in your golf course deal?"

Stein didn't answer.

"If you and he got together, you could make a deal on the land too, couldn't you? Did Fanny Dil know her son was thinking of selling their place?"

"I'm not going to discuss private business with you. You may be some sort of cop, but this hasn't got anything to do with that kid's murder," Stein said. He looked like he'd just been seized by acute constipation. His mouth was squeezed into a tight slit.

I gave him a hard cop stare…like I'd seen on NYPD. "I'll decide what's relevant to this case, Doc. You just answer my questions. Who owns the Krishna School? Adamji or his mother?"

His voice came out pinched. "I have no idea." He was lying.

I was beginning to get the picture. Francine Stein had screwed up a lot bigger deal than selling just her husband's spa when she took her share of the land. She'd split the joint property of La Sol and the Krishna School right in half. The pieces that were left would never add up to what everything together would have been worth as one package.

"Let's get back to Jerry," I said. "Has he been back to bother you since?"

"No. I told him I'd call the police if he showed up here again. Adamji scared the hell out of him anyway. Why the questions about Jerry?"

"I got into it with him couple of times. He did some vandalism on my car. I wondered if it was likely to be his idea or something your wife put him up to."

"Most of what he does is what she tells him to do. But you never can be sure with Jerry. He's very twisted. They both are." Stein had a distracted look on his face, like he was preoccupied.

"You'd like to get both of them wouldn't you?"

Stein jerked his attention back to me. I'd read his thoughts. "Sure I would, and Francine knows it. That's why you can find out more about what she's doing over there than I can. I've got a pretty good idea, but I'm gonna let you find it out for yourself."

"From Wang?"

"Wang's just a start. You see what he's got to show you, then I might be able to get you something more."

"I'm trying to find out who killed a teenage kid, not do an expose on your wife."

"Those might not be two different things."

I was suspicious enough about the Foundation to think he might be right. At least it was worth a shot. I told Stein I'd be in touch.

CHAPTER TWENTY-THREE

When I got back home I put in a call to Nils and left a message to call me and let me know if he'd made any progress finding the cow-murderers. Then I called Hillary Smythe and asked her if she'd seen Jimmy again.

"He's disappeared," she said. "He was supposed to have an appointment with me after school today, but he didn't show up. I called his house and his father wouldn't tell me anything. His school said he never showed up today."

I couldn't tell if she was worried or irritated. "Maybe it was the cow incident. Maybe that got him upset, though that ought to make him more eager to come and talk to you, not less."

"The cow?"

I told her about what I'd seen at the Litton's farm that morning, leaving out some of the more gruesome details.

"Christ," she said. "Why wasn't his father more worried when I told him Jimmy hadn't made his appointment with me? And the family must have been called when he didn't show up at school. That's standard operating procedure to call the house to see if the child is home sick."

Now she was clearly worried. And she had a point. Jimmy's parents should have been more worried, themselves. I sure was. Somebody had come after Jimmy once before and somebody had been at his farm mutilating the family's cow. If Jimmy was now missing, he could be in serious danger.

"I'm going to call Nils," I said. "Jimmy could be in trouble."

"I'll try the parents again," Hillary said.

"Thanks Hillary. I'm glad we're working together on this."

"You're starting to sound like a real human being, McGowan."

"Thanks for warning me," I said.

I called Nils again, but he still wasn't in so I left another message for him to call me. This time I said it was urgent.

Nils called just as I was polishing off my second beer. I told him about my conversation with Bernie Stein, about Stein's plan with Adamji Dil to sell the Krishna School and La Sol, and about my plan to visit Doctor Wang at UCLA tomorrow. Then I told him that Jimmy Litton might be missing.

I could hear the tension in Nils' voice. "Jesus Brian, Torres' killer already tried to get to Jimmy once. I think that killing the Litton's cow was supposed to have been a warning to him."

"And you think it scared him away?"

"Either he took off or somebody's already gotten to him. I sure as hell hope he took the warning and left."

"Where would he go?'

"Beats me."

"Would his parents know?" I asked.

"Maybe his mother. I don't think he'd tell his father anything."

I didn't know if Nils was right or if he was just expressing his competition with Ronald Litton. "Can you talk to his mother?"

There was a pause on the other end of the line. "Sure," Nils finally answered.

I told Nils that I'd be in LA the next day, checking out Francine Stein's past at UCLA. I'd call in to see what he'd found out about Jimmy Litton.

When I hung up I opened a third beer. It wasn't healthy for me and I knew it was no way to cope with things, but I was damned bothered. There'd been too many deaths so far. I didn't want Jimmy Litton to be another one.

CHAPTER TWENTY-FOUR

Early the next morning I wound my way down the mountain, hoping to avoid getting caught in the commuter traffic coming into the city from the San Fernando Valley on 101. I took the cut off just outside of Shambhala, which brought me down to the coast at Ventura, rather than Santa Barbara. It was faster and I didn't have to deepen my depression by passing the spot where Karin Stengaard had been killed. The heavy rains had caused some mud slides and the road was still covered with a sheet of brown muck in a few places that hadn't yet been reached by the highway department workers. By the time I reached the ugly stretch of flats on the outskirts of Ventura—where rusty oil derricks were stationed every few hundred yards or so, bobbing up and down like so many feeding horses— my rental car had a coat of mud that reached to the tops of the wheel wells.

The traffic was light until I started down the hill just past Camarillo and began picking up the steady parade of workers making their way in from the outlying valley towns like Thousand Oaks, Calabasas, and Northridge. By the time I exited onto the 405, heading toward the western side of the city, I was stuck in the "move ten yards then wait a half-minute before moving again," influx into the city. I'd forgotten what it was like to drive in LA.

Sunset Boulevard was backed up for nearly a mile so I

skipped it and continued on at the pace of a gimpy snail until I got to Wilshire which was only backed up for half a mile. When I finally got off in Westwood, everyone and his brother did too and I stood at the light on Wilshire and Westwood for ten minutes waiting to make a left turn. Dr. Wang's office was in the Semel Institute for Neuroscience and Human Behavior in the Medical Plaza just before the UCLA campus proper. I could have walked into the place, had my appointment and left in the time it took me to wait in the line of cars filing past the guard station to get to the patients' and visitors' parking lot. Once inside the Institute I headed straight for the staff directory posted on the wall only to find that there were five Wang's with their own offices. I was lucky his name wasn't Chen. There were eight of those. Only one of the Wang's was in the Department of Genetics, so I grabbed the elevator and rode it to the fourth floor where his office was located. When I walked into the small reception area, which contained a half-dozen or so uncomfortable looking green plastic chairs and a big metal desk manned by an intense horn-rimmed young man wearing jeans, a blue work shirt and a waist-length white lab coat, unbuttoned in front, I was only twenty minutes late.

The young man managed to tear himself away from the computer screen and looked at me skeptically. "Mr. McGowan?" He glanced at his watch then back at me, his eyebrows arched critically.

"I suppose Dr. Wang is late," I said, smiling as pleasantly as I was able.

"You're the one who's late," he answered, his tone fussy.

"It's all relative," I said, dazzling him with a little new-age physics. My eyes were glued to his eyebrows to see what they were going to do next.

He raised one skeptical eyebrow. I was deeply impressed. "I'll tell him you're here," he said. He picked up the desk phone and pressed the intercom button with a flourish, then announced loudly that, "Mr. McGowan has *finally* arrived," raising both eyebrows in my direction. I decided he could have handled the whole interchange with eyebrow signals.

In a moment a small, middle-aged Asian man came through a door off to my left. He was dressed in a white knee-length lab coat over a pair of cotton suntan pants and an open necked blue button-down oxford cloth shirt. It was the California doctor uniform... casual but all business. His round, tan face gave the same message—all business— only now he looked irritated. "You're late Mr. McGowan."

"Gee," I said. "Nobody mentioned it."

He looked at me with distaste, checked his watch and sighed. Then he held out his hand and ushered me toward the door he'd just come through. We followed a narrow hallway for about thirty feet, then he reached around me and opened the door to an office. I stepped inside and he followed. It was cramped. It wasn't intended for anyone other than Wang. The desk held two computers. Both were turned on. Papers were piled in every free space, including on the only chair other than Wang's. He cleared a place for me by lifting the papers off the chair and setting them on the floor.

"I've told Bernie Stein I can't talk about Francine," he said. His gaze darted around my face, like he was trying to memorize every line.

"That's OK," I said, glancing around the room. "The trip was worth it just to see your décor."

Wang chewed on his lower lip and gave me a long, hard look. "Why did Bernie Stein want you to talk to me?"

"He just said I should see what you were doing. He wanted me to see what his wife was doing when she worked here."

He leaned forward across his desk. "This is an NIH funded project. I don't give tours. Bernie knows that."

I smiled a smile of infinite tolerance. "I guess Bernie's worried that his wife may be continuing to pursue whatever kind of research she was doing when she was here. Whatever she's doing now could be connected to a murder. Maybe Bernie was trying to protect you."

The word murder had gotten his attention. He leaned anxiously across his desk. "Protect me. How? From what?"

I kept smiling. My face was beginning to hurt. "From getting caught covering up something that you knew could be dangerous. From being blamed for sweeping whatever Francine Stein was doing under the carpet."

He swallowed and looked at me suspiciously, licking his lips slowly. "I'm just trying to protect the university. I'm not covering anything up."

"Then show me your research. Tell me what Doctor Stein was doing when she was here. And what got her fired."

He looked confused. "I can't. The university…"

"Fuck the university," I said. "How's the university going to look if Francine Stein's research was responsible for a boy's death? How are you going to look if you could have helped and didn't? I know I seem like I'm just another pretty face, doctor, but I'm a lawyer… a very successful one. I've seen careers ruined and yours may be the next one. The university will leave you hanging out to dry. They'll claim ignorance of everything and blame you for covering up. It always works that way."

He looked panicked. "What is Francine doing?" he said in almost a whisper.

"She's altered the behavior of a bunch of kids. Aggressive delinquents have become meek and docile. The boy who was killed exhibited the same kind of meek behavior."

He looked alarmed. "How long have the delinquent kids been passive?" he asked.

"How long? I have no idea." I thought about it. When they were in town it was only Manuel Torres who'd been passive. "Not more than a few days, I'd guess. Why? Is that important?"

Wang got up. "I hope I don't regret this," he said, although whether he was addressing me or himself was unclear. "Let me show you something."

CHAPTER TWENTY-FIVE

We walked down a short hallway until we reached a set of double doors labeled *No Admittance*. Wang pushed through the doors with me shadowing him. Inside were rows of animal cages. It smelled like a kennel. Most of the cages were empty, but I could hear a general rustling...small sounds of metal rattling, an occasional vocalization. Nothing human. Near the back I could see that a few large cages contained monkeys, some of them pacing back and forth. In another corner were some smaller cages, and in them, large albino rats, their tiny red eyes glittering as they watched us.

Wang continued walking briskly until he came to a narrow door with a small window in it at face height. He peered in, then opened the door softly, walking slowly. I followed cautiously, half expecting some kind of animal to leap out. In the center of the room was a medium size cage. The monkey in it had bandages on his nose and ears. Stiff plastic hollow tubes held his upper and lower extremities in extension. Each of his fingers and toes was bandaged and some looked abnormally shortened. A rubber device ran beneath his chin, then between his teeth, holding them apart, and fastened behind his head. He was standing, but it looked more like he was balancing on his stubby bandaged feet and holding himself up by grasping the wires of his cage with his bandaged hands. His eyes searched us anxiously. He tried to open his mouth and make a sound but all that emerged was a stifled guttural noise. He started shaking then he fell over.

Wang stopped. "Easy, easy," he said in a low voice. I didn't know if he was talking to me or the monkey. "He's afraid I'm going to take off the devices," he said softly. "Easy boy, I'm not going to do it." Wang kept talking in that same low, soft voice. The monkey became less agitated. He hoisted himself up to a sitting position, staring at Wang.

"I want you to see his nose and ears," Wang said to me in the same soft voice he was using for the animal in the cage. He was unlocking the door and very slowly opening it. The monkey watched him warily. When Wang got his right hand inside the cage, the monkey drew back one arm and slapped Wang's hand with a ringing blow from the plastic tube. The pain showed in Wang's eyes, but he didn't remove his hand. Instead, he placed his left hand inside the cage and used it to grab the monkey's arm and hold it. He held the animal's other arm with his right forearm and used his fingers to pull back the bandage across the nose. Where the nose should have been there was only a mass of partially healed scar tissue. Wang pressed the bandage back and showed me one ear. It was a similar mess. He covered it back up and removed his hands from the cage.

"Willie did that to himself. He beat his own hands against his nose and ears. His fingers are almost all bitten off. So are his toes. If we take off the mouth guard, he'll chew off his lips. That's why he's afraid of me taking off his restraints. He doesn't want to hurt himself. He knows he can't control it."

"Why?" Was all I could think to say.

"Lesch-Nyhan disorder…created artificially."

"What?"

"Lesch-Nyhan disorder."

"You mean a disease that makes him self-destructive?"

"Not just self-destructive…aggressive. Remember the blow to my hand. If the mouth guard was off he'd bite me just as soon as he'd bite himself. If he could open his mouth wider he'd spit at us. If he were human, he'd swear and call us the most filthy names he could think of. Then he'd tell us he was sorry and mean it."

"People have this disease?"

Wang nodded. "It's rare, but people have it. It's what's known as an X-linked recessive disorder. Passed on through the female, but expressed in the male. Lesch-Nyhan is thankfully very rare, less than one birth in 400,000. An enzyme produced by a gene on the X-chromosome is absent. They are lacking an enzyme called hypoxanthine guanine phosphoribosyl-transferase or HPRT. The body needs this substance to recycle purines. Without it, abnormally high levels of uric acid build up in the body. We also suspect it has something do with the production of neurotransmitters, such as dopamine, adenosine and serotonin, but we don't know how. Serotonin is involved in a number of aggressive disorders. We can give a drug to reduce the uric acid, but it doesn't affect the behavior."

He might as well have been talking Swahili. "Doctor Stein was studying this disease?" I asked.

Wang nodded. He latched the door on Willie's cage and led me back out of the room. We crossed the large room to a far corner where several medium size cages sat by themselves. Each of them was occupied by a lone monkey. Wang began putting on a pair of heavy leather gloves.

"Francine made a discovery," Wang said. "She found that if DNA from Willie is implanted in a host monkey, the recipient reacts by increasing production of Serotonin and by becoming passive, extremely so. Watch." He opened one of the cages and reached in. The monkey inside shrank away from Wang's hands, but he was quick to scoop the animal up. Once he had him in his hands there was no resistance. Wang held the monkey under one arm while he opened the door to another cage. The monkey in the second cage approached the door eagerly. Wang place the first monkey in with the second. The latter monkey approached the other tentatively, sticking out his snout to smell him and reaching one hand over. The first monkey cowered in the corner. The second looked confused. He approached the other monkey again. The frightened monkey lay flat on the floor and covered his head with his arms. His body shook and a pool of urine spread out underneath his hips. Wang reached in and lifted the animal back out of the cage, placing him back in his own.

"This animal has had Willie's DNA for three weeks. The animal I put him in with is normal."

"This is Stein's discovery?" I asked.

"And more," Wang said. He was moving the 'normal' monkey's cage over next to that of another monkey. As soon as he was within a few feet of the other monkey's cage, the second animal rushed at the wire mesh. His lips were curled back over his teeth and his ears were laid back, like an attacking dog. Wang kept moving toward the angry monkey. He pushed the cage of the normal monkey within a foot of the other. The second monkey kept up it's attack. It began biting the wires of the cage, as though it might sever the wires and reach its target. Blood was beginning to appear from lacerations on his gums and lips. He was ripping at the wires with fingers and toes. Wang removed the other cage and threw a blanket over the cage of the agitated monkey.

"He has Lesch-Nyhan disorder?" I asked.

Wang shook his head. "He doesn't self-mutilate. He's only aggressive."

"What's wrong with him?"

"He had the same DNA transfer as the other monkey. Three weeks ago he was passive. Now he's like this. In another three weeks he'll be back to normal."

"So the passivity reverses itself?"

"Umhuh." Wang nodded. He was removing his gloves. When he got them off we walked back to his office.

Wang poured us both coffee from a glass pot that looked like it might be breeding some kind of new bacterial strain.

"How do you get DNA from one animal into another?" I asked.

"It's only temporary and it only applies to the DNA in blood cells. It'd be hard to make the procedure make sense to you, but it's a lot like a bone marrow transplant. The idea is that new blood cells are produced by the foreign DNA. The effects are limited to chemical reactions because the body's structure has already been determined by inherited DNA."

"So the new host develops chemical reactions that are like someone with Lesch-Nyhan disorder?"

"Some of the reactions. Actually, the body reacts by lowering the precursors to Serotonin production, among other things and there's a compensatory reaction that enhances the action of the smaller amount of Serotonin that continues to get produced. That's what decreases the aggression. Unfortunately, the body starts to reject the foreign bone marrow and the blood starts to return to normal."

I interrupted him. "Would the white cell count go up during the rejection phase?" I was thinking about Manuel Torres.

"Way up. It's the body's immune system reacting to a foreign agent. When the new DNA is finally inactivated, the brain receptors for Serotonin have become so used to the amplified effect of the neurotransmitter that they begin to habituate…they essentially won't fire any more. It's like a total depletion of Serotonin until that process, too, runs its course."

"And during that time the hyper-aggression comes out?"

"You've got it."

"How come Francine Stein got let go?" I asked, switching

the subject while Wang still had the illusion that I'd understood what he'd just told me. "It looks as if you're still carrying out the same line of research that she was."

He closed his eyes, as if he could shut me out. Sorry pal, I don't go away that easily. "I'm not doing what she did. That's not something I'm supposed to talk about," he said.

I looked at him hard. "I thought we had settled that," I said. "You and I both know what Stein is doing now. Those kids I saw reminded me an awful lot of that passive monkey. If they're going to become aggressive…"

"OK," Wang interrupted me. "She got let go because she tried out the DNA transfer on humans, specifically a retarded child up at Camarillo. The university hadn't okayed human research yet."

"What happened? I mean with the child at Camarillo."

He smiled, almost to himself. "It worked. The child was autistic, self-destructive like the Lesch-Nyhan monkey, but not nearly so bad. After the DNA transfer the self-destructiveness went away."

"Permanently?"

"For about a month. Then the reversal happened. He got worse. Almost killed himself by beating his head against the floor. He became aggressive too. It lasted another month."

"But your monkeys don't show self-destructive behavior, right?"

"This autistic boy was self-destructive in the first place. These were normal monkeys. It only makes them aggressive."

"Where did Stein get the DNA? Not from Willie, I hope."

Wang smiled bitterly. "No. Willie's DNA wouldn't have worked. There was another patient at Camarillo with Lesch-Nyhan, one who'd been there for years. He's an unusual case. Usually there's a fair degree of mental retardation and physical handicap that accompanies the disorder. This young man at Camarillo is only mildly retarded and he's barely physically handicapped at all. In fact he's frighteningly able and over six feet tall. He's aggressive, but he's only mildly self-destructive. Still he's always had to be kept isolated or he'd injure someone. Francine used his DNA."

I thought for a minute. "Is there any way to counteract the violent phase of the reaction? The kids I saw at Stein's place were all passive."

Wang shrugged. "That's what I'm working on...been working on for over three years. We've had some luck with SSRI's— specific Serotonin reuptake inhibitors like Prozac and a few experimental drugs that are stronger. We can reduce the aggression, but it doesn't go away entirely. It'll still get triggered by natural releasers for aggression, like another aggressive animal, or a wounded one, or competition for a female."

"Could Francine have found a cure for the aggressive phase?" I asked Wang.

He waited a few seconds before responding, thinking the question over. "It's possible," he said. "Francine is brilliant. I find it hard to believe she'd alter a whole group of delinquents if she knew they were going to become hyper-aggressive a month later. She'd never be able to contain them."

I thought about the barbed wire fences around the foundation office. Francine Stein was protecting herself in case her experiments produced more aggression than she could handle. I wasn't so sure she wouldn't try out DNA transfers with her kids.

"She'd need a supply of DNA from a patient with Lesch-Nyhan wouldn't she?" I asked.

Wang nodded.

"Could she have taken enough—blood samples or whatever— from the patient at Camarillo?"

He shrugged. "Maybe...that was several years ago."

"Maybe she's gone back."

"They won't let her in the door of that place," he said.

"A new patient?"

"Could be. It's a rare disorder. There are only a couple of hundred people with this disease in the whole U.S. Most of those with the disorder die at a young age."

"And if she did have a source of Lesch-Nyhan DNA and gave it to her kids," I asked. "How would they act?"

"Passive at first, then when their own immune system began to reject the foreign DNA, they'd go through alternating periods of passivity and aggression. Finally, they'd become hyper-aggressive."

"And during that phase?"

"They'd attack their weakest member…or anyone outside their group. If Francine is using Lesch-Nyhan DNA with those delinquents, she's playing with fire. Their behavior could get very nasty, very fast. I mean lethal. She could be creating a very dangerous situation up there."

"Maybe she already has," I said as I thanked him and left.

CHAPTER TWENTY-SIX

I had a few more stops to make before I could return to Shambhala. I went back down to the lobby of the Semel Institute and called Bernie Stein on my cell phone. Bernie had told me he could help if I thought that I had something on his ex-wife. I didn't have anything definite and I didn't think it really constituted a crime except insofar as it probably violated some laws regarding the use of minors as subjects in experiments, but it would sure shut Francine Stein's operation down in a hurry if I was right and the news got out.

I told Bernie about the likelihood that his ex-wife was conducting some kind of DNA transplant experiments related to making her delinquent charges less aggressive. That was about as far as I could go in explaining what Doctor Wang had said to me. Most of his explanation had passed right through my brain without leaving any trace. I did remember that she needed a source for the DNA she was using and I told Bernie that to make our case we'd have to find out where she was getting the Lesch-Nyhan DNA; either from a live human donor or maybe from a supply she had left over from her earlier experiments at Camarillo.

Stein didn't sound as if he were totally surprised by what I told him. He began to gloat. He finally had his ex-wife right where he wanted her. I tried to slow him down by explaining that I had no proof of any of this so far. The human DNA donor was only an assumption that I couldn't prove. He was undaunted. He said that if she was using a live donor or had an illegal supply of DNA on her property he'd get proof of it for me. For reasons he didn't seem eager to divulge, it turned out that he had keys to most of the locked gates and doors at the Foundation. The thought of Bernie Stein sneaking around the Foundation looking for evidence of his ex-wife's secret research made me nervous. Two people might have already been killed for being too curious about the Foundation. I warned him that he would be putting himself needlessly into danger since Nils and I could investigate as soon as I got back to Shambhala. He said he wouldn't mount a full-scale search of the Foundation, but he wanted to do some scouting after dark. We agreed to meet at his place around midnight to discuss what he'd found.

I called Ernesto Robles, an old friend from my LAPD days who was still a detective with the homicide division. There was a slim chance that Ernie was working on the Janice Le murder, but even if he wasn't he could fill me in on what had been found out so far.

Ernie wasn't directly involved in the investigation of Janice Le's death, but he knew the personnel who were and, even better, he was very aware of Manuel Torres' old gang, having investigated a few killings in which they were on either the delivering or the receiving end. He and I hadn't talked since my heart attack and we agreed to meet at Jerry's Deli in Westwood for lunch. The restaurant had been one of my favorite spots for making contacts and hobnobbing with potential future clients over the last several years. Ernie liked any excuse for getting out of his East LA precinct.

Walking into the crowded restaurant at lunch time, I kept my eyes on the floor and avoided scanning the room for familiar faces, not really wanting to see any old acquaintances and having to explain what I'd been doing for the last six or eight months. If Ernie was there, he'd see me and if he arrived later he'd find me. After all, Ernie was a cop.

I ordered a Caesar salad and a glass of raspberry ice tea and sat thinking about Doctor Wang's performance with his deranged monkeys. Except for the fact that I'd seen the meek behavior of the inmates at the Yearling Foundation, the idea of Francine Stein manipulating the DNA of a bunch of delinquents to reduce their aggression sounded too fantastic to believe. Seeing Wang's monkeys made the idea a little more believable, but a whole lot scarier. That any human being could turn into a source of pure aggression like the monkey, Willie, had become, was frightening enough, but to think that it might happen to a group of violence-prone street-toughs was horrifying. Of course I was letting my imagination get well ahead of the facts. All I really knew was that a bunch of the Foundation kids were uncharacteristically *un*-aggressive and that, from everything I'd heard, Manny Torres had been too.

My Mary Shelleyesque musings were interrupted by the dark, friendly face of Ernie Robles staring at me with a wide grin as he slid into the booth opposite me. He pointed at my tall, reddish iced tea. "You still sick, bro? What's with the tea?"

"I'm on duty," I said. "I'm working for the Shambhala Police Department. You know that cops can't drink on duty."

"Sure," he said. He turned and waved at the nearest waiter. "Bring me a beer." Then he turned back to me, the grin still plastered on his face, though I think he was forcing it to stay there longer than it would have on its own. "How the hell have you been? Where have you been?"

"Shambhala. Living the clean life. Clean mountain air, a mostly vegetable diet, almost no booze. Sex is only a memory."

He looked long and hard at me. "No shit man, you look a hundred percent better than the last time I saw you. Hell, you look ten years younger. If I'd known the clean life could do that for you I might have tried it myself." He rolled his eyes up and to the left, like he was thinking. "No I guess I wouldn't have, but it's helped you. How'd you get involved in police work? Has that got anything to do with your interest in Janice Le?"

The waiter delivered Ernie's beer and my salad. Ernie eyed the salad and then me, then told the waiter to bring him the same thing I was having. I told him about Manuel Torres' murder and Janice Le's role defending Jimmy Litton. I told him I was still involved in the Torres investigation, sort of as a favor to the Shambhala police chief.

"Torres' gang didn't do the killing," Ernie said. "Torres was big with them, and they'd probably like to go after whoever killed him, but there aren't many in his crowd with the balls to off somebody who was from outside the neighborhood, especially a lawyer. Everybody down there knows you don't get away with killing outsiders."

"You mean they can kill other Hispanics and get away with it?"

"A lot of my fellow boys in blue figure one less spic is a favor not a crime. They only have to worry when I get on the case…me or a couple other of my Latino bro's. But a young Asian lawyer from the Public Defender's office? My department's gonna tear the neighborhood apart on this one."

"What have they found so far?"

He took a long draw on his beer as the waiter set down his Caesar salad. I could see the shock on his face as he realized that the salad was all that was coming. "You sure this health diet is safe?" I smiled and nodded.

"So far nobody's found diddly. She was shot on the street, like a drive-by. Only whoever did the shooting just shot once and managed to take her out with the one shot. Gang gunnies aren't that good and they know it. That's why they always spray their victims with all the firepower they can. Besides, the bigger and messier it is the more powerful they feel. This killing was more like a precision assassination."

"Weapon?"

"Hunting rifle, 30 caliber, most likely a Blaser Jagdwaffen. I don't want to sound prejudiced against my own people, but I'm willing to bet they've never seen a .30 caliber Blaser Jagdwaffen. For one thing, it's a high powered German rifle that's only available in the big sporting goods stores. And it costs a hell of a lot of money…between two and three thousand dollars. Even on the street, like if someone ripped one off and was trying to unload it, it'd cost more than any of those Chicanos could afford. And then the most important thing is that they never buy rifles. You can't conceal 'em. What'd be the point?"

"So it's somebody trying to make it look like a gang drive-by?"

"Somebody who doesn't know anything about the kind of people he's trying to pin it on. Not very bright, not from the city, and with enough money to buy that kind of gun. That's who did it."

"I may know someone like that," I said.

"No kidding? You think it's got something to do with the case the Le girl was working on in Shambhala?"

I told him about Karin Stengaard and the threat against me. I told him about Jerry.

"Whew, bro! I think you'd better talk to the guys who are investigating this one for us. Sounds like you may have a suspect for them. This Jerry guy got a record?"

"Nothing."

We finished our salads and I got the name of the detective in charge of the Le investigation. I headed back to my car, leaving Ernie in Jerry's Deli ordering a hamburger and French fries.

CHAPTER TWENTY-SEVEN

Of course I'd managed to wait until the beginning of early rush hour to head back out of town so the drive back was as slow and fitful as the morning's commute. By the time I turned off the 101 and started the climb back up the mountain to Shambhala, dusk was settling. The heavy mud had been cleaned off of the road and the pavement was visible, which helped me see the road once the darkness enveloped the hillside. When I reached the valley I went straight home and had a beer and a turkey sandwich. There were still four hours before I was to meet Bernie Stein at La Sol. I decided it might not hurt to show up early. Besides, I could drop in on Malynda Price and see how her inner search was coming along.

I parked my car in the "visitors" lot and walked the quarter of a mile up the hill to the cottages. Miss Price was her usual effervescent self. She greeted me with an athletic hug, as though I were a long-lost friend. I was happy to be any kind of friend, she looked so inviting in a thigh-length, strapless sarong, and I started to step inside her bungalow when I sensed an unexpected resistance from her. "I've discovered my inner light," she said eagerly, one hand firmly planted against my chest.

"Uh huh," I answered.

"It was locked inside me all the time," she went on. "It only took the right key. I needed to develop my inner visualization."

Uh oh. I'd heard that line about visualization before. "Have you got an Indian in there with you?" I asked, cutting to the chase.

"He's marvelous!" she exuded.

Now I knew how General Custer felt. "Remember to keep hold of your hair," I said, leaving the porch and returning to the footpath. I began walking. The night air felt good. I hoped Malynda Price was happy with Chief Runningmouth. Her aura didn't really match mine anyway.

The cool air was laced with a hint of moisture. There was a light breeze that stirred the oak leaves overhead and I could see soft lights glowing in the windows of bungalows partially hidden through the trees. I kept walking until the last bungalow was well out of sight. The path was lit by electric lamps on tall poles every hundred feet or so. After a while I noticed a heavy chain link fence about ten yards off the path to my right. It was the fence surrounding the Yearling Foundation.

The fence and the pathway began to run parallel to each other. The lights on the path only cast their illumination about fifty feet in any direction and the thick trees cut down on that. I couldn't make out anything on the other side of the fence except that the forest ended as soon as the Foundation land started. Whatever was on the other side of the fence was enveloped in inky blackness. No buildings were visible at all. I was about to turn around and go back when I heard something. It was the sound of someone running, or maybe more than one person. I couldn't tell. The sound came from up ahead but beyond the trees and on the edge of the Foundation property. I hesitated a moment, remembering the savage beatings that had been inflicted on Manuel Torres and the jail guard by some superhuman killer. I thought about Doctor Wang's monkeys and what a human with that same disorder would be like, especially one who was a violent criminal to begin with. But I was looking for Bernie Stein so I sucked it up and headed in the direction of the sound. I'd only gone a few feet further down the path when something ahead caught my attention. It looked like a large shape hanging off the fence. I inched more slowly down the path toward whatever it was. When I was fifteen yards away I moved into the trees and toward the fence. I could just make out the object. A cold anxious feeling began to creep up to my throat from my stomach. In another couple of feet I was staring into the mutilated face of Bernie Stein.

He hung by one arm, which was grotesquely twisted through the links of the fence. It looked as if someone had pulled on the arm from my side of the fence until Stein's face and neck were tight against the chain. The man's face was a giant open wound. I approached him gingerly, alert to any sound or movement that would indicate that Stein's attacker or attackers hadn't left. When I got right next to him I stuck my hand through the fence and felt his neck for a pulse. I knew there wasn't going to be one, but I had to try. His skin was still warm. I wiggled the fingers on the hand that was sticking through the fence. The fingers hadn't begun to stiffen. Bernie had only been dead a short while. I instantly became more alert, listening for the sounds I'd heard before. I didn't hear or see anything.

Stein didn't appear to be carrying a cell phone or camera or anything as conspicuous as that to record whatever he'd found, if he'd found anything. There was no way to know if he was on his way into the Foundation or coming back out. I reached as far through the fence as I could and felt inside his shirt and pants pockets. Nothing...a few keys, his wallet, and some change. I looked at the keys. There were two key rings; one had an obvious Mercedes car key and four other keys that could have been house or office or anything. The other ring was an unadorned circular band of metal with three different keys. Two of them were the two-sided variety that usually fit a padlock. I pocketed the second ring. Then I decided I should call Nils.

The walk back made me feel creepy. What had been pleasant solitude a few minutes before now produced an eerie sense of loneliness. The gravel path was harder to follow. The dark stretches between the lights seemed longer than they had before. I tripped twice…over nothing. The faint lights from the bungalows in the trees reminded me that there were people here who were pursuing an innocent, if mindless, quest for self-improvement, or longevity, or good health or something. They'd paid their money and put their faith in Doctor Bernard Stein. Or maybe they just wanted a brief respite from the inexorableness of aging and dying, wanted to pretend that aging was only a chimera constructed by a world they had left when they entered La Sol. Bernie Stein's murder would remind them that the world's ugliness is something they couldn't escape. I felt bad for them, especially the old geezers. They could use a little benevolence at their age. They weren't going to get it looking for Shangri-La next door to the Yearling Foundation.

The lights were off and the door to the La Sol office was locked. I didn't see a pay phone anywhere around and I'd left my cell phone in my jacket in the car, which was about a quarter of a mile away. There was only one thing to do.

Malynda Price was still breathless when she opened the door. Maybe she'd just had a workout with the Chief. She tried to maintain her brightness, but I could tell she was confused to see me again. I must have seemed like the sort of sensible fellow who could take a hint. I told her I needed to use her cell phone.

She looked like she wanted to protest, but I took her gently, but firmly, by her pretty shoulders and steered her back inside her bungalow and over to the couch where I sat her down. "I'm afraid there's been a mishap," I said. "I've got to use your phone to call the police."

William Runningfoot came out of a back room. He wasn't dressed in full regalia, but he still wore jeans and moccasins and his shirt had a beaded design on it. Was it my imagination or was he zipping his fly? "What are you doing here?' he asked.

"Where's your phone?" I asked Malynda, ignoring Runningfoot.

She pointed to her purse on the kitchen counter.

"I asked you a question," Runningfoot said. He was doing his best to look fierce. "We were just having a lesson in visualization and you've interrupted it."

"Visualize this," I said, "your boss, Doctor Stein is about a half mile down the path hanging on the fence. He's deader than a doornail. I think I'd better call the police."

Malynda gasped. The Indian's face paled. "Dead?"

"Didn't I just say that?"

"But how?" he asked, his mouth hanging open.

"It wasn't from smoking," I said.

Malynda sat up straight. "Doctor Stein smoked?" she asked irrelevantly. It seemed to shock her as much as the fact that he was dead.

"I think he finally kicked the habit," I said.

Runningfoot looked devastated. He ought to. His meal ticket had just died. "Be serious," he said. "How did he die?"

I shrugged. "Let's let the police figure that out." I went into the kitchen and took the cell from the purse and called 911. The dispatcher at the station said he'd call Nils at home and have him come over. There was another cruiser out tonight and he'd send him too. I said I'd wait at Miss Price's Bungalow.

I was tense as a cat. "You don't have any beer, by any chance, do you?" I asked Malynda.

"This is a health spa!" she answered, looking at me like I'd just asked for an injection of heroin, or worse…maybe a Big Mac.

The chief went over to a chair and picked up a large leather beaded pouch. He unhooked the lid and reached in. When his hand came back out, he had a pint of scotch in it. He unscrewed the lid and took a swig, then passed it over to me. I took a healthy nip then offered it to Malynda. She looked at me like I was offering her a container of anthrax. I passed it back to the chief. The Indian had pulled a pack of Camels out of his pouch and was lighting up. He offered me one, but I declined.

Malynda began opening windows. "What about purifying our bodies and spirits?" she asked Runningfoot. There was a touch of hysteria in her voice.

He jerked his head up, like he'd forgotten she was there. His cigarette ash was half an inch long, but he didn't seem to notice. "Jesus lady, Doctor Stein's dead. Who gives a shit about all that crap right now?" he said.

"The noble savage," I said.

Runningfoot gave me an angry look. His ash fell off on the floor. Malynda looked at him disgustedly. He got up and walked to the door. "I'll smoke on the porch."

Malynda was waving her hands in the air as if to clear the smoke. Her nose was wrinkled up like somebody had farted. Her eyes were wide and scared.

I moved over closer to her on the couch. "The police will be here any minute. They'll figure out what happened to Stein. You need to relax."

"Stay here," she said, looking up at me with wide, frightened eyes.

"I have to talk to the police. That means I have to go back to where the body is. After that, I'll come back to check on you."

Her eyes became doe-like. She snuggled up against me. I had other things on my mind. I wished I could be on the porch smoking with the chief…or at least nipping from his bottle of scotch. I was beginning to respect some of the Indian ways. I heard the distant sound of a siren.

I pried Malynda's arms from around my waist and stood up. "I've got to show the police where the body is. It'll be awhile. I need to talk to Chief Larsen. Try to go to sleep."

Her look was both trusting and desperate. Her eyes were red and tired looking. I hoped she'd go to sleep.

CHAPTER TWENTY-EIGHT

Nils and his officers must have arrived at the same time. All three of them were coming down the path when I went out on the porch. Both of the officers had powerful flashlights, the beams of which played around the edge of the path. William Runningfoot was nowhere to be seen.

"It's a half-mile farther down the path," I said as Nils approached. "Stein is on the other side of the fence, the Foundation side."

We fell in step together, the two officers behind us. One of them was Halvorsen, the fat deputy who'd been at the desk when I'd visited Nils. The other was a young, well-built fellow with a Howie Long crew cut and a strong chin. Nils switched on his own flashlight and showed it on the path in front of us as we walked. "What the hell was he doing over there, I wonder?" he said. Off in the trees the doors to other bungalows were cracking open, aging, frightened eyes peering out, watching but afraid to get involved. The sirens had attracted people's attention. Some of the bolder guests came out onto their porches.

"He was trying to get some information on his wife," I said.

Nils looked at me suspiciously. "What kind of information? And how do you know what he was doing?"

"I talked to him around noon. Doctor Wang, the UCLA scientist he sent me to see showed me the kind of research that Francine Stein was doing. I thought she might still be doing the research and Stein said he was going to find some proof. He wanted to get enough on his wife to get her off the Foundation property so he and Adamji can go through with their sale."

"Jesus Christ. It just gets more and more complicated." Nils spat in the gravel as we walked along the path. "That Adamji is a weasel. I'm sure Fanny doesn't know anything about his plans." He seemed to get lost in his thoughts for a moment. Then he looked back at me. "What kind of research is Doctor Stein supposed to be doing?"

"I don't understand it completely, but it has to do with altering DNA or neurotransmitters or something. She's trying to modify her kids' aggression by giving them bone marrow from someone who has a certain type of genetic disorder. In Wang's monkeys it can cause either extremely meek behavior or violence, or both."

"You mean Stein's experimenting on those kids?"

"Maybe. This is all hypothetical. In order to do it she'd need a human donor with the right genetic disorder or a supply of blood from one. That's what Bernie was looking for."

We were near the spot where I'd first glimpsed Stein's body through the trees. "There…," I told Nils, motioning toward the fence. He shone his flashlight. The body hanging by one arm on the fence looked even more surreal in the beam of his light.

"Holy shit!" the fat deputy said.

We retraced my earlier path through the trees. When we got to the body, Nils walked back and forth in front of it before doing anything. He grasped the fingers on the hand that stuck through the fence. They'd lost their flexibility. Nils had to apply some pressure to extend the fingers. "Between one and two hours," he said.

"He was still warm an hour ago when I found him," I

volunteered.

Nils sent his fat deputy back to the cruiser for some wire cutters. Then Nils climbed up and over the fence, the same way Bernie Stein must have done to get onto the Foundation grounds. He had to jump the eight or so feet from the top. Nils made it look easy. The other cop, whose name actually turned out to be H. Long, and I, followed. The top of the fence was covered with coiled barbed wire, but Nils had thrown his coat across it. I grabbed hold as best I could, then followed Nils' lead and jumped across the top and down to the ground on the other side. Deputy Long followed me. When we'd made it to the other side, Nils made us stop before we went over to the body. He told us not to touch anything until the Medical Examiner got there. His gaze scanned the dark Foundation grounds.

"There's probably a road around here someplace, but I don't want the ME bringing an ambulance across this grass until we've looked for foot prints. That's why I don't want us walking around next to the body either." Nils turned to his officer. "We can't leave him hanging until morning so take your light and start looking at the ground but not too near the body. We'll wait until the ME can photograph the scene. We'll have him bring the ambulance down the path over on the La Sol side." His man nodded and got on his cell phone to the ambulance.

"You know what this looks like, don't you?" Nils asked me, staring at Stein's body from about five feet away.

"What?" I was a perfect straight man.

"Manuel Torres. The only difference is that Stein's on the inside of the fence."

It was an interesting thought. I'd been thinking of Torres' death as a crime of passion or at least of impulse. I was pretty sure that Bernie Stein was killed very deliberately.

The other officer was back with a giant pair of wire cutters; the kind they use to cut through the metal on cars after accidents. He'd driven his cruiser down the path and now he'd directed its floodlight on the scene, giving everything the appearance of a movie set. Despite the thickness of the chain link, he made quick work of it. Pretty soon there was a hole in the fence big enough for a man to walk through.

The Medical Examiner and his helpers had arrived. They began photographing the body and the entire area. An ambulance had backed down the path over on the La Sol side of the fence and after the ME had made his notes and had all of his photographs, the attendants put Stein's body on a stretcher and took him back out through the hole that had been cut in the fence, then up to the ambulance that was waiting to take him to the morgue. About that time, the headlights from a car could be seen bouncing across the grass toward us from the direction of the Foundation buildings.

"Looks like we finally woke somebody up," I said.

Nils moved toward the approaching headlights waving his arms. The car pulled up and two doors slammed. Jerry and Doctor Francine Stein came walking across the grass.

"What's going on here?" Doctor Stein said, the apprehension apparent in her voice. She was dressed in a pair of tight fitting jeans and a man's cotton shirt, loose at the waist. Her outfit made her look less severe from a distance. She looked tired, but her eyes were wide and alert.

Nils waited until she got close, then he spoke in a low, gentle voice. "It's your ex-husband, Doctor Stein. I'm afraid he's been killed."

"What do you mean, killed?" Her voice was shrill. She was biting on her knuckles. Jerry stood behind her, his gaze darting between Nils and me.

"It looks like murder. He was beaten," Nils said.

"Bernie…beaten?" She looked around at Jerry. He was watching the cops, who were examining the ground for footprints. She was struggling to regain her composure. Her gaze followed the receding, flashing lights of the ambulance that contained her ex-husband's body. She took a deep breath and, for the first time, seemed to focus on Nils and me. She glanced over at the gaping hole in the fence. "Bernie was on Foundation property?"

"Yes," Nils said. "He was next to the fence. We're trying to figure out if this is where he was attacked or if maybe he was attacked and got away but couldn't get over the fence."

"You mean attacked on our grounds?" Doctor Stein looked alarmed. Her shock still hadn't worn off.

"Yes ma'am. That's what it looks like, but we don't know exactly where."

"But what would Bernie have been doing here at night? And why wouldn't he have come to the office?"

Nils glanced at me, but I didn't offer him any help. "We don't know any of that yet, Doctor." He paused and took a breath. "We'll have to talk to your kids."

"And Jerry," I chimed in.

Jerry jumped like a startled rabbit at the sound of his name. He glowered at me in the dark.

"Why do you need to talk to anyone here?" Doctor Stein's tone was controlled, but strained. She was frightened. The tiredness showed in her face.

"They might have heard or seen something," Nils said. "And someone's responsible for this. Your kids are violent criminals."

"They used to be, Chief Larsen. They're not capable of doing this kind of thing."

"I understand, but we'll still need to talk to them."

"And why Jerry?" Francine Stein asked.

"Other than that he's a sadistic psychopath?" I volunteered. Nils frowned at me.

Francine Stein looked at me like I was someone's uninvited, obnoxious relative. "Why is *he* here?"

"Mr. McGowan found the body."

"Is he a suspect?"

"No."

"Why not? He's a violent person. He attacked Jerry twice."

Nils looked at her with his flat stare. "Did he?"

"He most certainly did. Jerry will swear to it. I think Mr. Detwiler witnessed one attack."

"I guess that was after Jerry slashed Mr. McGowan's car top and left his fingerprints all over the note he wrote." Nils looked over at Jerry, who was listening wide-eyed to the discussion about him. "Do you want to make a complaint, young man?"

Jerry shook his head and looked down at the ground.

"We'll talk to Jerry and your kids…tonight. You'd better get them up. By the way, Doctor Stein, do *you* have any idea what your ex-husband could have been doing on your property?"

Francine Stein looked uncomfortable. She shifted back and forth from one foot to the other, glancing irritably at Jerry. Finally, she shook her head curtly. "No. I have no idea."

Nils started to say something, but the cell phone in his coat pocket went off. He pulled it out and talked briefly. When he finished, he turned to Francine Stein. "We'll get your kids' statements in the morning. Jerry's too. My men will be here for awhile, but I've got to go." He gave me a look that said he needed to talk. I followed him over to the fence.

Nils' face looked strained, even frightened.

"What is it?" I asked

"Saraya Dil…she's missing. Kidnapped."

"Kidnapped? By whom?"

Nils' look was strange. His voice dropped to almost a whisper. I had to lean close to hear him. "Some kind of monster, a giant. He killed her dog, injured two of her classmates. Then he carried her off the grounds."

I stared at Nils. "You think it's our murderer, the one who did this?"

"Unless we've got two psychopaths on the loose tonight." Nils looked preoccupied.

"What else?"

Nils sighed. He looked tired. "Adamji's gone, too. He took off looking for Saraya. He's vowed to kill whoever it is who took her."

"Something else is bothering you," I said

Nils looked at me with what I might have mistaken as the worried eyes of a parent. "Jimmy…we still haven't heard from him. There's some kind of maniac out there. I hope he hasn't already got Jimmy."

I looked over at the cops milling around. Francine Stein and Jerry were watching us suspiciously.

"I'm going with you," I said.

"Good," Nils answered. "Let's go."

CHAPTER TWENTY-NINE

I followed Nils' cruiser from La Sol to the Krishna School. It was only about a mile as the crow flies but almost twice that long by the road that curved up behind the Yearling Foundation and along the foothills bordering the Foundation and school property then dipped down again to the valley floor. From there the road ran alongside a manicured Danish farm, visible in the darkness only as a precise row of white fence posts, gleaming in the headlights like polished ivory piano keys, until, off to the right, the entrance to the school appeared. Ahead of me Nils was hunched over his steering wheel like an old man, not his usual, ramrod straight self. After leaping the chain-link fence like a kid and directing the investigation of Stein's murder with diplomatic authority, the news about Saraya Dil had aged him. Or maybe it was the fear that her abductor had already killed Jimmy Litton. Whatever it was, Nils' feelings seemed to have overwhelmed him. More than anything else about the case, *that* had me worried.

We pulled into the parking lot of the Krishna school. Soft lights from the windows twinkled between the leafy branches of oak trees, creating filmy halos of moisture in their diffused glow. Long shadows enveloped so much of the pathway to the office that Nils and I both nearly tripped on the brick walkway.

I felt myself searching the shadows for movement, listening to the silence for a tell-tale sound. When we arrived at the office, its front door was open. Fanny Dil was standing in the lobby looking at a picture on the wall.

"My father was a pacifist," she said. I hadn't even thought she'd heard Nils and me come into the room. "He thought Ghandi was the greatest man he'd ever met. Once he told me that if Ghandi had been able to save himself by killing his assassin he wouldn't have done it. I wonder what he would have done if the assassin had had his gun trained on his child." She turned toward us. Her delicate face showed its age. There were bluish circles under her eyes and the corners of her mouth seemed weighted down, pulling her cheeks into loose folds. Her eyes had red veins that looked like crimson streaks of lightning spreading out from her coal black pupils. "Adamji will kill whoever took Saraya," she said quietly. "I'm going to lose them both."

"We'll find Saraya before Adamji does, Fanny," Nils said, gently. He began a movement toward her, then stopped himself, standing still and stiff, reaching out to her only with his gaze. "Tell us what happened," he said, softly.

"They were talking...Saraya and the two boys. He—the thing—came out of the shadows...he..." She looked confused for a moment, her words not coming. "I don't know what to call him," she said, looking at us helplessly. "Whatever he was, whoever he is, he came right at one of the boys and began hitting, biting, kicking him. The boy was surprised. He was injured before he could do anything. The boys' dog leaped at the attacker, but apparently he was just brushed aside. The monster killed the dog with one blow. Then the other boy jumped in, but he was no match for whatever it was. The.... whatever, knocked him down, then kicked him. The boys tried to get back up, but before they could, he took Saraya."

"Took her?" Nils asked.

"Freddy, the boy who was attacked first, said that the thing picked Saraya up and then ran off."

"Did he hurt her?" Nils asked.

"Not while they saw him. They tried to follow, but both boys were too hurt to go far. They came and got Adamji."

"You didn't see him yourself?" I asked.

She looked at me vacantly for a moment, as if she hadn't noticed that I was there and didn't understand why I was speaking. I wasn't sure she recognized me. Then she smiled absently, in reflexive politeness. "Mr. McGowan. I didn't notice it was you."

I waited, but she didn't seem to remember my question. "Did you see him, Fanny?" I asked again.

"No. But the boys described him to me, and to Adamji."

"We'll talk to the boys," Nils said.

I was more impatient than Nils. He was trying to be easy on Mrs. Dil. "Tell us what they said, Fanny."

She looked from me to Nils, then decided to answer. Maybe she needed to talk. "They said he looked like a monster. He was like a boy or a man, but he was deformed. His head was large and his nose was only partly there…smashed or ripped off they said. He was as big as Adamji. The boys said he was bent over, like he had some kind of handicap, and he limped when he walked, hitching one leg along like it wasn't as strong as the other. But he was strong. He must have been strong because of what he did to the students."

"Adamji didn't see him?" I asked.

"No. He was in bed. He heard about Saraya being taken at the same time that I did."

"Where did Adamji go?"

"I don't know. He left in the same direction the boys had said the 'thing' took Saraya. Into the woods, toward the Foundation."

"You said Adamji would kill him. Was your son armed?"

"My son can be more dangerous than any weapon, Mr. McGowan," she said, looking me straight in the eyes.

She was right.

"I'll get some more men over here," Nils said. "First I want to talk to the two boys, and see where it happened." He'd taken out his walkie-talkie and begun punching buttons.

"You go ahead," I told him.

Nils looked at me sharply, raising his eyebrows inquisitively. He was talking into the walkie-talkie. The room echoed with desultory static.

"I'm just gonna wander around a little," I said.

"Don't wander into the bushes," Nils said. "We might have to track him. I'm having one of the boys bring a dog."

"You've got your cell phone on you, right?"

Nils looked at me for a moment. He knew I had something on my mind. "You got an idea?"

"Just an idea. It's not worth diverting you or your men. You'll do better with the dog, but I want to be able to reach you if I find something."

"Should I come with you?" he asked.

I shook my head. I hadn't told him about taking the keys off of Bernie Stein's body, but I had a hunch. It was such a long shot that I didn't want to waste anyone's time but my own. "I'll call you if I need you."

Nils stood there looking like he wanted to say something else, but he didn't. He reached out and put his hand briefly on my shoulder. "Call me in an hour no matter what."

CHAPTER THIRTY

Going over the fence to the Yearling Foundation was no easier the second time than it had been the first, only this time Nils' coat wasn't covering the coiled barbed wire on the top of the chain-link fence and I got my pant leg caught and almost fell face first the eight feet to the ground on the other side. Luckily, my pants ripped and I managed to land on my feet. Ahead of me in the distance I could see the lights of buildings through the trees. That was my destination.

Occasional pines and clumps of oak trees dotted the terrain between me and the buildings ahead. I was walking in calf-length grass. As far as I could see there was no path among the trees and I fixed my gaze on the lights ahead and tried to maintain a straight line. As I got nearer, I recognized the back of the office building. The light I'd been following was a single porch light on the back of the building. The windows were dark. I realized that I was in the midst of the scene that could be viewed from Francine Stein's office. In a moment I would encounter the fence around the office building. I had no desire to go over another fence so I began circling to my right to give the office compound a wide berth. Soon I was even with the office and ahead I could see more buildings. Some had lights at several of their windows and others were dark, like the ghosts of ships tied up at night in their harbor. Just beyond the nearest set of buildings I expected to find my destination—the off-limits building that carried the extra warning signs on its perimeter fence.

The gate on the fence surrounding the building was unlocked. It shouldn't have been. The lights in the building were on, but I didn't see anyone around. I went through the gate. From inside the structure I could hear movement, then voices. One of them was a girl. I assumed it was Saraya. She was pleading with someone. I heard the sound of scuffling, then crashing. I hesitated outside the door for a moment, listening, but there was only a deathly silence. I slipped inside.

The room was dimly lit. I could smell the odor of sweating bodies. The floor was uncovered concrete. I reached a hand out to the side. The walls were cold concrete also. The room was longer than it was wide and ahead of me I heard the scuffling of feet. Then I saw him.

He was a gigantic boy, full bodied, and with straight black hair. He didn't have the sculpted muscles of a body builder, but his arms and shoulders were massive …massive and solid, like those of an NFL lineman. He wore a T- shirt and a pair of jeans, the Yearling Foundation uniform. But he wasn't one of the guards and I was sure he wasn't one of Francine Stein's delinquent kids. This was the patient from Camarillo with Lesch-Nyhan disease.

Adamji had him cornered, backed against the far wall of the room. The boy's large bony head was lowered, like a bull trapped in a bullring, knowing he had no way to escape. His face was the ruined face of a young man. His nose was nearly destroyed, and newly bloodied, where Adamji must have hit him in the face. The blood had sprayed like red paint across the top of his T-shirt, then dripped in a long solid swath down the middle of the shirt's front. The corners of his mouth were curled back in a snarl, like the monkey I had seen in Wang's laboratory. His eyes were narrowed, darting back and forth, looking for an opening, a way to get to Adamji. When he moved, he shuffled sideways, dragging his left leg as if it had been injured. Adamji was circling him slowly, his feet moving crab-wise, never off balance, never crossing one foot in front of the other. He was stalking the poor creature for the kill. Neither of them seemed to have noticed me.

I looked for Saraya. She was cowering in the corner. She didn't look seriously hurt. She tore her gaze away from the two circling figures and focused them on me, pleading for help. I gave her a quick smile of reassurance. Then I noticed what was behind her, barely visible in the shadows. It was the still form of Jimmy Litton, lying awkwardly on the concrete floor. He wasn't moving.

The hulking boy was moving along the wall in Saraya's direction. I couldn't tell if he was deliberately moving toward her or if that was just the way he was circling the room. He was coming toward me too, but I didn't think he'd seen me yet. He was too intent on watching Adamji, who was moving with him stride for stride, shadowing his steps from the other side of the room. Adamji's eyes were on his daughter as much as on the boy. His muscles tensed as the creature neared Saraya. I knew Adamji wouldn't let the boy get much further.

Saraya uttered a small cry…a strangled "no." The boy turned sideways to stare at her and Adamji started his move. He wasn't fast enough. I was closer. My foot caught the monster in the soft part of his stomach. He doubled over just enough for my right hand, packing the full weight of my body behind it, to catch him squarely between the eyes. The blow straightened him upright and I followed it with a short, quick right to the same spot. The punch didn't go far, but I'd managed to get my shoulder behind it. He went down like a felled oak, his crooked body straightened out as he lay comatose on his back. I stood over him, waiting to see if he moved and protecting him from Adamji.

Adamji Dil glowered at me and resumed his slow circling movement, with me as his target. I held my ground, though I was pretty sure I was no match for him. "Take care of your daughter," I snapped. He didn't respond. He seemed to be fixed into a trance, his entire being focused on completing the attack he'd started. "Go to your father," I told Saraya.

"Father?" She spoke softly, fear in her voice. Her plea was so poignant, I took my gaze off of her father for a moment and stared at her. Adamji stopped circling. His gaze swept the room like he was noticing his surroundings for the first time. When he rested his eyes on his daughter, he blinked, then moved stiffly across the room toward her, as if his muscles were resisting him. When he reached her side, he knelt and examined her. I watched. She appeared to be unharmed, speaking softly to her father, her eyes searching his face, as though she was as worried about him as he about her. I couldn't hear what she was saying.

I took out my cell phone and dialed Nils. I told him where we were. Then I went over to the body of Jimmy Litton.

Adamji watched me, his eyes smoldering. "This was not your business," he said in a guttural voice.

"Your daughter's safe. That ends your part in this, Adamji. This is police business. This person— whatever he is— may be the one who killed the Torres boy…and Bernie Stein and maybe this boy. " I nodded in the direction of Jimmy Litton's body.

Adamji's anger hadn't diminished. "That boy is not dead. I only knocked him unconscious."

"You?" I looked down at Jimmy Litton. He was breathing evenly. There was a large swelling on the side of his head.

"He and this monster were together. That boy was holding my daughter when I got here. He tried to stop me from attacking the other one."

I was totally confused. What did Jimmy Litton have to do with this?

Saraya was shaking her head at her father. "No," she said.

She looked like she wanted to tell her father something, but he wasn't listening to her.

"What is he?" Adamji asked, looking at the large figure still lying unconscious on the floor.

"I think he has a genetic disorder. It makes him aggressive. I think Doctor Stein is keeping him here in this building for her experiments."

"Experiments?"

I looked at Saraya. It wasn't the time or place to have this conversation. Adamji was a cold bastard. He should be thinking about his daughter. "Did he hurt you at all, Saraya?" I asked.

Her tiny face was tear-streaked, but her eyes were clear. She was staring at the unconscious hulk on the floor. "He didn't hurt me. I think he was trying to protect me. When we got to this building he kept telling me I was safe. The other boy…" she glanced over at Jimmy on the floor, "… he told me not to worry. He said he would take me back to my school."

"The other boy was being held here like you?"

She shook her head, her eyes large and shiny with tears. "I don't think so. He kept trying to calm the other one down. To talk to him. He wasn't afraid of him at all."

I looked at Adamji. "What did he say to you when you got here?"

"I didn't give him a chance to say anything. I hit him. Then I hit the big one. It should have stopped him, but he's strong. He fought back." Adamji looked at me with grudging admiration. "Your blows were more successful than mine."

The boy/creature was beginning to stir on the floor. He'd be a handful for even Adamji and myself together if Nils didn't arrive with some handcuffs and reinforcements pretty soon. In the distance, there was the sound of approaching sirens.

Adamji put his arm around his daughter's shoulder. She leaned her head against his side. I could hear Nils' voice outside, shouting to Halvorsen and Long. I opened the door and called to them. Then I went back to Jimmy. He was starting to stir. When he opened his eyes, he looked startled to see me. He sat up and quickly scanned the room. A look of relief crossed his face when he saw Saraya. He stared with alarm at the large creature on the floor.

"Mathew…he's hurt?" Jimmy said staring at the other boy.

"He's OK," I answered. "Mathew? Who is he, Jimmy?"

Jimmy looked back at me. His expression was a mixture of embarrassment and defiance. "He's my brother."

CHAPTER THIRTY-ONE

Getting the deformed boy into a squad car and transporting him to the station was no picnic. Nils' two deputies treated the boy like a wild creature escaped from the jungle or the zoo. While he was still groggy, they put two pairs of cuffs on his wrists and manacles around his ankles. When he tried to get up and found his feet bound together, he began to sob. He was surprisingly verbal. He begged to be let loose and promised to be good. He reminded me of an overgrown preschooler. Nils ordered Halvorsen, the fat deputy, to remove the manacles. The moment the kneeling deputy lifted the metal clasps from the boy's ankles, the young man delivered a vicious kick to the man's head. Nils had to restrain Halvorsen from attacking the still handcuffed creature, who immediately began to apologize and cry even more. And so it went. The boy would sob, whimper and cajole his captors until out of pity, one would come within reach of his feet or his head, then he'd kick, or butt, or bite the sympathetic deputy. Finally, Jimmy yelled at all of the deputies to leave him alone. He went over and took his brother by the arm and led him to the waiting cruiser. Mathew Litton bent his head and got into the back seat like a docile lamb. Although Jimmy wasn't handcuffed himself, he was also a prisoner. His part in Saraya's kidnapping would have to be sorted out later. He got into the car alongside his brother and the cruiser finally was able to pull away.

"That's Jimmy's brother?" Nils said. He appeared to be in shock.

"According to Jimmy, Mathew's been at Camarillo since he was a baby. He's got Lesch-Nyhan disease. I'll bet he was Francine Stein's donor in the experiments that got her booted out of UCLA."

"I thought the brother had a birth defect and died."

"I guess that's the story the family told everyone. Maybe it was easier than explaining that they'd given up their child to the state."

"How'd you know he was here?" Nils asked.

"A hunch, like I said. Doctor Wang told me that Stein would need a DNA donor if she was carrying on her experiments. She had used a violent patient at Camarillo before, and I suspected that she had either somehow brought him here or had found another person with the same disease. It's a disorder that causes such violent aggression that when I found out about it, I knew that it fit the picture we were getting of whoever killed Bernie and kidnapped Saraya. He probably killed Torres and your guard, too."

Nils looked dumbfounded. "Then Jimmy knew about him. He saw his brother watching Torres and Saraya. He knew it was his brother who came to the jail. Why didn't he tell us?"

"I think he was trying to protect him. Maybe that's why he was with him now. He was trying to control his brother's behavior. He told Saraya he'd keep her safe and bring her back to her school."

"But he didn't stop his brother from kidnapping her…or killing Bernie Stein. Why did the brother do it? Why Saraya? Why Stein?"

"We'll have to ask him…and Jimmy. It doesn't make a lot of

sense to me either."

"What about Francine Stein? You think she knows about this? She knows that she's harboring some kind of deranged killer on her property?"

"She must know about Mathew. She brought him here. Whether she knows he's killed people is another matter. But with Torres and her husband both being brutally murdered, you'd think she'd figure it out."

"And kill Karin Stengaard to keep it quiet?"

"And Janice Le." I told Nils about Ernie's hunch that the gang killing was a ruse. "Whatever Francine Stein did to get Mathew Litton here was probably illegal. And if she's using him for any experiments, that's illegal for sure. She'll lose her license and maybe go to jail if it can be proved. And if Mathew did kill Torres or anyone else, then she's partly responsible. She might kill to keep that covered up."

Nils just shook his head. "I want to talk to Jimmy and his brother…and their parents. Then I'm gonna haul Stein in and make her explain what's going on." He looked over at the tall gothic spires of the old Victorian house that was the Foundation office. "Funny she's not out here seeing what's going on."

"Maybe she knows what we found. She might not want to answer any questions right now."

"She'll have to answer them soon enough," Nils snapped, heading for his car.

CHAPTER THIRTY-TWO

I followed Nils' cruiser back to the jail. Both of the Litton boys had been taken inside and locked in separate cells. When Nils and I walked in Jimmy was trying to calm his brother down.

"Put him in with me," Jimmy said to Nils. "He won't hurt me unless he gets too excited."

Nils shook his head. "Sorry, Jimmy. It's too dangerous. The next cell. That's the best I can do."

"Has anyone called my parents?"

"I've called them. They're on their way here," Nils answered. He rubbed his eyes. He looked tired. I knew he was worried about having to talk to the Littons.

We were standing in the lobby of the jail, which was attached to the courthouse across the street from the police station. I was about to suggest that Nils go across the street to his office and wait for the Littons when Richard Detwiler came through the front door. He must have come straight from bed. He was wearing a pair of wrinkled slacks and a sweater with no shirt underneath. His black hair stood up at an odd angle on the back of his head, like he'd slept on it that way and hadn't had a chance to comb it. He frowned when he saw me. "Do you always have to call him first?" he asked Nils.

"He works for me, remember? Besides, he captured the boy.

He also found Bernie Stein's body."

Detwiler's mouth dropped open. "Stein's body? You mean he's dead?"

"I stopped reporting live bodies a long time ago," I said.

Detwiler glared at me. "How did he die?" he asked Nils.

"He was beaten to death…pretty viciously. He was on Foundation property. We found him hanging on the fence.'

"Jesus Christ!" Detwiler exclaimed. "This other Litton kid, the one who kidnapped the Dil girl, did he do it?"

Nils shrugged. "We're still investigating."

Detwiler's expression hardened. "I want to talk to the boy, the second Litton kid. And I want to talk to the parents. Their son's a suspect in both Bernie Stein's, and Manuel Torres' murders."

"The kid's name is Mathew," Nils said. "He's in a cell next to his brother. If I were you I'd talk to him from outside the cell bars. He can get pretty nasty."

Detwiler gave Nils a condescending look. "I know how to interview suspects," he said. Always the jerk.

"I'll take Jimmy into the conference room," I said.

We split up. Nils waited for the Litton parents to show up and I took Jimmy out of the cell block and down the hall to the conference room. It was the same room where I'd first met him.

Jimmy stared hard at me. "He wasn't trying to hurt that girl."

"Why did he take her?"

"He thought someone would hurt her."

"Who?"

Jimmy looked uncomfortable. Whatever he had to say, he was having a hard time saying it. "Matt doesn't explain things very well. He's not very good with words. He thinks there's kids from the Foundation who want to hurt the girl."

"Why? What kids?"

"I told you, Mr. McGowan, Matt doesn't explain things very

well. He just thinks they're going to hurt her." Jimmy dropped his gaze. "He thought that the other boy was trying to hurt her, too." His voice was so low I could hardly hear his last words.

"You mean Manuel Torres?"

Jimmy didn't look at me. "Yeah."

"Did he kill Torres, Jimmy?"

He didn't answer.

"There's been another murder. Doctor Stein from La Sol."

Jimmy's eyes widened in fear. "Matt didn't do that."

"But he killed Torres?"

"Yes," he said softly. "He thought Torres was hurting the girl. Matt thought he was protecting her."

"The person you saw watching Torres and Saraya Dil…that was your brother?"

"It must have been. I didn't know. I mean, I thought maybe it was, but I didn't know. He was staying at the Foundation, but I didn't know he could get out. He'd been watching them. He saw them have sex. Only he didn't know that's what it was. He thought Torres was hurting her."

"Why did he wait until Torres had left the girl?"

"I don't know." Jimmy raised his face to me. "He thinks like a little kid. And once he gets excited, he attacks everything, even himself. That's why he was at the Foundation. Doctor Stein's trying to cure him."

"You're sure he didn't kill Doctor Stein's husband?"

"He was with me the whole time except when he went to get the girl. I couldn't stop him. He snuck away when I dozed off. But he was only gone a half hour or so, honest." He still looked afraid. "What will they do to him?"

"Maybe send him back to the hospital at Camarillo. He's not responsible. Even Mr. Detwiler won't get a murder charge out of this one."

Jimmy's shoulders sagged with relief. "There's one more thing," he said.

"What's that?"

"He thinks they're coming after him."

"Who?"

"Whoever he's afraid of. Kids from the Foundation, I think. But he isn't very clear about it."

I nodded. "One more thing, Jimmy. What were you doing there with him? Doctor Smythe reported you missing."

He hung his head a little. "I'm sorry. I couldn't tell her about Matt. I was afraid for him. I knew he'd killed Torres and he came to the jail to try to get me out. I thought if I stayed with him he'd stop hurting people."

"So he killed the guard at the jail?"

"Yes."

"Let's go talk to your brother."

CHAPTER THIRTY-THREE

There was a crowd around Mathew Litton's cell. Jimmy broke into a run to reach his brother. I wasn't far behind. Richard Detwiler was standing beside a deputy, the DA holding a bloody towel against his face. His face was drained of color. Inside the cell, deputy Halvorsen and two guards were holding Mathew Litton on the floor. There was blood every place. The guards were trying to cuff the boy to the leg of the cot. The fingers on one of Mathew's hands were completely covered with blood.

Jimmy tried to push his way through to his brother. The deputy, Long, who was ministering to Richard Detwiler grabbed the boy. "I can calm him down," Jimmy yelled at the deputy. I grabbed the man's arm and twisted it away from Jimmy. Long jerked his head around to me, his free hand going for his weapon.

"Let him handle his brother," I said. "He can keep anyone else from getting hurt."

The deputy hesitated, the anger at my physical intrusion still evident in his face, but he was also thinking about what I'd said. We stared at each other. He took his hand away from his weapon and I let go of his arm. Jimmy was down on the cell floor next to his brother. Mathew's face was filled with terror and pain.

"He bit me then he bit off his own finger!" Detwiler, said.

I watched Jimmy help the guards cuff Mathew to the cot. Jimmy took a towel off the floor and stuffed it into his brother's mouth.

Detwiler was rubbing the blood off his face. The bite on his cheek was superficial. He'd live.

"You went into his cell, didn't you?" I said.

"Christ, nobody told me he was crazy. He's a fucking animal."

"And you're an asshole," I said. "What did he tell you?"

The DA looked like he was going to get angry at me, but he glanced over at Mathew Litton on the floor of his cell, and the fear was back on his face. "He killed Torres. He admitted it. He must have killed Bernie Stein too, but I couldn't get a straight story out of him. All he talked about was saving the girl."

"Did he say from whom?"

"It sounded like he was saying the kids at the Foundation. He wasn't making any sense. He kept trying to tell me something, then he got all excited and started biting everything in sight."

"Where's Nils?" I asked.

Deputy Long jerked his thumb in the direction of the end of reception area. "He's talking to the parents across the street, in his office."

"Put a Band-Aid on your face and come on," I said to Detwiler as I headed for the door. He held the towel against his cheek and followed me. I could hear him muttering behind me as we left the jail and headed across the street.

Nils looked up in alarm when we got to his office. He took one look at Detwiler and shook his head. "Christ, you went into the cell with him, didn't you?"

The DA just looked pissed. The two Litton parents were sitting wide-eyed, staring at Detwiler's bloody face.

"Mathew admitted killing Manuel Torres," I announced to Nils and the parents.

"Don't blame us. He was staying at the Foundation," Ron Litton said immediately. Ruth Litton bit her lip. She looked at her husband with disgust.

"Mathew's been at the Foundation ever since he came home from Camarillo," Nils said. "He visits his parents and brother every once in a while, but he always goes back the same day. He's only been home once since Torres' murder and they never asked him about it."

"That was the day I came over?" I asked.

Ruth Litton nodded. Now I knew who had thrown the stick at me.

"Why's he at the Foundation?" I asked.

"Doctor Stein said she could cure him," the father answered. "She'd worked with him at Camarillo."

"He's gotten better," his mother said.

"Better?" Detwiler interrupted. "He bit me! Then he bit off his own finger!"

"My God!" Ruth Litton exclaimed. "He hasn't done that since he's been back. Did you call Doctor Stein?"

"I called her," Nils offered. "She should be here any time, now."

"I'm charging him with Bernie Stein's death, too," Detwiler said. He glanced challengingly first at me then at the parents.

Ruth Litton raised her hand to her mouth, as if to stifle a scream. Whether it would have been of terror or protest, I didn't know.

"Chief Larsen said he didn't know who killed Doctor Stein," Ron Litton said, returning Detwiler's antagonistic look.

"Sometimes Chief Larsen is slow to admit the obvious," the DA said.

I reminded the DA that only a few days ago he'd thought it was obvious that Mathew's brother had killed Manny Torres.

Detwiler ground his teeth hard enough that his jaw muscles stood out. The effort seemed to increase the flow of blood from his cheek and he had to press harder with his towel. He looked at me with anger, but he didn't say anything.

"What are you going to do with Mathew?" Ruth Litton asked.

Nils shot me a glance. I shrugged my shoulders. "They've got him cuffed to his bed right now," I said. Nils rolled his eyes.

"Can't you put him in Doctor Stein's care?" Ruth Litton asked.

"That's whose care he was in when he did all this damage, Mrs. Litton," I said. "It'd be better to send him back to Camarillo."

"Not so fast," Detwiler interrupted. "Where he goes is none of your business, McGowan. I'm not letting him leave that jail until I've gotten a chance to finish questioning him."

"While he's chained to the bed?" I asked.

"If that's what it takes…yes!"

"How about getting Doctor Smythe in here to give you some help with him?" I offered.

Nils nodded. "Good idea. Jimmy trusts her. Maybe he can communicate that to Mathew."

Nils called Hillary Smythe, who said she'd be right over, and then he told the Littons that they could go home. Jimmy would probably be released in the morning since he hadn't really done anything except to try to keep his brother from hurting anyone.

Detwiler left to get his cheek attended to and Nils and I waited for Francine Stein.

I told Nils that Jimmy had said his brother had killed the guard at the jail.

"Christ almighty!" Nils exploded. "Doctor Stein ought to be charged with those deaths. What the hell was she thinking, bringing this kid out of Camarillo?"

"How'd she get him out? Did the parents say?"

"Hell, they just asked to have him come home. They'd put him there voluntarily when he was a baby because they couldn't cope with his self-mutilation. But they were free to take him out any time they wanted to. They just never told anyone that they were putting him in Stein's care."

"And it was her idea to take him out of the hospital?"

"She told them she could cure him."

"She'll claim she didn't know he killed anybody. She'll have to."

"But you think she knew," Nils said.

"I think she not only knew. I think Karin Stengaard and Janice Le were killed to keep the whole thing secret."

"That's going to be tough to prove."

"Not if she or Jerry owns a .30 caliber German hunting rifle and we can find it."

"A hunting rifle?"

"That's what killed Janice Le."

Nils clenched his jaw so hard the muscles bulged across his cheeks. "Those two were covering things up while Mathew went out and killed two more people."

"Maybe just one. I don't think he killed Bernie."

Nils looked at me like I'd lost my mind. "C'mon McGowan, Bernie Stein was beaten just as badly as Torres or my guard. Who else would have done that? Do you think Doctor Stein's got another one like Mathew out there?"

"Maybe a whole institution of them."

Nils' jaw dropped. "What are you talking about?"

I reminded Nils of what I had learned at Wang's lab. How Mathew's DNA could be used to alter the aggression in the other residents of the Foundation. I told him about the reversal that would happen after about three weeks, making the docile residents, hyper-aggressive."

"You really think Doctor Stein is doing that?" Nils asked.

"It would explain the violence to the Litton's cow. Mathew

didn't do that. And it would explain the way Bernie Stein died."

"But she'd be nuts to do that if the process reverses itself like it does in those monkeys. Her kids are already criminals. They're skilled at violence. If they lose all their inhibitions; they'll be homicidal maniacs."

"Maybe that's why Mathew Litton is scared. Maybe that's who he was trying to protect Saraya from."

Nils whistled softly. "Jesus, I hope you're wrong, McGowan."

Nils' intercom buzzed. It was the station's front desk. Francine Stein had arrived. Nils said to send her back.

She'd changed out of her jeans and baggy shirt and was wearing a tight black dress made from what looked like a light wool material. It was high at the collar, but sleeveless and short enough to reveal a bit of well shaped thigh above her knees. She had good looking shoulders, but she was starting to get a little upper arm sag, almost the only reminder of her age. Her face was made up, but it only heightened the sense of severity that reminded me of my first meeting with her. Her eyes flashed with irritation when she saw me.

"He doesn't belong here," she said to Nils, her eyes still burning into me. "This is about my patient."

"Mr. McGowan works for me. Anyway, I'll decide who belongs here. Right now you've got a lot of explaining to do, Doctor Stein."

She came the rest of the way into the room and took one of the chairs. She slung one leg over the other provocatively, showing more thigh and glancing at me defiantly. I couldn't help smiling. It was one hell of a show.

Nils kept his eyes on hers. "You've been harboring a very dangerous boy out there, Doctor. You had the parents bring him home from Camarillo and you kept him at your Foundation. Even after he killed Manuel Torres, you didn't tell anyone he was there."

Francine looked shocked. "He killed Manny?" She should have been an actress.

Nils nodded.

"Did he hurt the Dil girl?"

"No," Nils answered.

"He said he was protecting her from someone," I said.

Francine looked at me uncomprehendingly. "What does that mean?"

"It means that Mathew Litton isn't the only killer at the Yearling Foundation. Someone else killed your ex-husband."

Doctor Stein swung her head around to face me. Through her anger, there was a hint of panic in her eyes. "What are your talking about?" One of her heavily mascara-coated eyelashes had begun twitching.

"Mathew was only out of his brother's sight long enough to kidnap Saraya Dil. Mathew thought he was saving her from someone…someone from your Foundation."

She began swinging he leg angrily. "That's preposterous. I'm horrified that Mathew got away from the Foundation and that he harmed anyone, but there's no one he was saving that girl from. Bernie must have unlocked the gate to the building where Mathew was staying. Mathew wouldn't have recognized him and so he chased him back to the fence and then caught him and killed him. Once he'd gotten loose and become excited, he probably remembered the Dil girl from the night he killed Manny and he went looking for her."

"It's a nice story, Doctor Stein, but someone else killed your ex-husband."

Her face was crimson. She stood and glared angrily at Nils. "I demand that you release Mathew to me, Chief Larsen. He's my patient and it's dangerous to him and to others if he's not under my care at the Foundation."

"It seems to me that he's done all of this harm while he was in your care, Doctor," Nils drawled. "I can't release him. He's admitted two murders and he's charged with assault and kidnapping. As soon as the DA figures out what the charge is, I'll probably be arresting you for letting this whole thing go on."

She looked from Nils to me, narrowing her eyes suspiciously. "I see," she said. She started to walk out, then stopped and turned back. "You're a fool, Chief Larsen. If you keep Mathew here I'm not responsible for what happens." She turned her angry gaze on me. "You'll be sorry for this McGowan. You don't know what you've stuck your nose into."

I smiled back at her. "But you can count on me finding out. And by the way, nice dress."

Her face reddened even further. She turned and stormed out.

Nils' phone rang. It was the jail. Hillary Smythe had arrived. Nils and I got up and headed across the street.

CHAPTER THIRTY-FOUR

I was surprised when I stepped outside the police station to see that the first gray light of dawn was already visible above the tops of the mountains in the eastern sky. I looked at my watch. It was nearly six a.m. All of a sudden I felt tired. Nils looked old and exhausted. There were black circles under his eyes and a dark stubble of beard darkened his lower face. He blinked his eyes as he walked, but grim determination kept him moving toward the jail.

When we entered, things had calmed down from the earlier uproar. From the glassed-in guard station at the far end of the cell block, one of the guards waved at us and put his finger to his lips to signal us to keep quiet. To my surprise, Jimmy hadn't gone home with his parents and was sleeping in the cell next to his brother. The guard whispered to us that Jimmy wouldn't leave. Nils and I edged forward until we could see inside Mathew's cell . The boy was lying on his cot. He was no longer cuffed to the bed's leg and his fingers on one hand were wrapped with bandages. The towel had been removed from his mouth. Hillary Smythe sat on the edge of his cot, talking to him so quietly that I could see her lips moving, but whatever she was saying was inaudible. I grabbed Nils by the arm and began to back away. Hillary was doing just fine without us disrupting anything.

The guard came over to us. "She's a fucking miracle worker," he whispered. "She sent us all out and began talking to him. After a few minutes she came out and got the keys to the cuffs and some bandages. She told us to stay away and she'd tell us what to do later. She's got him eatin' out of her hand."

Nils and I waited. After a few minutes Hillary came out. Her face was deadly serious. She was wearing another one of her flowing dresses, a tan material with a print of small green flowers, belted at the waist. She was tiny in the middle. Her auburn hair looked wet like she'd just stepped out of a shower, and she'd drawn it back in a ponytail. She smelled like soap again. I peeked around behind her to see if she'd sprouted any wings.

"Somebody's going to have to prescribe him something," she said. "You'd better find out if Francine Stein had him on any meds. Maybe she can write another prescription for him if she did. If not, I'd try an SSRI like Prozac or maybe Risperdal, which will also sedate him."

"You know about his disorder?" I asked, impressed by the way she'd taken over.

"It's Lesch-Nyhan. I recognized it as soon as I saw him. I had a case in grad school. Mathew's less physically and mentally handicapped than most cases, but his self-destructive behavior is mild compared to most. It can get a lot worse. There's a specific behavioral treatment that I'm going to have to show everyone here. The only meds that make a dent in it as far as I know are SSRI's and some experimental use of L-dopa or a nonprescription drug called S-adenosyl-methionine. And you want to keep him from getting excited."

"How'd you get him calmed down?" I asked.

"As long as you stay very low key it won't excite him. I spoke to him, then I talked him through some relaxation. He's as afraid of his getting out of control as you are."

I was reminded of the monkey, Willie, and his fear of having his restraints removed. "Nice job," I said.

She gave me a thin smile. "I need to talk to everyone who's going to come in contact with Mathew," she told Nils. "Everyone's got to react to him the same way. That is, they can't react at all. If he hits, spits, bites, kicks, either himself or anyone else, nobody can react. They have to act like it never happened. Then he'll stop."

"You mean he's doing this to get a reaction from people?" I asked.

"I don't think it's that simple. All I know is that any reaction—from punishment to reward—increases his aggressive behavior. It's that way in all the cases."

"What if he injures himself?" Nils asked. "He bit off one of his fingers earlier."

"I saw," Hillary said. "If the bleeding is serious— life threatening—then you have to do something. You may even need to cuff him again. Otherwise, wait until he's calmed down and then go in and bandage him without saying anything about his behavior."

"I'll get my guys together," Nils said. Then he hesitated. "We change shifts at seven thirty. Maybe it'd be better to wait until shift change and talk to everybody at once."

Hillary looked at her watch. I looked at mine too. It was a little past six."Breakfast's on me," I said to both of them. Hillary smiled.

"You two go ahead," Nils said. I'm gonna file the paperwork on all this so I can go home and get some sleep as soon as I talk to my men. You'd better think about sleep, too, McGowan. You look like hell."

I looked at Hillary. "I didn't think that was possible," I said.

"It's always nice to have a reality check. Where are you taking me for breakfast?"

The only place that was open that early was the truck stop

down at the intersection of highways 150 and 33. It was a mile down the road from the station. We went in my car.

I filled her in on what I'd learned from Doctor Wang about the UCLA monkeys and my suspicion that Francine was using Mathew as a DNA source for her experiments. I told her that Bernie Stein was looking for incriminating evidence against his ex-wife when he was killed.

"If you don't think Mathew killed him, who did?" she asked. We were seated at a booth in the restaurant. Even though it was a truck stop, the majority of customers were business people who stopped in for breakfast and a morning paper before heading down the mountain to work in Santa Barbara or Ventura. There were some families who were vacationing and maybe there was one trucker. The young waitress had her blonde hair braided and she wore a stitched apron that mimicked a Danish farm girl's dress. The name of the place was Ole's Diner.

Hillary ordered Granola, juice and coffee. I looked around jealously at the commuters who were diving into their pancakes, fried eggs and bacon strips, then ordered Granola for myself. "I think some of those kids have turned aggressive. I think that's what Mathew was afraid of when he took Saraya," I said.

"Is Saraya in special danger from them?"

"I doubt it. I think Mathew is just fixated on protecting her. He thought Manuel Torres was trying to hurt her and he probably associates dangerous Foundation kids with her need to be protected."

"If you're right, then there's some very dangerous kids at the Foundation right now."

"And more of them will become aggressive each day. It'll wear off eventually, but Francine's gonna have a major management problem if she experimented with very many of those boys."

"How many kids do you think are involved?" The Granola had come and Hillary was digging into hers like it was duck l'orange. I looked at mine lying soggily in the bowl and took a drink of coffee.

"From what I saw when Detwiler and I visited the place, it's at least one cottage worth of kids. That's about twelve or fifteen of them."

"What does Francine say?"

"She denies any experimentation. She blames Bernie's death on Mathew."

"Mathew's capable of doing it, you know."

"I know, but Jimmy doesn't think he did. Then there's that thing with the cow. One person couldn't have done that...not even Mathew."

"Why the Litton's cow, though?'

"I have a theory about that. I think that Mathew may have gotten loose and gone home. Francine may have sent some of her boys to get him. If they were the aggressive ones, then they could have mutilated the cow just because it was there."

"That's a bit of a reach isn't it?"

"Maybe...maybe not. Francine said something odd when she left Nils' office. She said if Mathew didn't come back, she wasn't responsible for what happened. Jimmy said Mathew kept talking about people coming to get him."

"He said that to me too. That was one of the things that got him excited." I was poking my Granola with my spoon. "Don't be afraid of it, McGowan. It's just healthy food," Hillary said.

"I've got big muscles to supply."

She shook her head. "You're a real throwback, McGowan. You know that?"

"That's the trouble with this new generation, not enough real men."

She rolled her eyes, then looked at her watch. "I've got to get back."

I told her I'd drop her off. I needed to get a few hours sleep, then I had some things to do.

"You're going out to the Foundation, aren't you?"

"You're starting to worry about me, aren't you?" I gave her my famous leer.

Her face reddened. "You're an idiot, McGowan. At least take Nils with you."

"I do some things better alone."

She shook her head again. "Call me later, will you?"

I wiggled my eyebrows at her. "I knew you'd come around."

"Jesus Christ, McGowan. You're a case."

We got up and left.

CHAPTER THIRTY-FIVE

I was dead tired, but since I was already downtown, I thought I'd drop by the Jaguar dealer and see if my car was ready. It was only seven-forty and the shop manager was there, taking in drop-offs, though the rest of the shop was still closed. "Red," as everyone called him even though his head was bald as an egg, said the car was ready and if I'd wait a few minutes, he'd get it for me. I sat down next to him in the booth where he answered the phone and recorded the day's prospective repair jobs. I must have started to fall asleep because Red set a cup of coffee in front of me.

"Better drink this or you'll fall out of your chair. Rough night?"

I nodded and took a big hit of the coffee. "So this is how you dispose of your crankcase oil," I said.

Red grinned and shook his head. "Battery acid."

"You're soft top really had a job done on it," he said, pouring himself another cup of acidic coffee and leaning against the window of the booth. He was a big man, with thick freckled arms covered with red hairs, probably the same color as his head hair had been at one time. His white shirt with 'Red' embroidered on a blue oval patch over the pocket bulged out over his belt, but his shoulders still took up a lot of room and he had the look of someone who'd spent a lot of years doing hard work with his body. He had an open face with a smile that never seemed to leave completely. I could see why the dealership had chosen him to interface with the customers.

"Glad you could get it fixed so quickly," I said, not wanting to get into a lot of questions about what happened to the car.

"Vandals, huh?" He wasn't going to let it go so easily.

"Yeah."

"Any idea who did it?"

"Nope."

"I'd guess it was those kids from the Foundation. I don't know why anybody ever let 'em put that place here. We don't need a bunch of delinquents running around town."

I looked at his face. I couldn't tell whether he had something to say or was just passing the time. "Do they come to town much?"

He shrugged his shoulders. "Came to town that one night and started a fight with the Litton kid. He got charged with killing one of 'em. Everybody thought it was terrible, but now some of us aren't so sure it wasn't the right thing. Only it turned out he didn't do it. Don't know who did. Doc Lemon, the vet, says the Litton's cow was killed…tortured even. Might have been those Foundation kids retaliating against the Littons for what they thought Jimmy did. Then there's your car."

"There's a lot of 'ifs' in there. Nobody knows who killed the Litton's cow and I've got no idea who trashed my car top."

Red nodded knowingly. "Guess you're not as worked up about the Foundation as some of us are."

Red was hinting at something. I had an uncomfortable feeling about what it was. "Suppose I was…worked up, I mean. Is there something going on I should know about?"

He looked around, like someone might be listening to us. We were the only ones there. "A bunch of us are trying to get the Foundation closed. We've contacted Jim Slausen, our state representative. We put together a petition."

I breathed a sigh of relief that he was only talking about a petition. "I'll sign."

He looked around again. His smile was only a vague shadow and there was a cruel ugliness behind the look in his eyes. "Slausen's a pussy. He's probably not going to do anything. The word is that Doctor Stein made a big contribution to his campaign. We're gonna do something ourselves."

"Like what?"

"A little vandalism of our own. We figure if we can cost Stein enough money having to repair her place every couple of days, she might think about moving someplace else."

"What about Nils Larsen? He'll have to investigate and he'll probably figure out who did it. You'll end up in jail and the Foundation will stay right where it is."

Red looked around. My comment irritated him, but he was thinking about it. "What else are we gonna do?"

I didn't want to tell him everything I knew, but I could tell him enough to cool his jets a little. "Just sit tight. The Foundation is in hot water already. There's been some funny things going on there that Chief Larsen is looking into and last night Stein's ex-husband was killed on Foundation property. There's a pretty good chance the place will get shut down without you doing anything."

Red's eyes almost bugged out. "Bernie Stein got killed? Jesus H. Christ. How do you know these things?"

"I found Stein's body." That was all I wanted to tell him. His group sounded pretty volatile and I didn't want them learning about Mathew Litton or they'd probably turn on the Litton family again.

He let out a whistle. "This changes things all right. I'll have to tell the others."

"You tell 'em to sit tight. Any funny stuff from you people will work in the Foundation's favor. When Slausen hears about

Stein's murder and a few other things Chief Larsen has uncovered, he may reconsider your petition. No politician wants to end up on the side that gets bad publicity."

Red grinned. "You got it."

Another mechanic stuck his head in the door of the booth. "I'm here, boss. I'll open her up."

"Lemme get your car for you," Red said. Walking across the lot whistling, he looked like a happy man.

CHAPTER THIRTY-SIX

It was good to get my car back, but I was too tired to get much of a kick out of it. I drove home at an old man's pace and if I hadn't pushed myself to get out of my car, once I'd parked in my driveway, I'd have leaned back and fallen asleep behind the steering wheel. Decorum won out over exhaustion and I dragged myself out of the car, picked the morning paper up off the porch and staggered into my house. I ordinarily hate to go to bed when it's light outside, but I put my compunctions aside and peeled off my clothes, turned down the covers and groaned with pleasure as I let my head sink into the pillow.

The sun streaming through the bedroom window finally got me overheated enough that I woke up sweating. It had only been three hours since I'd crashed into bed, but I'd regained enough life to crawl out of bed and fix myself a cup of coffee just as if I'd woken up from a full night's sleep. My mind was already racing.

I didn't know what I hoped to find at the Yearling Foundation, but there had to be something there that would tell me if I was right about Doctor Stein's experiments. Mathew Litton's presence there was a fact, but that didn't prove he was being used to supply his DNA to other residents. Even if he was, it didn't prove that the Foundation kids were responsible for Bernie's death. I only had Jimmy's word that his brother hadn't killed Stein. And there was always Jerry as a possible candidate.

I quit thinking and headed for the shower. The hot water woke me the rest of the way up and by the time I'd dressed in a pair of jeans and my old *Southwestern Law* sweatshirt with the cut off sleeves, I felt like a new man. I put on my Nikes and grabbed the keys to my Jaguar. I was back in action.

I didn't bother to try the front gate to the Foundation. Even if I got past Jerry, I wouldn't be able to get to cottage C-3 without alerting them to what I was up to. They'd clear out any residents they didn't want me to see. I headed for La Sol. I was sure that they thought nobody would be stupid enough to use the same route into the Foundation that got Bernie killed last night. I'd show them.

The parking lot at La Sol looked like the last day of summer camp when the parents come back to pick up their kids. Except there weren't any kids. All of the old folks were hustling themselves to safer ground. I felt sorry for them, having their tranquility disturbed by the threat of violence. They'd probably go back to Reseda or Costa Mesa or wherever they came from and board themselves inside their houses for the duration. I was hoping *not* to run into Malynda Price. Not only had I not checked back with her before I'd left last night, but I couldn't afford any dallying now either. Malynda just might cause me to lose my focus.

I made it without incident down the gravel path to the fence where I'd found Bernie. The hole in the fence had been loosely patched by Long and Halvorsen with several strands of barbed wire running diagonally from one corner to the other and then from the opposite set of corners so that it formed a barbed wire X over the hole. The effect was more cosmetic than functional. Yellow crime scene tape was attached to the trees in front of the hole, cordoning off the area ineffectually. I slipped under the tape and edged my way past the barbed wire. Some barricade. I should tell Nils to add an IQ test to the screening procedures for his deputies.

Nobody saw me approach cottage C-3, or if they did, nobody reacted. Maybe I'd be surprised and find the same group of meek teenagers when I went inside. I wasn't. The cottage was empty. It was no longer livable anyway. All the furniture was smashed, water covered the floor, graffiti was sprayed on the walls. I guessed the residents of C-3 were no longer docile.

Paranoia had moved a little further toward the front of my mind when I left C-3 and headed toward the Foundation office. A dozen or so hyper-aggressive delinquents must be lurking somewhere on the grounds…unless they'd already split. They hadn't gone the route I'd come in, through the La Sol grounds, or the geriatric set packing up to go home would have been moving an awful lot faster. That meant the delinquents had gone out another way or they were still there, trashing and tagging their way through the Foundation and probably hoping to find some nice middle-aged unarmed victim like me on whom to take out their aggression.

The Victorian building that housed the office was visible across the grounds in the distance. It appeared untouched, but so had the cottage before I looked inside. As I made my way toward the office, I glanced between the buildings and could see the area where Mathew Litton had been kept. The fence around his compound was down, twisted into undulating waves of chain-link and barbed wire, punctuated here and there with gray metal poles that had been torn from the ground. I was glad Mathew was safely inside Nils' jail.

From the outside, the office looked intact. The gate was closed, sealing off access to the building, and from what I'd seen of the building where they'd kept Mathew, that meant that the rampaging residents hadn't tried to get in. If they had, neither the gate nor the fence would have stopped them. I wasn't going to let it stop me either. I didn't like the idea of standing there alone outside the fence waiting for a group of homicidal teenagers to show up. I'd climbed these fences before. I reached out to grab a good handhold in the chain-link and jumped back a foot from the sub lethal, but definitely painful, shock that vibrated through my body. No wonder this fence was still standing. It carried a good twenty volt charge.

I looked around me. I still didn't see anyone, but I sure as hell didn't like being so conspicuous. It was time for me to leave. My best bet was to go back the way I'd come in. Either that or take the route I'd taken last night through the trees and over the fence to the Krishna School. I debated just long enough to blow my chance for a clean escape. I could hear a car approaching along the road that came up from the front gate. There was no time to find cover so I waited, trying to remember what the best defense was when several hoodlums were coming at you from all sides. I remembered. There wasn't one.

The car was a black Camaro. It was one I'd seen before. Jerry was driving and he was going like a bat out of hell. He fishtailed the car to a stop in front of me and leaped out, looking at me in disbelief. He had a rifle in his hand. It was a .30 caliber hunting rifle. I couldn't tell from that distance, but I was willing to bet it was expensive and German.

"What the hell are you doing here?" He raised the rifle up to waist height, not really aiming it but not pointing it away from me either.

"I bet you wouldn't greet me like that if I was the Governor," I said.

"Cut the crap. How did you get in here? The gate's locked."

"There's still a hole in the fence where Bernie Stein went out horizontally last night, Einstein. There's not much point to your high tech locks on the front gate."

His jaw dropped. "Shit!" he said. "I forgot about that!"

"Where is everybody?" I asked.

"Right where they're supposed to be," he said, sticking out his chin belligerently.

I looked back at the building where Mathew had been kept. "Looks like you're training people to become a wrecking crew."

"What we're doing here is none of your goddamn business."

"What you're doing here is probably illegal as hell and I'm gonna make it my business, junior. How do I get past this fence?"

"You don't." He looked past me at the office. "You don't want to talk to them inside, anyway."

I turned around. The gate was still shut, but six more young guards had appeared, most of them looking like clones of Jerry, except for the big African-American I'd met before. A group of younger residents was behind them. They looked pretty tame so I concluded that these weren't the hyper-aggressive kids…just your garden variety thugs. All of them were gathering on the grass in front of the office. Francine Stein stood on the porch and looked over their heads at me. Her arms were folded and she looked like a queen watching her royal guard moving to intercept an intruder. The whole crew looked pretty brave considering that they all must have been huddled inside the building while the out of control residents demolished Mathew Litton's compound.

Jerry raised the rifle. Now it was midsection height. He sauntered toward me. I guess he knew he had an audience. "Still want to get inside the fence?"

I gave him my best unwavering stare and smiled just a smidgen. "You're about to make a fool out of yourself again, junior."

He brought the barrel of the rifle up toward my chin. It was a big mistake. Guns in my face are one of my pet peeves. I reached up and grasped the barrel of the gun and whacked him a solid enough blow on the side of his face that he staggered backward. Then I gave him the old fourth down punt to the balls and before he figured out why he was in so much pain, I hit him with a long right that came all the way from downtown. All of my anger about Karin Stengaard and Janice Le was behind that punch. Jerry was out like a light. I was startled by the sound of cheers. It was the residents behind the fence. I was sure that the cheer wasn't because I was that popular with the delinquents. It was because Jerry wasn't. Francine Stein yelled at her guards and they turned around and yelled at the cheering teenagers and then everyone was quiet. So much for freedom of expression.

I heard the click of the electric lock on the gate disengaging. Maybe it wasn't such a good time to visit Doctor Stein after all. Before the other guards could react, I took off running toward the trees that were between me and the fence separating the Foundation from the Krishna School. I heard shouts behind me but because Stein's people had had to come out through the gate, I had a good sixty yard head start. By the time I'd zigzagged my way between the oak trees and finally reached the fence, I'd doubled my lead and lost my pursuers, but I was exhausted. If I was going to climb the fence, I'd have to do it with my fingers crossed while I was pleading with the almighty to not let my heart fail me. But I was too tired to even try to climb the fence. I sat down to catch my breath. With my eyes closed, I could have drifted off into slumberland if I hadn't known that Jerry and his band of merry guards were hot on my trail. I needed just one more minute to gain back my full lung capacity and force the desire to slip into unconsciousness back out of my mind.

Two light thumps to either side of me brought me alert and brought my hands up in front of my face, my elbows tucked in over my stomach and ribs, and my legs ready to deliver a probably ineffectually weary kick to whomever had intruded on me. I opened my eyes to two somber looking teenage faces, both scanning me as well as the terrain on either side of me. Both of them wore the white dojo uniforms of Adamji's martial arts class. Despite their game faces, they both looked at me with concern. One of them had a bandage across his forehead and I guessed that he might be the boy who had tangled with Mathew Litton the previous night. Apparently satisfied that I was alone, they each grabbed an arm and pulled me to my feet. Then one of them bent over and the other one lifted me onto the first one's back. When he stood straight up I could grasp the top of the fence. I didn't need any more prompting. I put one foot in a link and threw the other foot over the fence, then swung the first foot on over too, so I ended up standing facing the fence from the other side, my feet in two of the links about a foot and a half down from the top. From there I inched myself back down the fence on the other side until I was about four feet from the ground. Then I let go. When I landed on my feet they collapsed under me and I fell heavily and tiredly on my back. I lay there with my eyes closed. Piece of cake.

The two students landed lightly on either side of me. When I opened my eyes they were standing quietly, waiting for me to move. I'd gotten enough of a second wind that I was able to scramble to my feet and give them both looks like I knew what I was doing. "Lead on," I said.

Adamji Dil was pacing on the front porch of the school office, dressed in white shorts and a crisp open-necked white short sleeve shirt. He had a startled look when I came around the corner of the building with his two students. His irritation at the students was obvious. "Why did you leave your posts?"

They looked at each other sheepishly. "He came from the Foundation," the one with the bandage said.

Adamji's eyes widened in surprise. "You've been to the Foundation?"

"Getting there was no problem," I said. "Getting out was a little hairy. Your boys helped me make it over the fence."

His look toward his students softened...but only a little. "Good job boys. Go back now and keep watch." They trotted off in the direction of the fence.

Adamji looked at me. His eyes narrowed like he was trying to decide if he could trust me or not.

"There's something going on over there," he said. "Two of their kids came over the fence. We caught them. They were badly frightened. They were talking about some of the kids going crazy. Trying to kill the others...wanting to go after Saraya and that Litton boy we caught last night." He talked stiffly, formally. I didn't know if it was his normal manner or because he didn't like having to talk to me.

"That fits with what I saw." I said. "It looked like some of the kids went on a rampage. They tore up some things and had the staff and a lot of the other residents hiding in the office behind an electric fence."

"And they chased you over here?"

I shook my head. "That was Doctor Stein and her guards. I don't think they want anyone to know what's happening over there. I didn't see any of the kids, except a few scared ones. I'd like to talk to those two you've got here."

He didn't say anything but nodded his head and turned and went into the office building. I followed. The little old lady in the sari wasn't around. Two of the chairs were occupied by a couple of teenage kids. Both of them were the typical tattooed, street punk Foundation resident types. One of them was long and thin and had a jagged edged *18* on one arm, which I recognized as the sign of LA's infamous eighteenth street gang. The other, shorter and pudgy, looked milder, except for the three tear drops dripping down his cheek...each one representing a gang kill. They'd been tough hombres once, but now they looked scared. Three of Adamji's students were hovering around them, watching them suspiciously. All three were baby-faced white boys dressed in their white pajama-like martial arts outfits. They wouldn't have been able to hold the two delinquents, except the Foundation boys considered themselves asylum seekers, not prisoners.

I asked the two Foundation kids what had happened. The eighteenth streeter did all of the talking, though the little fat guy occasionally prompted him with comments in Spanish. He told me pretty much what I'd expected to hear. The C-3 kids had been getting more and more violent over the last week. There were fights within the cottage and then they began to go after the other residents and some of the guards. Apparently, they mounted their attacks in packs. When they caught someone they beat him severely. The Foundation guards had told all the other residents to stay away from C-3 and its occupants but last night they'd gone completely amok. They were roaming the grounds, claiming to have caught and killed an intruder, then they talked about going after Mathew Litton and Saraya Dil as revenge for Manuel Torres' death. When my phone call had brought the cops onto the grounds, that had put an end to things until sometime this morning, when the C-3 residents had come out of their cottage again, as one group. This time they were dressed in gang colors and they had weapons…knives, clubs, everything but guns. They trashed their own cottage and the building where Mathew had been kept, then went after the other residents and the guards. According to these two, there were at least three dead kids in the cottages that I hadn't looked into. Everyone who could make it had fled to the office, but these two hadn't made it in time. The gate had been locked and the fence electrified and they took the same alternate escape route I had…over the fence to the Krishna school. Neither of the boys knew where the C-3 gang had gone. That meant about a dozen violent teenagers were on the loose somewhere.

I asked the two kids if they knew where Mathew Litton was. They both nodded. "In town, in jail," the tall skinny one said.

I figured if they knew, the other Foundation kids did too.

"I've got to call Chief Larsen," I said. "Those kids could be headed for town. You'd better keep up your guard here, just in case."

Adamji had heard everything the two Mexican-American kids had said. He looked puzzled. "What's going on with those other kids?"

"Doctor Stein has turned them into a bunch of Mathew Littons, only worse. Mathew has a genetic disorder that makes him aggressive but— I know it sounds crazy to say it— he's not a mean-spirited kid. These are psychopaths who were already bullies and killers. Now they've got Mathew's genetic disorder."

Adamji stared at me uncomprehending. "How?"

"Stein gave them Mathew's DNA," I said, knowing I had no idea how that was possible. I hoped Adamji wouldn't ask.

"How is that possible?"

I looked at Adamji's skeptical face and weighed my answer carefully. "I'm not sure how to explain it at a level you'd understand."

He looked at me suspiciously but didn't ask any more questions.

. . .

I got Nils on the phone. None of the kids had shown up in town, but Francine Stein had called and told him she had twelve residents on the loose. She hadn't told him they were probably out ravaging the countryside. I explained the situation to Nils and told him I'd be there as soon as I got a ride to my car. Hillary and Jimmy were with Mathew. I told Nils to send Hillary home and triple his guard.

CHAPTER THIRTY-SEVEN

I sensed something was wrong when I noticed the lack of traffic on the street leading into town. When I reached the first strip of shops I became aware of the absence of shoppers walking from store to store. Then I saw the smashed storefront windows. A crowd of people was in front of Jorgensen's liquor store. They stared at my car as if they were checking whether I was friend or foe. I pulled up to the curb.

The Indian maitre d' from the Taj Mahal restaurant came over to the car. The liquor store was across the street from his restaurant. "They killed Harry Jorgensen and his wife," he said breathlessly.

"Foundation kids?"

"A whole gang of them. They beat Harry and his wife to death…for no reason. They took liquor and started drinking it. They took Harry's gun, too. They were shooting it off when they left."

"Which way did they go?"

"Toward the jail. Why aren't the police here?" he asked, angrily.

Remembering the size of Nils' little force, I didn't even want to think about the answer to that question.

I gunned the engine and spun rubber leaving the curb. I

headed down the side street that contained the police station and the jail. The street was deserted but there was a body on the porch of the station. It was the fat deputy, Halvorsen. I jammed on the brakes and leapt out of the car. The deputy wasn't moving. I couldn't tell if he'd been shot, but his head had been caved in by something harder than a fist and his shirt was in tatters in front and along the side, revealing glimpses of torn and bruised skin where he'd probably been kicked repeatedly. I took his pulse. There wasn't one. Then I noticed that his gun was gone. Now they had two.

A couple of shots were fired across the street from the direction of the jail. I waited to see if anyone was going to come out of the building and when no one did, I sprinted across the road. The entrance to the jail was in the back. Maybe there was access through the courthouse, but I wasn't sure. The jail and courthouse were part of the same building but a jail wouldn't have very many back entrances. I decided to ignore the courthouse and moved cautiously along the sidewalk leading around back to the jail. Ahead of me, someone was standing at the jail's entrance. Ducking behind the azaleas that lined the side of the building, I could just make out two figures. One looked like an African American, tall and slim, and the other was a short white kid. Both of them were young—maybe fifteen or sixteen— and armed with two-by-fours.

I looked around for something to use as a weapon. Leaning against the building among the bushes was a long handled shovel. I slipped between the plants and took the shovel, then inched forward along the side of the building. I could see the two at the door. They were pacing and talking in an agitated way, as if they were on speed. Each of them had an open bottle of whiskey in his free hand. It sounded as if they were arguing. If I waited long enough they'd probably go after each other, but I didn't have the time. Both of them had their backs to me and I managed to get within six feet of them without being detected. I took one step out of the bushes and swung the shovel at the head of the African American. He was my height and I arched my swing a little upward, like I was a long-ball hitter. The flat part of the shovel caught him in its upswing, squarely on the occiput. He went down without knowing what hit him. The other boy spun around and dropped into a crouch. He was a freckle-faced white kid who was no stranger to fighting with sticks and clubs. He held the two-by-four in both hands, ready to use it to block a blow with the shovel. His eyes glittered like an animal's.

I took a step toward the freckle-faced kid and drew the shovel back over my right shoulder, as if I was going to swing it like a club. He shifted his arms to the same side, ready to ward off my blow. As soon as he did, I reversed my grip on the shovel so I was holding it like a spear. Instead of clubbing him, I jabbed straight ahead, aiming for his chest. He managed to get his two-by-four up high enough to deflect my blow, but that only swung the shovel blade around so that it hit him in the face about eyeball height. The blade of the shovel sank a half inch into the bridge of his freckled nose then lacerated both eyes. He groaned and dropped his two by four, covering both eyes with his hands. He was enough of a bloody mess to almost turn my stomach, but I couldn't afford to be delicate at the moment. I drew the shovel back and clubbed him full force in the face with the flat side of the shovel. He dropped to the sidewalk and lay unconscious, leaking blood from his nose and something clear and watery from both eyes.

I traded my shovel for the two-by-four that had dropped from the African American's hand and was lying on the sidewalk. I'd be able to move more quickly with a club than with a shovel. From inside the building I heard another shot. The front door was glass and if more of the runaway kids were inside the lobby, they'd have seen me fighting with the two sentries and come running out. I opened the door and went inside. The lobby was empty, as I'd expected. I'd need to go behind the front desk and buzz myself in. The buzzer made quite a racket, but there wasn't much else I could think to do.

It was a small jail and there was only one cell block. When I opened the door I could see three bodies on the floor. Two of them were close enough for me to see that neither of them was one of the Litton kids. They looked like Foundation residents. I couldn't tell about the third body. From the far end of the cell block, Nils yelled at me to go back out. He was holed up inside the guard's room behind a desk that had been shoved into the doorway. The glass upper half of the room's wall had been shot out. There were at least two other people in the room with Nils. One looked like one of the guards and the other was the deputy, Long. The cell doors to Mathew and Jimmy Litton's cells were open and more than a half dozen kids were crowded inside. Mathew Litton was one of them. I didn't see Jimmy.

I started down the cell block toward the guard room. Nils saw me coming and laid down some cover fire. Even so one of the young toughs came toward me out of Jimmy's cell, a long, thin knife in his hand. He was a small African-American kid with no shirt and tattoos on both of this shoulders. Even without reading the name on his tattoo, I recognized 'Runt' from the cottage. His pants were pulled low and he came at me in a fast rush, the knife held low and in front of him. His eyes were wide, like he was on something. He didn't look like he recognized me and I decided he wasn't just trying to renew our acquaintance. Anyhow, we'd not really been that close. I dispensed with any formal greeting and used my two-by-four to clock him with a swing that would have made Miguel Cabrera proud.

When I got to the door of the guard station I dove head first over the desk. Nils caught me before I drove my head into the floor on the other side. Then I noticed the third guard. He was crumpled in the corner, a gaping, bloody hole in his forehead. I crouched down behind the desk, Nils next to me.

"We can't hold them much longer," he said. "If they come out of the cells we can get to them, but they've got Mathew. They've got a couple of guns. They shot Bill."

"Your deputy's dead across the street."

Nils shut his eyes and took a deep breath. "That's why he hasn't been here to help us."

"Where's Jimmy?" I asked.

"I sent him home with Hillary."

"How about if we rush them?" I asked.

"We have to," Nils said. "If they get started out of here, we'll only be able to stop a couple of them before they get through the door."

I looked at the other guard and deputy Long. They both nodded. I crawled over and took the gun from the dead guard's holster. "Let's do it," I said.

Nils started firing and led the rest of us across the top of the desk. The kids had gotten the idea to leave at exactly the same time. They rushed for the door as we ran toward them. They had Mathew Litton, his hands tied together with a belt, between us and them, stopping us from shooting. One of the kids had a key from the front desk and they crowded through the door while we pulled up and watched helplessly.

"Shit!" Nils said. "Wait in here for a minute or they'll pick us off as we come through the door."

We waited, feeling frustrated. I looked at the third body on the floor. It was another of the kids, a Mexican-American boy with a red rag tied around his arm, and half of his other shoulder blown off. I looked down at Nils' gun. It was a .44 magnum, not police issue. He wore it in an old fashioned cowboy holster with the bullets strung along the back of the belt.

Runt had recovered enough from my home run on his head to get up and flee with the rest of them. That meant there were nine of them left, although the freckled-faced boy I'd blinded outside wouldn't be much help to the others. They had Mathew, but he was their prisoner, not their ally.

"I've never seen kids fight like that," Nils finally said. He was staring at the three kids on floor. His face was blank.

"They've been physically altered," I said. "They've got some of Mathew's defective genes in their systems and it makes them destructive…more than they usually are. They killed at least three kids at the Foundation and the Jorgensons who own the liquor store."

Nils winced. "What do they want with Mathew?"

"Revenge, I think. For killing Manuel Torres."

"So what do you think they're gonna do?"

I shrugged. "My guess is they'll go back to the Foundation. That's the only place they know around here. Or they could stay in town."

My last statement alarmed Nils more than he already was. He muttered, "Fuck it," and threw open the door to the lobby and walked out.

CHAPTER THIRTY-EIGHT

The calls to the police station were coming in fast and furious. The Foundation kids had cut a wide path of destruction in their exit from town. The worst disaster was at the high school. Nils and I cursed ourselves for not anticipating it. A school would have been these kids' most familiar territory. Other teenagers would be their most familiar targets. School was out or they'd have done even more damage. The only kids at school were some sports teams practicing and a group of cheerleaders. The Foundation residents had walked onto the high school grounds and demanded car keys and females. Apparently a few of the football players had had enough guts or few enough brains to challenge them. Two of them had been shot and two more beaten severely. Everybody else had fled, except four girls who hadn't made it away fast enough. Every kid with a car had gotten away so the Foundation crew were still on foot, but they'd taken the four girls with them and were last seen headed across the park in the direction of the Yearling Foundation.

One of the calls was from Hillary. She and Jimmy had gone to her office, rather than her house and they had heard the shots coming from the jail. Jimmy was worried about Mathew and had become so agitated that Hillary couldn't keep him inside the office, and now she didn't know where he had gone.

"He'll come here," I told Nils.

"He should be here by now."

"Quit worrying," I told him. "Jimmy is the least of our worries." Nils looked dubious but nodded grudgingly.

The calls kept coming in. Red Hovland, the manager from the Jaguar dealer called to offer help. He and some others were willing to serve as deputies and go after the kids.

I shook my head. "They're trouble." I told Nils. "Red and his group are loose cannons. You'll never control them."

"I've got to get the girls back. And Doctor Stein and the other residents at the Foundation are in danger. I've only got one deputy and two jail guards."

"And me."

A hint of a smile flickered briefly across his face. "And you."

"Call the state police, the county sheriff, the Governor. Wait for some backup," I told Nils.

He thanked Red and declined his offer, then called the sheriff, the CHP and the Governor's office.

Nils was still worried about Jimmy, so I called Hillary to ask if he'd come back. He hadn't. She said she was coming down to the station. If Jimmy showed up she might be able to calm him down.

Frankly, I was glad she was coming. I thought she might be able to calm Nils down also.

Nils and I waited. He made sure his guards and his remaining deputy had the right armaments and we watched the ambulances take away the bodies from the jail. The day was starting to lose light. I walked outside and felt the cool evening air. Looking around me, everything seemed calm and serene. Shambhala was a quiet mountain village, a haven for artists, philosophers, gurus and now, mad scientists like Francine Stein. She'd certainly ruined the neighborhood.

While I paced back and forth in front of the police station. Hillary Smythe pulled up in her forest green Pathfinder. I was surprised by how glad I was to see her. The danger had made me acutely aware of her safety. I felt a sense of relief to see her in front of me and unharmed. She looked more lissome, beautiful, and more vulnerable than I had remembered her.

"Are you OK?" she asked, looking at me strangely.

I must have been standing there looking like a half-wit, watching her get out of her car. "I'd have post-traumatic stress disorder, except the trauma isn't 'post' yet," I said.

"Did Jimmy show up?"

"No."

"What's Nils doing?"

"Waiting for reinforcements. The gang bangers went over to the high school and killed a couple of kids then took some girls with them. They seem to be headed back to the Foundation."

"Jesus!"

"Exactly."

"There's a bunch of townspeople grouping together over at the Nordstrom's Jaguar lot," she said.

"Shit! I thought they'd quieted down. Nils told them he didn't want their help."

"They looked like they were getting ugly when I drove by. A lot of them were armed with guns. Some of them had baseball bats or axes."

"How about pitchforks and torches?"

She smiled grimly. "Not yet."

"I'd better tell Nils."

Nils didn't want to leave the station until the county cops or the CHP showed up. He asked Hillary and me to go talk to the crowd at Nordstrom's.

The streets of the little village were still mostly deserted as we drove in Hillary's Pathfinder toward the auto dealership. It was like a town under siege. There were only a handful of people at the Jaguar lot when we got there. One of them was the mechanic I'd seen that morning when I was waiting for my car. I asked him where everyone had gone.

"Ol' Red's got them all worked up," he said. He seemed to be in awe of his manager.

"So where'd they go?"

"To the Foundation."

"Oh shit," I said. "How many were there?"

"Hell, there was a whole shitload of 'em…couple dozen at least."

I looked at Hillary.

"Did you see a kid…Jimmy Litton?" she asked the mechanic.

"Sure, he was with 'em."

Hillary spun her Pathfinder around and we headed back to the station.

•　•　•

Four green and white County Sheriff's cars were parked in front of the Shambhala Police Station when we pulled up in front of it. The lobby of the station was crowded with uniformed men. There were six deputy sheriff's, one police deputy, a guard from the jail, and Nils.

Nils was addressing the group of deputies. He stopped talking when Hillary and I walked in. "What's the word on the local crowd?"

"Two dozen of them are headed toward the Foundation," I said. "Jimmy's with them."

"Are they armed?" Nils asked.

I looked at Hillary. "Some were when I saw them earlier," she said.

"We'd better get moving," Nils said to the assemblage.

I looked at Hillary. She could see I was going to ask her to stay behind.

"I'm going to be there in case I can do anything. Both Jimmy and Mathew respond to me better than they do to anyone else," she said.

She was right.

Nils must have thought so too. "You two ride with me," he said.

CHAPTER THIRTY-NINE

Nils led with his siren screaming and the other local and county cars followed suit. I knew cops knew how to drive fast, but Nils took the dark curves leading to the Yearling Foundation at a speed that had me terrified. I was thinking what a shame it was going to be that I had fought my way through so many of those crazed teenagers only to be killed when Nils wrapped his cruiser around an oak tree.

The gate to the Foundation was knocked flat to the ground, the fence attached to it twisted and uprooted for the space of two of its poles on the hinged side of the gate. Red Hovland and his followers must have driven right through it. Up ahead there were a dozen cars and pickups lined up around the Foundation office. Nils kept coming full speed with lights and siren going until he was almost on the townspeople. Everyone scattered and he hit the brakes. It was an effective way to break up the crowd.

The office fence had floodlights mounted on it every ten yards or so. I'd never noticed them before. They lit up the perimeter around the building and caused long shadows that gave an eerie cast to the whole scene.

Red and several of the men had rounded up about a dozen of the residents. The kids were sitting on the ground with a half dozen armed men pacing around them and looking important.

Some of the kids looked like they'd been roughed up pretty badly. I didn't know whether that was Red's group's work or that of the returning hoodlums. Red looked serious, but he was obviously happy with himself. He strode over to Nils. Red was carrying a gun. "We caught a bunch of 'em, Chief. They didn't put up too much of a fight."

Nils gave Red a cold stare. "Those aren't the right kids."

Red's smile disappeared and looked at Nils suspiciously. "What do you mean?"

"Those kids haven't even left this place. The ones we're looking for are only about nine of them. I've seen 'em all and none of these kids are them."

Red glanced over at the kids being guarded by his men. "They look pretty damn dangerous to me."

"Where's Doctor Stein?" Nils asked.

"In the office, I think. When we got here she came out on the porch. A bunch of those delinquents ran inside the fence and chased these others out. Then Stein closed the gate and put a charge into it. We fired a few shots at her and the kids, but they all went inside."

Nils' face reddened and his eyes blazed. "Jesus Christ. You shot at Doctor Stein?"

"I figured she was harboring the kids that killed all those people in town."

Nils gave him a withering stare. "Get your friends out of here," he said.

Red didn't move. "If these are the wrong kids, then the right ones are here someplace…probably inside that big house with Doctor Stein."

"And we've got enough uniforms here to take care of them."

Red had his chin stuck out. He looked Nils in the face and smiled cynically. "Hell, Chief, they took that Litton kid right out from under you at the jail. I'd say you shouldn't be turning down any offers of help."

Nils balled up his fists. His eyes narrowed and Red's sardonic smile disappeared as he stepped back nervously. I thought Nils was going to hit him. Instead, he asked him where Jimmy Litton was.

Red let out the breath he'd been holding then shrugged. "He was with us, but I haven't seen him since we got here."

Nils shot me a worried look.

"We'll find him," I said. I motioned to Hillary to follow me. I had a pretty good idea where Jimmy would have gone.

I took Hillary's hand and pulled her away from the crowd and into the shadows. I could hear Nils on the bullhorn trying to coax Francine Stein out of the office building. The county cops were gathering up the kids that Red had captured, but none of the townspeople looked like they were leaving.

"Where are we going?" Hillary asked. She wasn't resisting my grasp on her hand so I kept hold of it.

"The place where they kept Mathew is just behind these next buildings. I bet that's where Jimmy went to look for his brother."

"You think the violent kids are in that building?"

I was surprised by the lack of fear in her voice. "No. But Jimmy might be."

"Where are the delinquents and Mathew?"

"I don't know. In the house with Doctor Stein, I guess. At least not close by, I hope."

It occurred to me that holding Hillary's hand wasn't an effective defense. I still had the dead guard's pistol. I dropped Hillary's hand and pulled the gun out of my pocket.

Up ahead, the lights were on in Mathew's building. It was eerily quiet, although we could still hear Nils' amplified voice behind us. I put my fingers to my lips to silence Hillary and pointed out the twisted pieces of fence around the building so she wouldn't trip over them. When I stopped moving, I could hear someone moving inside the structure. Suddenly the light went out and it became quiet again. I pulled Hillary over close to me, then stepped in front of her.

"Jimmy!" I called out.

There was no answer. I called again.

I got a call back. "Is that you Mr. McGowan?"

"I'm here with Doctor Smythe."

I could see him coming out of the building.

Hillary came around me. She waited until Jimmy got close then reached out and put her arms around him. "You were looking for Mathew, weren't you?"

"I heard they took him." His eyes told me he hoped he'd heard wrong.

I nodded.

"I thought if he got away he'd come back here. Mathew's hard to keep hold of. It'd take a lot of them."

"There's a lot of them, Jimmy," I said.

"Where are they?"

"We don't know."

"Is Chief Larsen here?" he asked hopefully.

"He's here and he'll be glad to see you," Hillary said. "Let's go find him."

The sound of shots came from the direction of the office. All three of us flinched, then I gestured for Hillary and Jimmy to duck down and I nodded in the direction of the office. The three of us picked our way back through the fencing and crept cautiously toward the bright lights that were still lighting up the area around the office. The deputies and the crowd from town were crouched behind their cars and trucks.

Everyone startled when Hillary and Jimmy and I came out of the shadows and some of Red's group raised their guns in our direction. Nils bawled at them and they lowered their weapons sheepishly. Nils came scuttling over, keeping his head down and motioning for us to do the same. He looked relieved to see Jimmy.

"Looks like they're inside," Nils said to all of us. "They won't let Doctor Stein come out to talk. I'm trying to get them to send one of their own out to talk to us. They've got several residents and guards in there with them. The girls somehow got away before they went into the building. Some of the townspeople are taking them to the hospital. They were hurt pretty badly."

"Goddam those bastards!" Hillary said, surprising us all.

"Is Mathew in there?" Jimmy asked.

Nils looked at him softly. "I guess so. We haven't heard anything directly." He looked up at me. "All they do is yell obscenities and fire at us every once in a while."

"Anybody been hit?" I asked.

"Not yet. We can't shoot back cuz we don't know who we'll hit."

It sounded like a standoff.

There was a lot of murmuring from the men around the cars. Someone yelled for Nils. The door to the office was open. A scared looking guard edged his way out, his eyes wide with fear. He was one of the muscular, blonde surfer types, but it wasn't Jerry. Whoever it was, his white T-shirt had blood all down the front. He was waving at us to not shoot. When he got to the edge of the porch he turned around, as if he'd heard someone say something to him. A shotgun blast lifted him backward off the porch. He landed on his back in the grass, leaking a pool of blood and not moving.

"Get the hell out of here or another one gets the same thing," a voice shouted from inside the door, which was still cracked open a half a foot. The civilians from town looked like they were in shock. Nils grabbed the rifle from a speechless Red and fired a single shot. The bloody head of the speaker from behind the door pitched forward into the crack between the door and the frame, then slid to the floor, just the head and one shoulder protruding onto the porch with the rest of the body inside. Then somebody pulled the body back inside and slammed the door.

Red and the others, including the deputies, stared at Chief Larsen. "That'll show 'em who calls the shots here," Nils said.

"That leaves eight," I said.

"We might be able to take 'em if we could get in," Nils said.

When I'd come past the back of the house the night before looking for Mathew, I'd seen a transformer box on a pole behind the house. I told Nils about it. If the transformer were knocked out, the fence would go dead and the electronic gate would disengage.

"I'll send a man," he said.

"I remember where it is," I said. "Give me a rifle. Something that'll crank off a lot of shots in a row."

Nils looked down at the rifle of Red's he was still holding. He handed it to me. Red started to object, but Nils and I both glared at him.

"Got more bullets?" I asked.

Red looked at me sourly but dug into his pocket and pulled out a box and handed it to me.

I looked at Hillary. "I'll be back in a while."

She smiled thinly and reached out her hand to touch mine briefly. Then she put her arm around Jimmy and drew him closer to her.

"How about giving me a little less light," I said to Nils. He began issuing orders over his walkie-talkie. In a minute, gunshots started and the big lights on the fence posts blinked out one after another. It took another minute for my eyes to get used to the dark, then I took off around the edge of the compound and headed for the back of the house.

The transformer was between the house and the fence. It must step down the voltage from that used in the building to the twenty or so that went through the fence. It was about twenty feet up and another thirty yards inside the fence. I kneeled down and rested my right elbow on my upraised right knee, aiming the rifle with my left hand. I figured I'd pump enough bullets into the transformer in every place I could hit, that it ought to do something. The rifle was semi-automatic and I pulled off nine rapid shots before the whole transformer went up in a cascade of sparks. I'd drawn enough attention to bring a hail of bullets thumping into the ground around me, and I took a couple of quick rolls to the side then jumped up and dove behind a small pine that was just thick enough to hide my body. The bullets kept coming for another five seconds then stopped.

When I got back to the parking lot Nils was organizing his troops. The gate was open about a foot. I'd been right that when the power shut off, the electric lock on the gate had disengaged. I looked at the office. When the transformer went, it had taken out about half the lights in the building with it. The whole place looked creepy. A faint moon peeked occasionally from behind high, rapidly moving clouds, giving just enough light to make the old Victorian house with its peaked roof and turrets, look like a gothic manor. Over the tops of the turrets I could see that the trees behind the house were lit up periodically by the flashes of arcing electricity from the still sparking transformer.

Nils was trying to get Red to keep his people in line. The deputies had on flak jackets and helmets. They were forming up for their assault. Nils was worried that, once the uniformed officers went in, the mob from town would start pumping lead into the house randomly and his own men would become casualties of friendly fire. I wasn't part of the assault team so I took it upon myself to issue threats to anyone who was even thinking about firing a gun while the deputies were in the house.

Nils had his first man ready to push through the gate and open it wide for every one else. The plan was that the others would rush in all at once and then fan out up close to the building. From there, they'd throw in some tear gas, then go in the front door if nobody came out first. Nils started a countdown.

Someone yelled, "Shit! It's on fire!" We all looked up. Flames were just visible, licking the air from the back of the house near the transformer.

"Mother of Christ!" Nils swore softly.

We stood transfixed as the roof of the structure began to send flames skyward. Three figures came running out of the house, headed for the gate.

"Don't fire!" Nils yelled.

As the running figures got closer I recognized Jerry. He was leading two other young guards. When he'd gotten to within thirty yards of the fence I could see he recognized me. The look on his face was terrified and pleading. Ten yards from the gate he and the other two went down in a volley of bullets from the house…stumbling and reaching out in a final desperate attempt to reach safety. The townspeople behind the cars fired off their own volley at a shadowy figure that had remained on the office porch. The figure lurched forward. There was just enough light from the flames above to illuminate the person's identity. It was Francine Stein, her black wool dress nearly in shreds, her shoulders and breasts white and exposed in the strange light. She took an uncertain step off the porch, but her eyes were unseeing. It was only her lower motor centers moving her limbs automatically. Her already dead body twitched grotesquely in mid-air then collapsed in the dirt at the foot of the front steps.

"Goddamit!" Nils yelled, and turned and fired a warning shot above the cars. "No more shooting, you assholes!"

We waited. I felt a hand in mine and looked down to see Hillary's head next to my shoulder. She was still clutching Jimmy. He was staring wide-eyed at the office, the entire roof and back of which were now in flames. Nils was on the phone to the fire department.

"Mathew's in there," Jimmy said quietly. He looked like he was in a trance. Hillary and I both reacted at once. She tried to tighten her grip and I reached desperately for Jimmy's shirt, his shoulder, his hair, anything. But we were too late. He was running full speed toward the house. I took off after him.

Jimmy was fast, but I was gaining. I knew we were both perfect targets for anyone inside, but it couldn't be helped. One more step and I'd be able to reach him with a flying tackle. Then I felt a sharp pain in my thigh and my right leg collapsed under me. Going down, I could already see the blood spurting from the artery that had been severed from the gunshot. Jimmy was on the porch. I hit the ground and rolled, hoping to get close enough that no one inside would be able to get an angle on me for a second shot. I heard footsteps behind me, then saw Nils as he took the front steps all in one stride and tried to grab Jimmy before he made it into the house. The two of them ended up entwined in a hurtling ball that smashed right through the front door. I heard the gunfire from inside. Nils' powerful .44 boomed four times, then the rest of the shots were from other guns. Finally there was silence.

I waited unbelieving, staring at the broken door and expecting to see Nils and Jimmy appear. There was only the roar of the fire and the smoke billowing from the front door, exiting the house like an evil spirit exorcised from its host.

I shut out the reality around me and focused on my own body. I could hear the blood from my leg squirting rhythmically against the side of the house. Pressing as hard as I could with my right thumb on the artery above the wound, I used my left hand to awkwardly unfasten my belt, then wrapped it around my leg above the severed artery and cinched it tight. I wasn't sure I could walk. I heard footsteps, but before I could get myself set for an assailant, two sheriff's deputies in flak jackets appeared. Each of them threw one of my arms over his shoulder and they dragged me back through the gate.

Hillary was at my side. "Jimmy...," she began. Her voice cracked.

"I know," I said. "Nils too. They didn't make it."

We both stared at the burning office building. No one could be alive in the inferno it had become. How many kids and guards were still inside was anybody's guess. Mathew and Jimmy were in there. And so was Nils Larsen.

CHAPTER FORTY

The bullet I'd taken in my leg hadn't broken any bones but an artery was irreparably damaged and a fair amount of muscle had been shredded. I didn't look forward to a lifetime of dragging one leg around behind me so I called a surgeon friend of mine who was also a former client and he had me transferred to Cedar Sinai where a small committee of doctors fixed me up so well that, according to them, I'd be better than when I started. Between the plastic artery running from my heart and the one in my leg I was becoming another six-million dollar man.

Hillary visited me daily but my lengthy recovery had made me miss the funerals for the Litton brothers. I was sorry. Hillary said there weren't many townsfolk there. The rest of the town had plenty of other losses to mourn. Despite their central role in the whole affair, the Litton family quickly faded back into their marginal status in the community. A couple of the high school boys who'd been killed were members of the football team and their deaths garnered the spotlight.

The Yearling Foundation was closed and the surviving residents sent back to more traditional penal facilities. The press had descended on Shambhala, calling for an investigation, but since all the Foundation's records had gone up in smoke and its director was dead, there wasn't much to investigate. The whole story about Mathew Litton and the use of his DNA in experiments with other residents never surfaced at all. There was no one to tell it. Nils was dead and so were both of the Steins and Mathew, himself. Hillary and I talked about it and we decided that focusing media attention on poor Ruth Litton, who might then get blamed for letting Doctor Stein use her son in her experiments had zero upside to it so we didn't say anything. I could pretty well count on Robert Wang and the UCLA community to not bring anything up.

I was determined to make it to Nils' funeral and hoping to see Ruth Litton there or find a way to visit with her. Hillary had done a lot of counseling and hand-holding with both parents, but I felt I owed them something from me personally. If I'd been a little faster or luckier, Jimmy might not be dead at all.

I got myself discharged the day before the funeral, which was planned to be a pretty big civic event in Shambhala. Nils had a lot of friends and a far-reaching reputation in the Santa Barbara/Ventura area. Besides that, the loss of an officer in the line of duty always brought out a massive response from law enforcement groups all around the state. Shambhala had lost three officers, including their Chief.

Hillary brought me home and loaded me and my wheelchair into her Pathfinder to head to the cemetery. I'd skipped the parade and speeches. I was sure they had more to do with who was trying to get him or her self elected or re-elected to something than with Nils. Anyway, I wasn't sure how I felt about my fellow Shambhalaans yet. Red Hovland's group had been treated as heroes who'd responded to an attack on their town by beating their plowshares into swords and bearding the lions in their lair. Even if there was some truth to that characterization, I knew that the group from town had been more of a nuisance that night than they'd been a help. Anyway, I preferred attending just the funeral and paying my respects to

Nils more privately.

I was surprised to find that Nils had no family at all. I knew he wasn't married, but I guess I'd thought that someone like him must have had some blood ties to the community. I suppose the citizens of Shambhala were his family. The line of traffic going into the little mountain cemetery was at least a mile long. Everybody was coming to say their last goodbyes.

I sat in my wheelchair on the periphery of the crowd and listened to the faint voice of the minister reading a service over the gravesite about fifty yards away from me. Hillary had moved closer so she could actually hear what was being said. I felt a firm but gentle hand on my shoulder. I looked up at Fanny Dil. She gave me an encouraging smile.

"I kinda had my eye on Nils," she said wistfully.

"He had his eye on you, Fanny. You would have been a pretty good pair."

"Everything changes," she said.

"Your school doesn't change much."

Her face started to dissolve into sadness. Then it stiffened. "The school is closing. Adamji has decided to sell."

"Sell? But the Yearling Foundation has closed. They'll be no more trouble."

"I know. We've regained possession of the Foundation property...and La Sol."

"How?" I asked, though it was starting to make sense to me.

"When my father divided the property, he only leased it to Bernie Stein. Stein's wife could divide it in their divorce, but if neither of them were alive it reverted back to us. Adamji found a buyer who wants all three properties for a country club and spa. I made Adamji the legal owner several years ago so that when I died there wouldn't be any problems."

"You mean if one Stein died the property went to the other, but if they both died, it came back to Adamji?"

She nodded. "I never thought Adamji would sell the

school."

"What will you do?"

"My son will give me enough money to live very comfortably. I'll stay here, somewhere in the valley. I've lived here all my life."

They were lowering the casket into the grave. Fanny and I became quiet. She touched my shoulder again, then slowly moved off toward the parking lot.

People were walking back past me. One or two of them smiled. Most of them looked at me as if they thought they should know me but couldn't remember from where. One or two stared at my wheelchair. Hillary was walking slowly, talking to someone. As they approached I saw it was Ruth Litton.

My impulse was to stand, but I caught myself before I put any weight on my bad leg. I told Ruth Litton how sorry I was about her boys. She thanked me for what I'd done for them.

"I know you risked your life for Jimmy, Mr. McGowan. That's why you're in a wheelchair now."

I told her the wheelchair was only temporary and that I wished I had been successful saving Jimmy. It probably would have saved Nils too, since he died trying to save Jimmy himself.

Mrs. Litton started to cry— softly and shyly— looking around as if she were embarrassed, even though we were at a funeral. "Nils loved Jimmy," she said. "Even though I never told him. I think he knew."

"Knew what, Mrs. Litton," I asked.

"Jimmy was his son." She looked at me and then at Hillary, a bright, proud look in her eyes.

"Whether he knew or not, Nils seemed to care about Jimmy like he was his son," Hillary said. She didn't look surprised.

"He knew," Ruth Litton said, more sure of herself this time. She seemed buoyed up by her certainty.

I thought back about Nils' behavior. All the times he seemed overly concerned about Jimmy…enough so that I'd asked him about it more than once. I'd thought it was because of his concern about Jimmy's mother, but maybe she was right. Maybe he knew.

"You're probably right," I said.

Ruth Litton forced a smile and blinked back her tears. She shook my hand, then Hillary's and walked away.

"How's the leg?" Hillary asked. She was pushing me across the thick grass of the cemetery lawn.

"I can't leap tall buildings yet, but it's getting stronger. There were more casualties from this affair than just those who were killed or wounded. Fanny Dil told me her son has sold the Krishna School."

Hillary stopped pushing. "Sold the school? Her father's place and what it stands for are the heart and soul of Shambhala."

"I think its soul is soon to become golf."

"I guess Nirvana is only temporary," she said, resuming her pushing. There were a few other cars in the parking lot and an occasional lonely figure could be seen among the headstones, remembering someone. In the distance, the round pine covered crests of the Santa Ynez Mountains were a dark green splash of color framed by the pale blue sky.

Purchase other Black Rose Writing titles at www.blackrosewriting.com/books

and use promo code PRINT to receive a 20% discount.